DEADLY SENSE

Max Jeffries

Paperback ISBN: 978-1-7636835-0-1

Ebook ISBN: 978-1-7636835-1-8

Book cover by The Illustrators Australia

ALSO BY MAX JEFFRIES

Altered Sense

For Jude

ONE

In a dimly lit studio apartment shrouded in darkness with its sealed and blacked-out windows, William Denham navigated through an assortment of clutter strewn haphazardly across the chipped concrete floor. The air was filled with an eerie stillness, disrupted only by the quiet bubbling emanating from test tubes and beakers on weathered wooden workbenches. These vessels held mysterious concoctions subjected to the intense heat of bunsen burners, transforming their contents into a slowly thickening, grimy paste.

As Will's eyes attuned to the pervasive darkness, he saw half-filled bottles of acetone lurking in his path, scattered amongst heavy nylon sacks bearing labels, indicating the contents were iodine crystals. With every fumbling step, he winced at the acrid sting of the pungent solvents assaulting his eyes and nostrils.

Upon adjusting to the toxic bouquet of chemicals, Will was confronted by another assault on his senses – the overwhelming stench of decomposing food. The source of the putrid odour revealed itself as an overflowing garbage bin positioned beside a boarded-up door and the only exit from the small apartment.

The four others inside worked in silence under white sterile face masks, measuring different chemicals and decanting the contents of larger beakers into several smaller ones. They didn't notice Will walking behind them, inspecting them as they worked, and he knew they couldn't. Technically, he was not even there.

The room's contents suddenly dawned on Will with a chilling realisation as he surveyed the clandestine operation before him. Although he had limited knowledge of drug production, a surge of awareness informed Will that the chemicals being handled included volatile substances like lithium and red phosphorus, and he realised he was inside a meth lab. As Will passed one of the benches, a middle-aged worker, his face mostly covered by a white mask and engrossed in handling a clear liquid, abruptly looked up at an overflowing beaker. Attempting to traverse the room quickly, he stumbled over the disarray on the floor, colliding with a workbench. In an instant, a cascade of glass beakers toppled, their contents spilling uncontrollably, hurtling towards the exposed flame of a bunsen burner. The immediate consequence was a spectacle of azure flames engulfing the entire workbench, rapidly spreading with an unrestrained ferocity.

Before Will or the four workers could react, a sequence of chemical reactions unfolded with a menacing rapidity. The building convulsed in a deafening eruption, engulfed in a chaotic symphony of fire and rubble, leaving no room for escape.

In a jolt, Will catapulted awake, his body drenched in a clammy sheen of sweat, the echoes of a pained gasp still lingering in the dimly lit motel room in the city of Taree on the New South Wales Mid-North Coast. The musty air hung around him, accentuating the disoriented haze of his abrupt awakening. With a groggy slowness, he shifted in bed, reaching for the lamp on the bedside table. The feeble light revealed an old digital alarm clock, its luminous numerals proclaiming the hour of 4:45 a.m. He sank back into the pillow, the cool fabric offering a fleeting respite as he wrestled with the aftermath of what he just experienced. A fumbling hand roamed the sheets, searching for the air conditioning remote. The oppressive January night outside, laden with humidity, crept through the poorly ventilated confines of the roadside motel. The remote, entangled in heavily bleached white sheets, was eventually found, and Will activated the split system air conditioning unit, craving the relief of the cool air. He kicked his legs out from under the sheets, and knowing he would not fall back to sleep, he got up and headed for the shower.

***

It had been six months since Will's first premonitory vision, which began in the aftermath of a brutal attack on his way home from work. The unsettling premonitions had begun with obscure glimpses of the future, beginning with a haunting arson attack that claimed the life of an elderly woman. These precognitive episodes unravelled into a tapestry of horrifying scenes, leaving Will grappling with the mysterious nature of his newfound ability.

His confidant and best friend, Doctor Ravi Sandeep, a colleague at City South Hospital in Sydney, had earnestly attempted to dissect the phenomenon. Their collaborative efforts, however, yielded no tangible understanding. The visions persisted relentlessly, each more frightening than the last, occurring abruptly during deep sleep or inconveniently during daylight hours. His mind projected eerie clues in everyday objects, transforming them into something cryptically related to an actual future event, or he found himself thrust into a completely new environment. Each of these experiences was daunting and often confusing.

When they first began, the visions were a source of perpetual torment for Will, and Ravi ultimately had him committed to the psychiatric ward at the very hospital where they both worked. The evidence mounting in favour of Will's premonitions convinced Ravi, without a doubt, that something very unusual was happening to his friend. The more arduous task was convincing Aubrey Woods he had developed this new ability. Woods, the detective assigned to investigate his assault, showcased her competence when she arrested and charged all three offenders within days. She had a determined yet sensitive approach to her work; however, when Will confided in her, he was pushed away and labelled as crazy. Woods was finally convinced when his visions led to the safe recovery of kidnapping victim, Abby Sullivan. Will's continual persistence in proving his visions were accurate made him solely responsible for leading the police, with pinpoint accuracy, to where she was being held for ransom, allowing for her safe recovery. However, even after gaining Aubrey Woods' trust, she and Ravi were the only persons privy to Will's abilities.

Several months ago, Woods had transferred out of the Surry Hills Detective's office after taking a job at the Robbery and Serious Crime Squad of the State Crime Command under the experienced and burly Detective Sergeant Ian Yule. Woods had impressed Yule during her work on the Sullivan kidnapping. As soon as a vacancy on his team opened up, he made sure to give Woods the position.

That is what brought Will to Taree. Woods and her entire team, plus Will, travelled from Sydney in response to an urgent extortion investigation, which, thanks to him and a series of rather confronting visions, was now likely to be resolved in a few hours.

After she transferred to work under Yule, Woods discreetly introduced him to Will in a quiet little cafe in South Sydney, where she explained he was one of her most valuable informants. Will felt he made an interesting first impression on Yule. At twenty-eight years of age, he was scrawny, his frame draped in baggy clothing, and hiding his bony face was a mop of thick, black hair. While he thought Yule was not impressed with his appearance, it seemed that he trusted Woods and, after the meeting, she later explained that he would continue to act as a police informant.

Prior to the meeting, Woods told Will she had briefed Yule that he was a cyber whizz, privy to sensitive information, and had access to chat rooms via the dark web, which unscrupulous individuals used to discuss and brag about planned illegal activities. According to Woods, Yule was not tech-savvy enough to ask follow-up questions, and appeased; he agreed for their relationship to continue.

After this meeting, Will was told he could contact Woods when he had information. However, over the next several weeks, what was the most significant concern to her and the team was what Will saw occurring in Taree.

TWO

His friends and family had warned him about dealing with Shaun Neilson and his crew, but David Finnegan was desperate. His construction business was suffering, and the banks refused to extend his line of credit or offer a small business loan. He had to lay off his staff and was now working on his own, managing the physical labour and administration, often working eighteen-hour days. With the economy slowing and opportunities for high-paying work drying up, he had to accept simple and lower-paid jobs, mostly handyman work, and his income for the past six months was not even close to paying his mortgage and business insurance. He maxed out his credit cards and was quickly running out of options. He tried his best to shield his wife from the financial strain, but she realised something was wrong when her own credit cards were declined while buying groceries.

David Finnegan met with Neilson at his auto repair shop just south of Taree. A bulky thug of a man, who was probably on the books as a mechanic escorted him to an office above the busy workshop. The rumours surrounding Neilson's business suggested this man worked as an enforcer. Employed purely to reclaim debts and take care of anyone Neilson needed him to. The huge man, wearing a tight white t-shirt and covered almost head to toe in tattoos, wearing thick, gold jewellery, invited Finnegan to sit on a wooden chair opposite a desk too large for the small room while Neilson finished a phone call in the room down the hall. Finnegan squirmed in his chair and had second thoughts about the meeting, but before he could get up and leave, Neilson entered the office and took his seat behind the desk in a huge leather executive-style chair. When Neilson sat down, the weight of the enormous man tested its suspension, and it seemed to sink a few inches. The massive stomach of the fifty-year-old entrepreneur hung over his belt, and he was out of breath and sweating from what must have only been a ten-metre walk. He collected the sweat from his red forehead and ran it through his thinning grey hair, slicking it back before offering the same hand to Finnegan to shake. While repulsed, he reluctantly accepted it out of politeness.

'So what do you know about my business?' Neilson asked, leaning back in his chair and resting his hands on the back of his head. The sweat marks under the arms of his light blue business shirt almost ran the length of his torso.

'Well, I know you lend money to people,' Finnegan replied nervously. His fingers twitched, so he quickly put them in his pocket to conceal his nerves.

'No. I operate this auto shop, a panel beating company, a towing company, and also the fish and chip shop around the corner,' he said without subtlety or any attempt to hide his arrogance in correcting Finnegan.

After only a few minutes in his presence, Finnegan loathed the man. Still, he remained out of desperation, so he let him continue to stroke his ego.

'I do pretty well for myself,' Neilson said.

'Okay,' Finnegan mumbled.

'I'm not a bank. Now, who told you I would loan you money?'

'Just a rumour. I guess I heard it at the pub.'

'Hmm. Well, you're right, I suppose. I do occasionally offer small cash loans. Is that why you wanted this meeting?'

Finnegan entertained Neilson, but he had heard the man loved loaning money to people struggling to stay afloat as though he had the power of their fate in his hands. The rumours were he loved to exert his power and dominance over those who became completely financially vulnerable to him. He had also heard several horror stories about what happened to people who failed to repay their debts. In any normal situation, Finnegan could hold his own against someone like Neilson. He was thirty-three years old and fit, rippled with muscle from more than a decade of backbreaking labour, but in this meeting, he felt like a small child, completely isolated and hopeless.

'Honestly, yes, it is. My business isn't doing too well at the moment.'

'I see. How bad is it?'

Finnegan cringed at this question and paused for a moment. Neilson smirked, apparently getting off on seeing his distress.

'I just need a bit to pay some bills and get back on my feet. Just something short term.'

'Now you understand this is my own money, don't you? I'm not a charity, so I charge more interest than the banks. You probably already know that, I suppose. If you could get a bank loan, I imagine you'd be there instead of my office.'

'I've had some problems with the banks in the past.'

Neilson smirked again. 'How much do you want to borrow?'

Finnegan sighed before answering, '$40,000.'

Without a reply or even so much as a flinch, Neilson opened his top desk drawer, produced a bundle of paperwork, and slid it across the desk toward Finnegan.

'Standard contract,' he said.

Finnegan began reading the document while Neilson turned around and fumbled with the dials on a safe behind his desk. Finnegan got to the end of the contract and felt sick when he saw the rate of interest he would have to pay was 20% per month over the three-month loan period.

'I don't know about this. It's a lot of interest.'

'Well, you see, I'm taking a risk on you. You clearly have bad credit. No one else will loan you the money for a reason. You're a loser, Mr. Finnegan,' Neilson said as he placed a stack of hundred dollar bills on the desk. Finnegan's face went pale. He hated this man, but he needed him.

'You'll make weekly repayments, understand?'

'I don't know,' Finnegan said, avoiding eye contact.

'Well, the cash is there, take it or leave it, but my conditions are not negotiable.'

It didn't take long for Finnegan to decide to take the money. He thought of his wife, five-year-old son, and the house he would lose if he missed more mortgage repayments. With tunnel vision and thinking of only his short-term money problems crippling his family, Finnegan decided that this $40,000 would mend his immediate insolvency. He would then work as hard as possible to clear this debt quickly and quietly. What he failed to consider was the violent greed Neilson was capable of.

THREE

Just before leaving work at the hospital for the day, Will was finishing up his maintenance duties by fixing the last of several loose door hinges in the paediatric ward. Once he finished, and just as he was packing a screwdriver back into his toolbox, the vision came to him.

It came on fast and without warning, starting when he felt his knees buckle as he was forced into the dark night of his new surroundings. His mind was transported to an old gravel car park. He found himself kneeling next to a man who was also on his knees, and when he turned to look at him, all he could see was a mop of sandy-coloured hair covering the man's face as blood dribbled from his mouth. Looking down, he saw the man was wearing khaki cargo shorts with the logo 'Finnegan Construction Taree' on the left leg, near the knee where it met the gravel ground. The man wearing these shorts offered his hands outstretched in a plea, and his entire body trembled.

Will tried to stand, but his mind would not allow it.

'*Stand up,*' he said, urging himself to move, but he couldn't. He knew all he could do was stay kneeling and watch.

A large, muscular man with arms like tree trunks and covered in tattoos was standing over the top of the man beside Will, while a fat man in a baggy grey suit was standing nearby with a smirk on his face, smoking a cigarette.

'The first repayment was due yesterday. I'm surprised. I thought at least the first payment would be made,' the fat man said as he threw his cigarette butt at the kneeling man, hitting him in the arm. He flinched as it burnt his skin.

'I'm doing my best, I promise,' he said. 'I'm just not getting the work I thought I would. Please, I just need more time.'

The fat man smiled and nodded to his associate. Another powerful punch landed on the kneeling man's jaw, knocking him onto his back.

'Please,' he begged again as he winced and lifted himself back on his knees, his head hanging down toward the ground. 'I can get you the money.'

'Now, when we first met, I thought we sorted all this out,' Will heard the fat man say while he still tried to look past the kneeling man's shaggy hair to see his face.

'I know, but someone cancelled the work I had scheduled at the last minute, so I couldn't have prepared for that.'

'Not my problem,' he replied, his voice now raising.

Given up trying to identify the kneeling man, Will did his best to take in his surroundings, but all he could see was that he was in a car park with two cars in the distance. One was a ute, the other a dark sedan. The weather was warm, and the night was clear, but large, bright spotlights surrounded them, creating a glare and making him unable to see past the standing men. While he couldn't work out where he was, he thought maybe he was in the car park of a local sporting ground.

Since these bizarre visions started several months ago, Will had experienced enough to mask the fear and do his best to absorb as much information as possible. He had no control over what he saw or when, and all he could do was carefully observe and take in as much as he could. He could not always see everything he wanted, and while frustrating, the more complex and detailed the strange visions were, the more they exhausted him. So whatever he could see, no matter how limited, he tried to burn as much as possible to his memory.

The fat man continued. 'This is just a friendly reminder. Now, I'm going to give you some additional time. You have an extra four days, and we will have our money, with added interest, now an extra ten percent by the 14th. I am going above and beyond for you, so what do you say?'

'Thank you,' the kneeling man said, choking on the words.

Will shuddered in disgust at the torment he was witnessing.

'You're welcome,' the fat man said with a sly grin. 'Now, if the next payment is late, things will get much worse. We wouldn't want something to happen to your delightful little house, would we? Especially when your wife and boy are home.'

Before the kneeling man could speak, the muscular associate of the fat man kicked him in the chest with the underside of his boot, directly in his solar plexus, forcing him back on the ground again.

Will's head spun uncontrollably, and his vision became grainy. He quickly found himself back in the paediatric ward, on his knees and struggling to breathe.

'Are you okay?' A young and now startled girl lying in a colourful bed on the ward asked.

'Oh yes, I'm fine. I'm sorry. I just tripped,' Will replied anxiously as he caught his breath and looked at the ward's exit. He needed to get out and call Woods as soon as possible.

FOUR

Will rose to his feet, his face adorned with a forced smile as he acknowledged the children on the ward. A peculiar air enveloped the space as the youngsters diverted their attention to the disoriented maintenance worker, many of whom were now giggling at him. Silently, Will retreated from the room, ensuring he was out of sight before sprinting down the expansive hallway – his destination: a secluded and private area within the labyrinthine corridors of the hospital.

Alone at last, he fished out his phone with a sense of urgency. He dialled the number, and the device emitted a soft hum as it connected. Now devoid of the playful laughter from the children's ward, the hallway served as a silent witness to the clandestine call about to unfold. In this moment of solitude, surrounded by the hushed hum of the hospital, Will prepared to unravel what he had seen during the unsettling vision.

Woods picked up on the third ring. 'Hey Will, I'm just about to leave for the day. How are things?'

'Hey Aubrey, I was having a normal day until I saw something. If you know what I mean?'

Woods gasped, then replied in a hushed whisper. 'What did you see?'

'A guy wearing shorts with Finnegan Construction Taree written on them. He was getting roughed up by two guys. I think he owed them money, that's what they were talking about.'

'Taree? As in the town of Taree?'

'I guess. That's what was on the logo. I couldn't see his face, though.'

'Where was he?'

'All I know is that I was in a car park or something similar. It was dark, and I couldn't identify anything, but it looked like this guy was going to be in real trouble. He was getting knocked about a bit. But Aubrey, this one was different.'

'How do you mean?'

'I know what day it was. They told him he had to make a repayment before things got worse. He said he would give him four days, until the 14th, to pay whatever debt he owes. But today is the 9th, so I've worked it out, and I think what I saw just now will happen tomorrow night, the 10th. Then, four days from this incident, unless this guy pays, something bad might happen.'

'Hold on,' Woods said, 'Let me jump on the computer and do some checks. There may be some intel on our system. We might have an ongoing organised crime situation, or someone could have reported something about one of Finnegan Construction's employees.'

Woods searched the web browser for Finnegan Construction Taree and identified a low-budget website with basic contact information. The company, however, was based in Taree, as expected. The website listed the proprietor as David Finnegan, followed by contact information and his construction licence information.

'Maybe it's the owner, David Finnegan,' Woods said. 'I'll call him and see if he can tell us if he knows anything. Woods dialled Finnegan's phone number on the website. The call went directly to voicemail.

'You still there?' she asked.

'Yeah, I'm here,' Will replied.

'No luck with the phone. Is there anything else you can remember?'

'No, that's it.'

'Okay, hold on.'

Woods logged into the police database and began searching for any reports made by David Finnegan of Taree. There was nothing. She found a report on the system that he was involved in a minor car crash a few years ago, but there was nothing else.

'I'm not finding anything on my end, Will.'

'Damn, yeah, look, that's all I can tell you for now.'

'Okay, well, let me know if you see anything else. For now, there isn't much we can do. We don't even know who these people are, and for all we know, who you saw may not even be this David Finnegan.'

'I think I knew that when I called, but I needed to check,' he sighed.

'Absolutely. Take care, Will.'

***

Will changed out of his uniform and collected his bag from his locker. Before leaving, he walked past the psychiatric ward to see if Ravi was still in his office to debrief with him about what he saw, but he had left for the day. As he left the hospital alone, a pang of frustration echoed within him as he contemplated the limitations of his visions. The yearning for control gnawed at him, and he wanted to be more than a passive observer in his cryptic visions. He didn't want to be a mere spectator; he desired a stronger connection and mastery over his visions to provide Woods with a complete narrative of what he saw, not just puzzling tidbits.

FIVE

Another day passed, and Will did not have another vision. He did his best to forget what he saw yesterday, but he couldn't. His earlier vision taunted him. He knew something would happen to the mysterious man in the Finnegan Construction shorts, and he knew it would happen tonight, but without another vision, he felt frustrated and powerless.

When the weekend rolled around, Will slept late on Saturday morning. Having spent the previous night gaming online and losing track of time, he got to sleep after 2 a.m. and by the time he dragged himself out of bed, he made lunch instead of breakfast. His cramped little apartment in Sydney's inner south suburb of Surry Hills was steaming hot as the full strength of the summer's day was heating the building. The inside walls were hot, and the thick, carpeted bedroom and living room floor seemed to trap all the heat. All that relieved him was an old ceiling fan rattling with every rotation and the cool water from his shower.

After he ate a sandwich, Will showered and dressed in shorts and a singlet. He wandered back into the living room, closed the blinds to keep the glare and heat to a minimum, and sat in his old leather recliner. After mindlessly watching TV for a while, he switched it off and looked for his phone. He slowly lifted himself from the chair, but his shoulders were sweaty and stuck to the hot leather. As his skin peeled off the chair, he felt himself being dragged back into it as though weighed down by an invisible force. He tried to lift himself, but his head was forced back, and his eyes faced the white ceiling of his apartment and began to sting and water.

His eyes then shut, and Will was no longer in his apartment. He could hear trees gently rustling in the soft breeze, which was quickly interrupted by a low buzzing sound growing louder, and he could just make out a shadowed figure moving closer to him. As his vision focused, he saw a postal worker on a motorcycle wearing a yellow high-visibility shirt and helmet. On the back of the helmet, Will saw a bumper sticker that read, *'Taree Historic Motor Club Inc.'*

'Taree?'

The postal worker was on his rounds, dropping off mail in the letter boxes on the wide, tree-lined suburban street where Will found himself. He looked up and saw the street sign. It read 'Flores Drive.' The houses lining the street seemed identical, as though he was standing in a newly built estate.

His mind took him further down the street until it arrived at a house which looked exactly like each of the ones he had just passed – a red brick single-story house with a single-car garage and a small, neat garden out the front filled with brightly coloured flowers. All recently planted. A large bay window at the front of the house had its yellow curtains drawn open, but nothing was remarkable about the place. His eyes focused on the bay window while a man walked past carrying a small black pistol. It was a brief image, but there was no mistaking what he saw. Shortly after, Will heard a child crying from inside the house. At the sound of the crying, Will felt pressure tightening around his torso, followed by the feeling his waist was dragging him. The next thing he knew, he had been pulled to the inside of a house, standing in a modern-style kitchen with white cabinets and wooden countertops.

The same three people he saw days earlier in the gravel car park then surrounded him. This time, the fat man sat at a round wooden table in the centre of the kitchen with a crying woman and a child beside him. Next to them sat the man whom Will assumed to be the same one assaulted in the car park. Will now saw his face. Rugged and unshaven, with a broad jaw. His eyes, while glassy and red were filled with terror. Standing over him was the muscular man from the car park. He pointed a small pistol at the man's temple who started gently weeping in between panicked and shallow gasps for air. Bruises, both old and new, covered his face. Will guessed that some of the old cuts on his face, likely inflicted the other night, had reopened.

'You said I have until the 14th?' The man pleaded.

'Yes, but I thought I would just drop by to show you how serious I am,' the fat man said as he unbuttoned the first button of his white business shirt and fanned his sweaty, red face. He turned to face the woman holding the small child. She was petite, with long dark hair and thin arms which were trembling.

'Mrs. Finnegan, when I gave your husband money, it wasn't a gift. It was a loan. I am trying to run a business here, but things become complicated when repayments aren't made.'

The woman and child continued to cry.

'So what are we going to do now, Finnegan?' Neilson said.

'We will work something out. Just leave my family out of it. Please, I'm begging you.'

The fat man stood up. His smirk was now replaced with a look of fury. He slapped the cowering man with a powerful open hand palm to his face. It caused a red welt on the left side of his face. The woman yelped, and the child continued to cry.

'You brought them into your mess when you disrespected me. Our agreement was straightforward,' he spat.

Panicked quickly engulfed Will, but his resolve solidified. He needed to watch and listen carefully to learn more about this family teetering on the precipice of an ominous fate.

The fat man and his muscular associate, who was again wearing a white t-shirt that was too small for him but allowed him to show his bulky frame, seemed to enjoy their work. To Will, it looked as though they had been involved in these kinds of discussions many times before, and they carried themselves with a sense of authority and confidence. While it couldn't have been the first time they had been in these situations, he assumed it was the first time for this young family. This was the second time he had seen these two vile men, and things were escalating quickly. It was clear there was some debt involved, but he couldn't take his eyes off the terrified woman and child.

'Why did you let this happen?' the woman asked as she continued to sob.

'Because he's a hopeless businessman,' the fat man said as he pulled a gun out of his pocket and joined his associate in aiming it directly at the terrified man's head. 'Consider this your last warning. I'm a man of my word. I'll be back on the 14th before midday. You lose a kneecap if you don't have my money by then. If you go to the cops, your wife and boy will also lose one. Do not make them pay for your mistakes. Understand?'

'Ye.. yes,' he stuttered.

Will's head spun, and he was losing the ability to stay focused on what was happening. He tried to slow himself down by concentrating as hard as he could, but he was losing sight of the people in the room. The voices were becoming distorted, and the sound of the fat man was becoming warped and deeper. He could no longer make out what was being said. As his head spun faster, the dizziness built up, and he felt a wave of nausea wash over him just before his eyes snapped open. He was back in his leather armchair. He was trying to calm himself and control his breathing.

Will scrambled to his feet and fumbled for his phone. After a few rings, Woods answered, and he recounted all he had seen in this second vision, including the name of Finnegan he had just heard.

'Right, let me recheck the system,' Woods said. 'The team and I are on call and working the entire weekend, so hopefully, we can follow up on this. Flores Street is where our system records David Finnegan living, but there's still no report about any of this. But that's him, the owner of the construction company we found the other day.'

'Well, this is happening. The 14th, I'm sure of it.'

'That only gives us a little bit of time. And you're sure you saw the guns?'

'Absolutely.'

'Okay, I'll have to tell Yule and see what we can do. Technically, my team has jurisdiction over dangerous and urgent extortion matters like this, so I'm hoping we can stay on the case. Timing will be crucial too,' Woods said. 'Let me make some notes and put a plan together. I'll brief him first thing tomorrow morning.'

'What will you say?'

'Well, these types of matters usually involve some level of organised crime, and it sounds like this guy got himself in debt to some pretty serious people. I'll tell him you were chatting with some people on an online forum where they mentioned an illegal debt collection organisation in Taree. I'll say they were boasting about themselves online and are targeting a local. Unfortunately, these things aren't that uncommon, so it should work.'

'Okay. What else can I do?' Will asked.

'Nothing for now. Just sit tight. I'll call you tomorrow. Let me know if you see anything else.'

Will ended the call and rubbed his eyes. They were stinging, and he suddenly felt exhausted. Sinking deeper into his recliner, he sat in silence for what felt like hours, going over everything he had just seen, and hoping to see something else that would help Woods and her team before it was too late.

SIX

David Finnegan washed his face in the kitchen sink. He slowly dried himself with paper towels, carefully to avoid the swollen and tender parts of his face still aching from two separate beatings. His wife Marie and five-year-old son Zachary remained at the kitchen table, cuddled up to each other. The two men had gone, but the fear lingered in the house like a foul smell. Finnegan looked at his family and felt sick when he saw their frightened faces. Marie said nothing and stared at him in shock, disbelief, and contempt. He had not told her about the company's financial crisis, instead chose to deal with it alone. His decision was now evidently a mistake that may cost them their lives.

'I'm so sorry,' he said, still keeping his distance, unsure of how to proceed and whether he should try to console them physically.

'What have you done?' Marie said, still trembling and clutching Zachary.

Finnegan didn't respond and just kept his head down.

'What have you done?' she repeated with raw fury, now standing up and charging toward him. Still crying, she began hitting his chest and kicking his shins. Finnegan said nothing and accepted each strike from his wife, feeling he deserved the punishment.

'How could you do this? You borrowed money from them?'

'Yes, I'm sorry. I had no choice.'

'You had a choice. We could have borrowed money from my parents. Now, look at what you've done.' Marie soon ran out of energy and stopped striking her husband. Her adrenaline had crashed, and she collapsed on the ground, crying. Zachary ran over and consoled her. When Finnegan tried to put his arm around her, she brushed him away.

'Maybe you should stay with your parents for a while. I don't want you getting hurt,' he said. 'I'll come up with a way to get the money.'

'You need to call the police.'

'I can't call the police. They'll kill me. They'll kill you and Zac.'

Marie stood up, took Zachary by the hand, and led him into his bedroom. She began packing a bag of clothes.

'Marie, please. Talk to me,' Finnegan pleaded as he watched her pack a bag for herself once Zachary's was packed.

'Just leave me alone, David! I can't be around you right now.'

He gave up and let her continue packing. The damage was done, and he knew he couldn't change his wife's mind. It was his mistake, and he knew that. What was important to him now was to make sure they were safe, and deep down, he knew that leaving was their only option for now.

As Marie walked down the hallway to the front of the house, pulling behind a travelling suitcase on wheels, she turned to face her husband again.

'I'm going to speak to my parents about getting the money you owe.'

'I don't want them involved.'

'Well, they became involved when you didn't think about your wife and son! They will loan us the money to get out of this mess, and don't you dare say anything more.'

In her rage, Marie took Zachary by the hand and led him out the front. Two minutes later, they had the car packed and were gone without once looking back.

***

After a routine team meeting at police headquarters, Woods pulled Yule aside to update him on Will's recent encounter.

'I got a call from Will Denham,' she whispered.

'Yeah, what did he have to say?'

'He has some pretty reliable intel that a guy in Taree is being extorted. Apparently, the guy owes some money, and Will says they are going to visit him to collect it on the 14th. He said they are bringing guns, and it could get pretty nasty.'

'Who's the victim?'

'David Finnegan. He's a local builder from Taree. We have an address for him, and that's where this is going down.'

'What else did Will tell you?'

'He spoke to some people online. Apparently, he's in debt, and this crew were talking themselves up in an encrypted group chat, discussing how they would come down hard on the guy if he can't make his payments. Threatening him with a firearm. They were bragging about it.'

'What do we know about Finnegan? Involved in any sort of drugs, organised crime?' Yule asked.

'Not that we know of. He's a local builder. His phone has been going straight to voicemail, too.'

'What do you want to do?'

'I think we at least get up there, sit off the place covertly and wait and see what happens. Will's not wrong about this stuff. His intelligence is reliable. Trust me.'

'I do trust you. I don't know if I trust Will yet.'

'I know you've just met him, but let the previous successful information he's given speak for itself.'

Yule nodded. 'Fine. Brief the team and we travel up there in the afternoon of the 13th. I'm giving it one day. If it doesn't happen on the 14th, we leave, and you can get the locals to follow up with Finnegan to see if anything is going on.'

'Thanks, Sarge. It'll go to plan, you'll see. I want to bring Will up with us. He can bring his computer and give us live intel. It'll be easier than being on the phone.'

'As long as he stays away from the house. Get prepared to brief the team. You'll be running the show.'

SEVEN

The remnants of the explosive vision lingered in the recesses of Will's mind as he climbed out of the motel shower. Wearily, he pushed aside the heavy motel curtains on Crescent Avenue in Taree, greeted by the crisp morning light that leaked into the room. As he took a deep breath, the weight of anticipation settled on his chest, exacerbated by the looming date – the 14th, the day his premonition forewarned. The motel room, though modest, bathed in the morning sun, projected a deceptive tranquillity. The vibrant hues outside contradicted the ominous scenes etched in Will's vision. Despite being far removed from the hustle of Sydney, the town's main road proved unexpectedly lively, with a constant stream of passing trucks creating a distant hum that permeated through the thin windows.

Will took a chilled water from the mini fridge and drained the bottle. The cooling drink served as a brief respite, a fleeting moment of calm in the face of what was to come, but sitting on the edge of the bed, his anticipation intensified as he anxiously waited to hear from Woods.

A light knock echoed through the motel room a tad before 7 a.m., and Will moved to answer the door. There stood Woods, wearing light blue shorts and a crisp white singlet. Her usual pale face was flushed red, and she breathed heavily, evidence of her usual morning exercise routine. Woods was a year older than Will but bore a youthful appearance thanks to her healthy diet and regular exercise, something he had neglected over the years. While her presence carried a sense of professionalism and authority, she also had an underlying energy that hinted at her disciplined training regime. As she stood at the threshold, the unspoken weight of the impending day hung in the air, and the shared concern etched on her features mirrored Will's apprehension.

'Sleep well?' she asked, letting herself in.

'Yeah,' Will lied. He decided not to tell her about the explosion he saw overnight just yet. She had enough on her mind this morning.

'Good. I just went for a jog. I couldn't sleep. I'm just eager for this to resolve, so a run takes away some nervous energy.'

Woods removed her hair tie and carelessly combed her fingers through her long blonde hair as her kind, bright blue eyes looked directly at him.

'So I'm going to shower and then meet with Yule and the rest of the team to go over the final plans for the day. Are you okay to drive?'

'I guess so.'

'I want you to take my car,' she said as she handed him the key to a silver Toyota Camry. Wood's work car, which they shared on the drive from Sydney to Taree yesterday.

'I'm a little rusty, but no problems. What do you have in mind?'

Will had a driver's licence but never needed to use it. Truthfully, it had been years since he had driven a car, but Woods didn't need to hear of his anxiousness about being behind the wheel.

'In the next few minutes, drive down to Flores Drive and see if anything comes to you. I want you to see the scene in person to see if you can pick up on anything. But be careful, and don't get noticed. Keep your phone with you, too, but say nothing to Yule. He doesn't want you near there, but I need to know if you see anything else that may endanger the operation.'

'Okay. So what's the plan on your end?

'We will get there just after 8 a.m and wait. When we see the guys you described, we will stop them before they get inside. When we search them and find the guns, we arrest them for possession of the firearms and we take them away, cleanly and safely. Away from Finnegan and the house. We will then chat privately with Finnegan later in the day to find out what's happening. We'll do this after we have our two targets safely in custody.'

Will nodded. He thought it was a sound plan.

The car was parked directly behind his room in the main open car park area, however, the shape of the motel required him to walk along an old concrete walkway connecting the many ground-floor rooms, including Yule's. Although he didn't work directly for Yule, the man gave off a surly vibe and had an intimidating aura, so Will preferred to sneak past his room quietly to avoid being questioned.

After a ten-minute drive, Will found Flores Drive. It was a long, straight road, and as he slowly drove down, the street became very familiar to him from his vision only days earlier. As he arrived in the middle of the street, he saw two men get out of a black Mercedes parked on the side of the road. It was the two men from his vision. There was no mistaking the fat man wearing a sky blue business shirt and dark trousers, followed closely by the muscled associate, again in a tight, white t-shirt. Will panicked and swerved to the side of the road. Hitting the brakes hard and stopping the car about fifty metres away from them.

With a lingering sense of anxiety, he observed the two men crossing the street, hoping his sudden halt and display of reckless driving had gone unnoticed. His gaze remained fixed on them, nervously tracking their movements. The fat man assumed the lead, trailed closely by the bulky associate, who had his hands concealed within the folds of khaki cargo shorts. From his vantage point, Will watched as they marched up a concrete driveway, heading towards a house he immediately recognized as the Finnegan residence. The gravity of the situation settled heavily on his shoulders as he fumbled to extract his phone, his fingers navigating the keys with urgency. The air was thick with anticipation, and with each ring, the stakes heightened, the need for intervention pressing upon him as the scenario he had foreseen unravelled in real time.

'Pick up, Aubrey,' he whispered desperately.

The call went to voicemail.

He tried again. Will pleaded with her to pick up the phone. Whatever was going to happen inside the house was happening right now. He knew the fate of those inside hung in the balance, and each unanswered ring stretched into an agonising eternity.

The phone went to voicemail again, and he left an urgent message.

'Aubrey, you need to call me back! I'm at the house, and they are here!'

Will sat back in the seat, turned the ignition off, and tried to think of what to do.

***

Neilson banged hard on the Finnegan family's front door. When he received no answer, he continued even louder.

A short time later, David Finnegan answered the door, shirtless but still wearing his flannel pyjama bottoms. Before he could say anything, the bulky associate pulled out a silver revolver from the side pocket of his cargo pants and pointed it directly at Finnegan's forehead. He whimpered, and his knees buckled as he lowered himself to the ground at the threshold in complete fear and surrender. Neilson smirked as the gun tracked Finnegan to the ground.

'Get up!' Neilson demanded before walking past Finnegan and entering his home. The associate picked him up with one hand and pushed him through to the living room while pressing the firearm into the small of his back. The chilled kiss of the metal barrel made his legs tremble with each weak step.

Neilson entered the living room as though he owned the place, sat on the couch, and crossed his legs.

'For your sake, Mr. Finnegan, I really hope you have my money for me right now.'

EIGHT

As nervous tension coiled within him, Will remained in the car, his eyes darting anxiously as the two men disappeared from view and advanced towards the house. The gravity of the situation intensified, prompting him to dial Woods for the third time, his fingers moving swiftly over the phone's keypad. Woods finally picked up after several rings. A wave of relief washed over Will as the call connected.

'It's happening right now,' he blurted out. 'Not in a vision. Right now!'

'What?' she answered urgently, breathing hard into the phone.

'Yep, right now. Two men walking up the driveway. You need to get here urgently!'

'Did you see a gun?'

'No, but it's definitely them. One of them was wearing bulky cargo shorts, so I suppose there was enough room for a weapon. What do I do?'

***

Woods took a deep breath. This operation was her responsibility. She had to make a quick decision, and she knew that part of being an excellent investigator was adapting to unexpected changes and responding accordingly. They had no choice but to force their hands. Their tactics quickly changed. They could not stop the two men on the street anymore. They would have to go in and face at least one potentially armed offender.

'Okay, here's what we do,' Woods said. 'I need you to get away from there. Drive back here as fast as you can. Will, I mean that, as fast as you can. I don't want you anywhere near there if something happens.'

'Got it.' Will said, starting the car.

Woods continued as he drove. 'We will bust through the front doors ourselves. There's no time for any other plan, but to do this without a warrant, we need solid information that there is some emergency or breach of the peace there. Originally, all we knew was these two would visit Finnegan before midday. I'll tell Yule that you have now heard through your sources online that they went into more detail about their plans and will now collect their debt just after 7 a.m. I'll say they were bragging online about having a firearm. Okay?'

'Sure, I can back that story up.' Will replied.

'Once we leave to go to the address, use the motel phone to make an anonymous call to the police to say you saw two men with guns enter the Finnegan residence. They live at number 79 if you didn't know, okay? Our records on the family are up to date. We will have our radios on and will hear the job coming over the air. This is important because your anonymous call will support our probable cause to enter the house.'

'Yep, got it.'

Will drove back to the motel as quickly as possible and met Woods in the car park to return her keys. A few seconds later, Yule and the team were rushing to their cars, and without acknowledging Will, they got in and sped off.

'Remember the plan,' Woods said to Will as she tightened her belt, adjusted her firearm in the holster, and started the car. Just before she sped off, Woods watched Will run to the motel's small foyer and pick up the receiver of an old white phone stuck to the wall near some tourism pamphlets.

***

As Woods headed to Flores Drive, the urgent call came over the police radio. *'79 Flores Drive, Taree, a witness saw two men enter the property, one possibly in possession of a gun, crews to respond.'*

Woods smiled. *Nice work, Will.*

She knew Yule would have heard that over the radio, and now the team had grounds to burst into the property unannounced and without a warrant. Two local Taree Police car crews also responded urgently to the call and advised they would arrive in ten minutes, responding code red – lights and sirens.

Woods and her team would be there in less than five.

Each of the team's six members had their own unmarked police car. The original plan was to jam the two offenders on the street before getting close to the Finnegan residence, blocking any chance they would have to escape. Now, however, Woods and her colleagues raced in convoy to the address, knowing their unknown targets were already inside.

When they approached Flores Drive, they sped toward the house as quickly as possible and slammed on the brakes, across the driveway or on the front nature strip directly in front of the house. There was no time for a soft or subtle approach. They all threw open their car doors, slid into ballistic vests and charged toward the front door, guns drawn. Yule led the team, and just as they were grouping up at the door, they heard a piercingly loud scream from inside. With no hesitation, Yule leant back, used all his weight on his solid frame and drove the sole of his boot directly at the lock of the front wooden door, shattering it before charging inside. The team followed closely behind. They were in perfect formation, covering every part of the entry hallway, lined with happy family portraits of the Finnegan family while moving fast and efficiently toward the kitchen and living room at the back of the house.

Yule and Woods saw Finnegan first.

He was tied to a dining room chair in the living room. Rope fastened his hands behind his back, and he struggled against the restraints. Both fresh and older dried blood covered his swollen face, and he looked at the group of strangers who had forced their way into the house with guns aimed directly at him. His expression reflected pure terror.

'Police,' Woods whispered, presenting her badge.

'Outside,' Finnegan said with a pained groan, using his head to point toward the sliding glass doors leading to the backyard.

'Guns?' Yule asked quietly.

Finnegan nodded.

The team members took a deep breath while Woods grabbed the handle of the large glass sliding door. As quickly as she could, she threw it open, sliding it all the way back on its rails. Her heart pounded in her chest, anticipating the danger she would face outside.

NINE

The detectives burst through the open door out onto a wooden verandah. Half the team turned left, and the other half turned right.

Two men stood on the right-hand side of the deck in the far corner. One muscular man holding a small silver revolver and leaning on a BBQ, and the other, a shorter, fat man talking on a mobile phone. Their shirts were covered in small droplets of blood, speckling both of them.

'Police don't move!' Woods screamed. 'Drop the gun now.'

The muscular man holding the gun panicked and froze.

'Do it now!' she repeated, this time even louder.

Following the direction, he immediately relinquished his grip on the revolver in a panic. The metallic clatter reverberated through the tense air as the weapon thudded onto the deck, symbolising his surrender. Without even being told, the formidable-looking man dropped to his knees with his arms raised. Like a scared child, he offered no resistance.

'Now you,' she said to the fat man. 'Take the phone away from your ear and slowly place it on the ground.'

He also complied with the directions, but displayed an arrogant expression. As he lowered the phone, he gave Woods a sly grin before standing back upright, never breaking his gaze.

'Do you know who I am?' he asked, still staring at Woods.

'I don't give a shit who you are. You're both under arrest for an aggravated break and entering with a firearm. Guys, cuff them, please.'

Woods motioned to the members of her team to move in while she and Yule kept their firearms drawn and level at both men. The remaining four members of the team re-holstered and moved in to secure the arrests. They gave both men a frisk search, during which they found a black Glock 23 buried in the belt of the fat man, hidden beneath a large roll of fat. After handcuffing both men and securing the firearms, the team marched them down the stairs of the wooden deck to the grassy backyard and pushed them face down onto the ground. In the distance, the sirens of the approaching uniformed car crews responding to the initial radio call rang through the air.

Yule and Woods returned inside the house and untied Finnegan just as four local uniformed police arrived. After brief introductions, Woods explained they had been watching this house as part of one of their investigations and would take custody of the two offenders.

Yule said, 'I'll get you guys out into the backyard to help my team with the offenders. Keep them separated and take them in your caged trucks back to the station. Once we are done here, we will head back there.'

'No problem, do you need anything else?' one officer asked.

'Just an ambulance to check up on him,' Woods said, pointing to Finnegan, battered and bruised, still whimpering in the corner of the living room.

The uniformed officers used their radio and called for an ambulance before they left the house via the backdoor. Woods and Yule helped Finnegan stand up and walk to the softer lounge in the back of the living room.

'I'll get you some water,' Woods offered.

Yule followed Woods into the kitchen. While she was at the tap filling a glass, he helped himself to a clean glass from a cupboard above the stove.

'Great work, Aubrey. I have to be honest, I doubted Will's reliability, but he convinced me today.'

'Thanks, I told you he was the real deal. I'm just glad we got here before anything worse happened.'

'Yeah, and now they're going to put these two away for a long time, and as you know, with these types of stand-over extortion matters, people usually report things to the police when it's too late, so well done.'

'So I can report back to Will later?'

'Yeah, that's fine, but don't give him too much. We still have to complete our investigation, and it has to go before the courts. Just give him the basics.'

Woods returned to the living room and sat next to Finnegan. He finished his water and held the empty glass in shaking hands. Woods helped him put it back on the coffee table and introduced herself.

'An ambulance will be here soon, but I'd like to ask you some questions first. My name is Aubrey Woods. I'm a detective with the Robbery and Serious Crime Squad.'

Finnegan stared at Woods with a puzzled expression. 'How did you know what was happening? I didn't report anything. Was it my wife?'

'No, nothing like that; we just had a report about men coming into this house with guns. So why don't you tell me your name and what this is all about?' Woods took out a pen and notepad, anticipating being told what she already knew. However, she played down her team's involvement to keep up appearances with Finnegan.

'David Finnegan,' he said. 'I recently borrowed some money from Shaun Neilson. My business is tanking, and he offers small loans to people the banks won't lend to. So I borrowed $40,000 from him, but when I couldn't pay it back on time, he and that big oaf roughed me up. My wife found out, and she took my boy away to stay safe. They threatened them too.' Finnegan choked a little and then sobbed. His tears mixed with the blood on his face. Woods sat silently and waited for him to continue when he was ready.

'I really wish I never took the money, but I was desperate.'

'So what happened today?' Woods asked.

'Late last night, my father-in-law dropped over the money I owed them. That's what the bruise below my eye is from. He wasn't thrilled with me, and he let me know it, but he still bailed me out. They had to empty their savings to cover for me.' He paused and took another sip of water.

'I'm such an idiot,' he muttered.

'Look, it's over now. We have both of them in custody. You're safe. They can't hurt you anymore,' Woods said. 'What happened next?'

'Well, they came here today like I knew they would. I gave them the money, but it still wasn't enough. They said I owed them extra fees for *"their trouble"*. Because I was a bad customer, they said, and that they had to chase me for repayments continually. I had to pay another twenty grand. I gave them all I had, but it didn't stop them from roughing me up again and tying me to a chair.'

'Unfortunately,' Yule added. 'These types of people are all the same. Once they have you, they feel like they own you, and there's a good chance they would have kept stringing you along for a lot more money than that.'

Finnegan nodded. 'Can I call my wife?'

'Of course,' Woods replied, 'but the ambulance will be here soon. I want them to check you out. I expect they will take you to the hospital because you might have a concussion. Maybe she can meet you there.'

'I don't know if she'll even want to see me after what I've done.'

'You made a mistake. It's over now. I'm sure she'll come around.'

Moments later, an ambulance arrived, and after a quick assessment, they decided it would be best for Finnegan to be taken to the hospital. With the help of the two ambulance officers, he plodded back through to the front of the house and stepped over the debris of the once previously intact door, which Yule had all but destroyed with his size thirteen boots. Walking toward the ambulance, he hesitated a little as there was now a sizable crowd of local onlookers in the street trying to get a glimpse of what was happening. Woods told him to ignore it all and helped him into the back of the ambulance van. Inside the van, they attended to Finnegan's cut face and neck, patching him up. Before the ambulance left, Woods informed him that she would take a formal and more comprehensive statement once he was released.

'Aubrey, these two are now in the docks at Taree police station. Let's meet up there and get them interviewed and charged. Good work again,' Yule said.

'See you back there. I'm just going to give Will a call.'

Woods walked through the crowd of nosy neighbours and got in her car, where she dialled Will's number once her phone connected to the Bluetooth.

'Are you okay?' Will said as soon as he answered the call.

'I'm fine, Will, it's all over. We arrested both of the men you had been seeing, and it turns out Finnegan was being extorted, just like you said. Also, Yule's pretty pleased with you.'

'Is Finnegan okay?'

'He's fine, but I'd hate to think about what would have happened if we never got to him. I suspect they were just going to keep extorting him. He was a simple family man and an easy target. It could have gotten far worse, especially for his wife and son. So thank you, Will, you did great.'

'Thanks, Aubrey. And thank you for trusting me. So what are you doing now?'

'Well, we will interview these two, and we plan to charge both of them. They won't be able to go near Finnegan for a long time. Still, I will recommend he move far away as soon as possible. Plus, it won't take long for the whole town to discover what happened, and his family could do without the rumours. Anyway, we may be here for a while. Are you okay to wait around for a lift back?'

'Oh, don't worry about me, I'll take the train.'

'Are you sure?'

'Yeah, I find them peaceful. I might head to the station soon. I need to be back at work tomorrow.'

'Okay, no problems. Well, thanks again, Will. You were incredible today. I'll talk to you soon.'

TEN

The train rocked Will into a hypnotic, sleep-like trance on the long ride back to Sydney until the loud, high-pitched squeal of the brakes startled him wide awake. As he walked back home in the afternoon heat, he felt his t-shirt stick to his back, and the bright summer sun pierced his eyes with a sharp glare as he shook himself loose from the sweaty shirt. There was not a cloud in the sky, and Will knew how hot his old one-bedroom unit would be, having sat for nearly two days without so much as a window open, so he detoured and headed for City South Hospital at the far most southern edge of Surry Hills to catch up with Ravi before he finished for the day.

The ten-minute walk felt exhausting, primarily because of the heat, but the walk from Central Station was mainly uphill. As he approached the hospital, he saw the fantastic modern building bustling with energy. The main entrance doors were continually opening and closing as foot traffic came and went, and the ambulance bay saw a frequent rotation of vans, which was not unlike a busy taxi rank.

The hospital recently promoted Will to assistant maintenance manager, which came with a slight pay rise and the ability to control the roster for more balanced shifts. A few months ago, Ravi also received a promotion in the hospital's psychiatric unit, which gave him a larger office and moved him into a position where he, too, had greater decision-making capabilities.

This promotion also allowed a new resident psychiatrist to take Ravi's old position on the gruelling graveyard shifts.

Navigating through the bustling main patient entrance of the hospital, Will slipped past the frantically busy triage team. The flurry of medical professionals attending to urgent cases prevented any notice of his arrival, allowing him to move forward without pausing for obligatory exchanges. Continuing past the waiting room, Will made his way through the extensive expanse of the hospital, heading towards the rear of the building, where a long, sterile hallway led to the psychiatric ward. Without his hospital maintenance master key, he approached the security door leading into the unit. A button press on the bell served as a signal, prompting him to look up at the security camera overhead. With a subtle hum and the discernible sound of locks disengaging, the heavy door unlocked.

Entering the ward, Will encountered the security guard stationed there – a burly man named Bob with a broad nose and a thick beard whom Will had known for years. He carried a constant smile that accentuated his crow's feet. A silent acknowledgement passed between them, recognising the routine nature of this interaction. Bob's role was clear: ensure that no one left the ward without the explicit direction of the medical staff within. This initial checkpoint marked the beginning of Will's journey into the controlled environment of the psychiatric unit.

'Hey, Will, what are you doing here?' Ravi said as he paused his conversation with the nurse at the front counter. Ravi was of Indian descent and in his early thirties, and like Will, he was tall and thin. Disregarding the traditional doctor's lab coat, he wore a blue shirt and tie with grey trousers.

'Hey Ravi, I just wanted to say hi. Maybe we can chat in your office?'

Ravi entered his office first and sat on an oversized black chair behind a thick mahogany desk. Will took a seat opposite the desk.

'I just got back from Taree on a job with Aubrey,' he said.

'Oh, you went away with the police?'

'Yeah, she wanted me on the scene just in case, but they arrested a couple of people for a home invasion and extortion.'

'That's great, Will,' Ravi said as he unlocked his top desk drawer with a key he always kept in his pocket and produced a small red leather notepad.

This was the notebook Ravi used to document every vision Will had. To catalogue them, and try to understand more about what was happening inside his mind. So far, all he felt like was a glorified note taker as nothing was evident about what was causing the visions. All prior testing upon Will, including several MRIs, proved inconclusive. What interested Ravi, however, was the time between visions, their clarity, and whether they were presenting as dreams or if they were happening during the day. Will recalled each vision involving David Finnegan while Ravi wrote notes and occasionally paused thoughtfully.

'So that's about it,' Will said. 'The police think Finnegan would have continued to be extorted.' It could have ended badly for his family, but Aubrey tells me they will be put away for a long time.'

'Aubrey must be happy.'

'She was, and so was her boss. I think he's starting to trust me, even though he knows nothing about the visions.'

'Brilliant, Will. Congratulations,' Ravi said as he re-capped his pen after finishing his notes. He fumbled with his thick glasses, pushing them further up the bridge of his nose. 'What about headaches or fatigue after the visions?'

'Fatigue, yes, but nothing unusual.'

Ravi locked the diary away and straightened his tie while he looked back at Will.

'Hey, Ravi, while I was away, there was another vision.'

'Oh?' he said, reaching once again for his book.

'Yeah, but wait to write this one down. I'm still trying to figure it out. I haven't told Aubrey anything, either. I will soon, but she's still busy at Taree, and I don't have much information yet.'

Will wrestled with the memory of the vision involving the chemicals and an impending explosion. Frustration and helplessness settled upon him as he attempted to recall the intricate details without being able to discern any solid information about where or when the explosion would occur. Will's frustration soon echoed a sober truth – there wasn't much he could do unless further revelations unfolded within his visions. He was simply caught between the desire for more clarity and the stark reality of his constrained visions.

'You'll let me know if you see anything else?' Ravi said.

'Yep. I'm back to work tomorrow, so I'll see you then.'

'I'll be here. See you tomorrow. Nice work again, Will. Really, well done.'

ELEVEN

Will woke the following morning at 7 a.m. to the sound of his phone's alarm. He quickly dressed in his maintenance uniform, gathered his bag, and left his building on foot for the short walk back to the hospital.

In his new role as assistant manager, he began his morning duties with a sense of purpose. His first task involved delving into the overnight maintenance log containing reported issues and repairs that awaited his attention. Swiftly scanning the report, he assigned his team members to various hospital sections requiring their expertise and reserved a task for himself: a faulty elevator stuck in the basement. He gathered his tools from the maintenance shed next to the rear loading dock, and choosing the fire escape stairs, Will descended into the dimly lit basement.

Although the heatwave continued above ground, the basement remained cool because of the surrounding damp rock wall. Three elevators fed to the basement from the right wing of the hospital, and Will found the faulty one quickly enough as someone had stuck a post-it note to the door and written *'fix me'* on it in red pen. He set down his tool bag and opened the doors with a crowbar to get a better look.

When he applied force to the doors, a strange rush of smoke and intense heat forced him back. Will closed his eyes and coughed, and when he opened them, he found himself inside the same dirty drug lab he first saw a little over a day ago. A series of small explosions happened around him as the highly flammable chemicals leaked over the floor, causing the fire to spread so fast that there was no way anyone could escape. The four workers inside scrambled as best they could, but debris and the rapidly growing fire blocked their only way out. Piercing screams of pain and terror ran a cold shiver up Will's spine as all he could do was watch. Less than a second later, the building exploded with a loud bang, and the powerful force lifted Will off the ground. For a fraction of a second, he felt weightless until he found himself at least thirty metres away from the burning old granny flat, standing in the driveway of the main house in front of it, watching as the roof caved in and the pungent chemicals continued to burn. It was pitch black, and an eery silence filled the night, broken only by the crackling of burning metal and wood.

The flames destroying the small granny flat showed no signs of easing, and Will knew it would only be a matter of time before the fire spread or another explosion happened when the flames reached another drum of chemicals.

He stood still in horror as the screaming eventually stopped.

He knew everyone inside was dead.

Will's vision pushed his eyes down at the ground. He saw a burnt piece of paper in his hand. He picked nothing up from inside and didn't know how he came to possess it. He looked down, and he saw it was a sealed and stamped envelope. Despite being mostly destroyed, he was able to identify the receiving address - '46a Newington Street, Sefton, NSW.'

As soon as Will read the address, his eyes flew open and he locked his gaze on the silver doors of the basement elevator. He quickly collected his tools and left the elevator. He would re-assign this job to another team member later. For now, he needed to speak with Ravi.

He sprinted up the stairs and exploded into the hallway, heading straight for Ravi's office. This time, instead of ringing the buzzer, he used the keys on his belt clip to let himself inside the psychiatric unit. Without so much as a glance at the security guard watching the door, he ran down the hallway, past the ward, and found Ravi's office door open. He entered without knocking and slammed the door behind him. When Ravi heard the door slam behind him, he was startled, and glanced up from his laptop, looking slightly irritated.

'Will, I have to see a patient in a minute. What's wrong?'

'Another vision, just now, the same explosion,' Will said as he gasped to catch his breath.

'Slow down,' Ravi said, now fully alert and ready to give his full attention. Here sit. What did you see?'

Will spent the next five seconds inhaling as much oxygen as he could before he continued.

'I know where the drug lab explosion is. It's in Sefton, not too far from here. I have to call Aubrey and let her know.'

'You saw the address?'

'Yes. It was nighttime too, so fortunately, we've got time.'

'How do you know it's tonight?'

'I don't, but I can't risk it. Can I call her from here?'

'Yeah, of course. What exactly did you see?'

Will walked through his recent vision step by step in as much graphic detail as possible. When he finished, Ravi simply said, 'Call her now,' and slid the phone toward Will.

He left the office to go see his patient and closed the door, leaving Will to make his call in private. After a few rings, Woods answered.

'Where are you?' Will said before Woods could even greet him.

'Whoa, hold up. What's this all about? I'm still in Taree, chasing down a few more loose ends. What's with you?'

'I didn't want to say anything yesterday because we were busy with Finnegan, but I had a vision while we were away. It was a drug lab exploding and killing four people inside. I saw it again just now, except now I have the address, and we've got to do something.'

Will finished recounting his vision with as much detail as he gave to Ravi while Woods listened without interrupting.

'So what do we do?' Will asked.

'Well, I'll be up here all day. Let me make a couple of calls, though. I'll get in touch with the Chemical Operations Team. They are the ones who manage meth labs.'

'I just hope they can get there as soon as they can. I don't know when this lab is supposed to explode, but I know it was dark, so it could be tonight.'

'Don't worry, I'll pass on the information and they will bust in and arrest whoever is inside and pull apart the lab carefully before anything happens.'

'Okay, thanks, Aubrey,' he said, and a sense of relief washed over him, knowing that Aubrey would do something to prevent the impending disaster.

TWELVE

W hen she ended the call with Will, Woods advised Yule of this information and called the Chemical Operations unit team leader, who works within the Drugs and Firearms Squad. Detective Sergeant John Plume took all the details and advised he would send a chemical diversion team to the address to look for any signs of a meth lab in operation. The team had extensive training in recognising signs of a clandestine lab in operation and would be best equipped to respond accordingly. Coupled with what Woods advised was reliable intelligence, the team would have a walk-up start in making significant arrests and keeping a lot of dangerous drugs off the streets. Before ending the call, Woods warned Plume about the reported instability of the lab, based on the informant's intelligence and suggested it would be safer to investigate during daylight hours.

Plume replied nonchalantly and sounded slightly irritated, 'Detective, all labs are dangerous and highly volatile. We deal with nasty chemicals on a daily basis but we are well trained and well equipped to manage it.'

'Just be careful, is all I'm saying.'

Plume ended the call before responding.

***

Just after 8 p.m, and concluding their previous job, Detective Sergeant Fredericks, a stocky middle-aged man with a thick moustache and thinning black hair, addressed his team. 'I just received some information. We need to stop by an address at Sefton and look at a possible meth lab. Apparently, there's a pretty large-scale operation with as many as four workers currently working inside. Lots of chemicals may be involved, so we will wear all our safety kits. Let's check out the address and take it from there.'

His team of five jumped into two separate vans and made their way to their new job. About twenty minutes later, they slowly turned onto Newington Street at Sefton and crept toward number 46a. As they neared the neighbouring address of number 44, Fredericks identified a middle-aged man leaving a late model white Toyota Camry, which was parked outside the main house of number 46, a large two-storey double brick house. He walked down a long driveway toward what Fredericks assumed was number 46a, the small unit at the back of number 46.

'Did you see that?' Fredericks said to Detective Phil Jones, a thin, thirty-year-old investigator with spiky blonde hair and the newest member of the team sitting in the front passenger seat of the van.

'Yeah, I did; he's carrying an enormous bottle of acetone.'

'Yep thought so.'

Frederick picked up the police radio, which was tuned to a private back channel used by his chem ops team.

'Team, gear up! We are going in. We have sighted an unknown Asian male carrying a large bottle of acetone. The intel has been confirmed, and it is highly consistent with manufacturing methylamphetamine.'

'Copy that,' was heard repeated over the radio several times by the rest of the team.

Within two minutes, the team assembled at the top of the driveway, clad in full protective hazmat suits that shielded them from the potential hazards contained with meth labs. The air crackled with a silent tension as each member, armed and determined, drew their guns. In unison, they began a disciplined march, navigating the long concrete driveway with a precision that bespoke their training.

At the bottom of the driveway, Fredericks addressed his team one more time. 'We knock and announce our office. As soon as they open the door, we verify it is a lab. Once we have visual confirmation, we secure everyone and clear the place. Yes?'

The team nodded in unison.

The team, led by Fredericks, approached the front door of the granny flat. He knocked loudly on the door.

'Police! Open the door now!'

Nothing.

'Police! Open the door!'

Fredericks heard some shuffling from inside the unit and took a step back from the door. A few seconds later, the old door opened slightly, getting caught in the amount of garbage inside. A small, frail-looking Asian male stuck his head out of the small opening.

'Hello,' he said nervously and barely audible in a thick Mandarin accent.

Fredericks ignored him and peered past him into the flat, locating what he confirmed was a well-established meth lab. Barrels of chemicals covered the floor, and beakers bubbled under bunsen burners.

'You're under arrest for manufacturing prohibited drugs,' he said, responding to the scene immediately as he reached through the door and pulled the male outside.

A sharp yelp escaped the man, fracturing the eerie silence that had enveloped the scene. The unexpected sound rippled through the air, creating a stir within the unit. From within the confines of the structure, a loud rummaging ensued.

The sudden disturbance added an element of unpredictability to the unfolding situation, and the remaining members inside began rummaging around quickly inside, casting a shadow of uncertainty over the hazmat-clad team as they braced themselves for the unknown. The air crackled with a blend of anticipation and apprehension.

'Get in and clear it quickly. There are more people inside,' Fredericks directed.

They pushed through the door to find three more people inside, now trying to hide amongst the putrid rubbish and large empty bottles. The room was poorly lit, and the team used their torches to light it up. The lab was large, probably able to produce a very high volume of methamphetamine, and while it wasn't the most disgusting lab they had seen in terms of poor hygiene, it was close.

As the team quickly made their way through the lab, charging toward the workers, one of the male cooks panicked and knocked over a highly flammable substance on a table, right next to a lit bunsen burner.

The following happened in an instant.

The table caught fire, and it followed the trail of clear liquid as it poured onto the concrete floor. The intense flames stretched along the floor and toward several large drums containing flammable liquids. Before anyone in the room could react, the first explosion happened, pursued by the second and then a third. Within five seconds, fire engulfed the entire unit, and the roof caved in from the largest of the several explosions.

The sudden eruption shattered the stillness, and a devastating force engulfed the chem ops team in an instant. The violent aftermath bore witness to a tragic and instantaneous fate as the lethal impact claimed the lives of each member. Simultaneously, the three meth cooks within the unit met a similar grim end.

The devastation continued as Fredericks and the man he had forcibly removed from the studio apartment met a harrowing fate. A fireball erupted with ferocious intensity, obliterating the area around the front door.

THIRTEEN

Laying in bed, Will tossed and turned in frustration, unable to sleep. The heat in his apartment and his distracted mind prevented him from falling asleep. He got up and went out to the living room, where the large ceiling fan would hopefully provide some relief. After carelessly flopping back onto his recliner, he found the remote under the cushion and turned on the TV. It was nearing 11 p.m., and the late-night news was just starting. The news anchor began the broadcast with breaking news from South West Sydney, reporting that an explosion at a suspected drug manufacturing laboratory had resulted in the deaths of five police officers and four civilians. It was a brief story, as the details were still emerging, and they were unable to release the names of those who died in the accident. The tragic report ended with a short and grainy video file captured on a mobile phone, which a neighbour filmed showing the small granny flat completely ablaze and its walls destroyed, accompanied by the background noise of frightened bystanders screaming in a horrified panic.

A jolt of recognition surged through Will as he fixated on the house displayed on the TV screen. It was unmistakable – the house where he had orchestrated the police dispatch. The eerie familiarity of the setting, now presented on the television, sent shivers down his spine. The consequences of his actions, now broadcasted on the screen, made him feel sick.

He clutched at his stomach while his head spun, trying to process everything he saw. Although the inside temperature of the apartment was uncomfortably hot, Will felt stone cold. Confronted by the undeniable truth that the tragedy was a direct consequence of his actions, he felt the weight of guilt bear down on him. In a desperate attempt to comprehend the scope of the repercussions, Will forced himself to revisit the vision in his mind. The scenes played out like a haunting reel. Trembling and overwhelmed, tears welled up in his eyes. There was no denying it. He knew his vision, and his subsequent reaction to it, sent those police officers to their deaths.

He took out his phone and dialled Woods immediately. He didn't even know what he was going to say, but he needed to hear her voice. As soon as she answered, he could tell from the fragile tone of her voice, she too had heard the news.

'Will, I don't know what to say,' she said, her voice breaking.

'It's all my fault,' was all Will could muster.

'Will, please don't say that.'

'No, Aubrey, don't. It's my fault. If I had never said anything, all those people would still be alive.'

Woods said nothing, but Will could hear her breathing becoming laboured.

'Why did they go in at night?' Will asked. 'I told you the explosion happened at night.'

'I don't know, Will. They had all the information.'

'Did you know any of them?'

'No, I didn't, but I know people who did. From what I heard, they were great cops.'

Overwhelmed by the weight of his culpability, Will gasped and rushed to the bathroom, leaving his phone behind in the living room. The urgency of his emotions manifested physically, and he vomited into the toilet. After the heaving subsided, he splashed water on his face, attempting to regain composure. The reflection in the mirror betrayed the toll the events had taken on him, his eyes still clouded with tears and his face etched with the weight of remorse.

Returning to the living room, he picked up his phone but didn't speak.

'Will, listen to me very carefully,' Woods said. 'This is not your fault. You gave me the information about what you saw, and a terrible accident happened. You can't blame yourself. There is always an enormous risk going into these types of situations.'

'I can. And I will. I need some details, Aubrey. Please. What else do you know?'

'Honestly, not much at this stage, and we may never know how the explosion happened with no survivors to interview, but Will, these labs are so dangerous, and the team would have known that.'

'What if me sending them there actually caused the explosion? Had I not said anything, everything might have been okay.'

'No, Will. We aren't going to do this, and you can't think that way. Listen, let's talk more face to face. I'll be back in Sydney tomorrow by lunchtime. Let's meet up, have some food, and talk through everything. I can't let you blame and punish yourself for this.'

Will didn't reply. His phone was six inches away from his ear, but he was miles away in his mind.

'Will, can you hear me? Will?' Woods said desperately.

He dropped the phone and sank back into his chair. He had never felt this distraught and lifeless before.

FOURTEEN

In the early afternoon of the following day, Will was alerted to the loud ringing of the buzzer in his apartment. In the later hours of the morning, he must have dozed off while still sitting in the armchair and standing up, his back and neck felt stiff. The shrill sound of the buzzer continued, and it shattered the stillness, rousing him from what had likely been an unintentional nap. Upon waking, reality crashed back with brutal force, the weight of the previous night's tragic news hitting him anew. A groan escaped him as the persistent ringing of the buzzer echoed through the apartment. Slowly, he peeled himself from the chair.

'Yeah,' Will groaned, pressing down on the talk button.

'Will, it's Aubrey. Can I come up?'

'No, I don't want to talk about it.'

'Please, come on, let me up.'

Will released the talk button slowly, dragged his feet away from the door back to his armchair, and collapsed in it. He let out a heavy sigh and wished he was back asleep, but with the moaning buzzing in the background, he knew sleep wouldn't come. Woods rang the buzzer for another five minutes while Will remained consumed in his grief, with no intention of moving from his chair.

Woods's attempts to reach Will extended beyond the buzzing intercom as the day unfolded. Text messages and voicemails peppered his phone, each plea for a response going unanswered. Ravi, concerned by Will's absence from work, joined the chorus of attempts to make contact. Each call met the same fate – unanswered and ignored. Will's retreat into his armchair became a refuge from the outside world as he neglected food and human contact in a continual self-punishment.

***

Ravi's growing concern deepened as the second day passed without a sign of Will at work. The gravity of the situation had become palpable, especially after a detailed update from Woods on the traumatic events that unfolded. The graphic details sent shivers down Ravi's spine, and he couldn't fathom the impact it must have had on Will. After several unanswered calls and text messages, Ravi decided to check up on Will. With no more appointments in the day, he left the hospital and made the quick trip to Will's apartment. From the street, he glanced up at the second floor and noticed that Will had closed his street-facing window and pulled the curtains shut. Ravi sighed and pressed the buzzer for his apartment.

Will didn't respond.

He buzzed again, this time holding it down for ten seconds.

There was still no answer.

He was getting more anxious with every passing second, waiting for a response. Woods had told him how devastated Will was when he received the news – blaming himself and refusing to speak further about it. Until Will was ready to acknowledge his grief, Ravi knew the pit of self-torment and pain would be relentless.

He tried to open the double glass doors at the front of the building, but he found them locked. Ravi then circled the building, hoping to find an open window to call out to Will, but he discovered everything was locked up tight. After he completed a full lap of the building, he buzzed again. As he neared the intercom system, another resident from within the building came out, and just before it locked shut again, Ravi stuck his foot in the door and entered. He walked up the stairs and knocked loudly on the door.

'Will, it's Ravi. Come on, open the door.'

Ravi heard Will groan from the other side of the door. 'Ravi, go away,' he mumbled. 'I don't want to talk to anyone.'

'I'm not leaving until you open the door.'

'I just want to be alone,' Will said from behind the closed door.

'Come on, just let me inside. I'm worried about you, and Aubrey is too. Come on, open up. Have you slept much or even eaten in the last few days?'

'A little,' Will said, opening the door.

'Geez, Will,' Ravi said as he looked him up and down before letting himself inside.

The neglect that had settled over Will in the past few days manifested in the visible toll it took on him. His dishevelled appearance told a story of physical exhaustion. Greasy strands of hair obscured most of his face, even more so than usual, and the dark, swollen bags under his eyes betrayed the restless nights he had endured.

'Let's open the windows. A little natural light will be good for you.'

Ravi drew the living room curtains and lifted the window as a gust of warm, but welcomed fresh air entered the apartment. Will returned to his armchair, slumping down and saying nothing.

Ravi surveyed the small unit and witnessed a scene of disarray unfolding before him. Clothes lay strewn across the floor and coffee table, and food wrappings were scattered about, another testament to Will's current state of mind. An empty bottle of bourbon stood as a witness to the solitude Will sought within the confines of his apartment, and Ravi couldn't help but feel the weight of his friend's pain.

'How much have you been drinking?'

'I don't know,' Will mumbled.

Ravi dusted off some crumbs from the couch and sat opposite Will.

'Aubrey told me everything that happened. But you know deep down it's not your fault. Aubrey has told you that, and you know it. I know you are hurting, and I understand why you are in pain. I truly do. But doing this to yourself will not help. You can't stay locked up in here.'

'Five police are dead, Ravi,' Will said, choking on his words.

'I know.'

'With everything that's happened since I started getting these visions, I promised myself I would never ignore one again, but I don't know what I'm supposed to do now. Everything I thought was good about what I do has now turned to shit. Every time I close my eyes, I see them, Ravi. Five innocent police officers, all dead because of me. Now that vision of the drug lab constantly replays itself in my memory, mixed with the news footage. I can barely take it.'

Will clenched his fists, and his eyes flooded with tears.

Ravi sighed and gripped Will's shoulders. 'You have an incredible gift, Will, and you've helped so many people. You need to remember all the lives you've saved.'

'I saw the explosion at night. I told them to go in during the day. Why didn't they just go during the day like I said?'

'You have no control over how they would respond to what you saw. You did everything right.'

'I don't want another vision. I'm done. And you need to leave.'

'You know as well as anyone you can't control what you see.'

'Leave, Ravi. Please.'

'I can't leave while you are like this. I'm worried about you.'

'I'm not going to hurt myself, if that's what you mean. But I'm staying here and ignoring anything I see. I have plenty of sick leave at work, so it's fine.'

'Can I come back tomorrow?'

'What for?'

'Just to hang out.'

Will sighed. 'I guess.'

'What's for dinner tonight?'

'I'm not hungry.'

'I'll order you a pizza and have it delivered here.'

Will shook his head. 'Bye, Ravi, see yourself out.'

Ravi thought about protesting but stopped himself. He knew Will just needed time to heal.

FIFTEEN

The following day, Ravi returned to Will's apartment building after work. Looking up at his unit, he saw the living room window had been closed again, and the curtains pulled tightly across. When he rang the buzzer, Will answered almost immediately, not by a greeting, but by simply unlocking the front door. When Ravi heard it click open, he pushed through and walked up the stairs to the unit.

The apartment was still dark and had a pungent stench, so Ravi repeated what he had done the previous day by walking straight over to draw the curtains and open the window, while Will didn't budge from his armchair.

'How are you feeling today?'

'About the same,' Will responded, not looking back at Ravi. 'Aubrey tried calling me last night, but I couldn't speak to her.'

'She cares about you. She's just checking in.'

'It doesn't change what I did.'

'Will, I heard there will be a memorial for the police officers tomorrow. I'd like you to go. I think paying your respects and getting some closure will be good.'

'That'll be hard for me.'

'I know it will be, but I want you to be able to move on properly. You can't dwell on this. Did you sleep last night?'

'Not really?'

'What about eating?' Ravi asked as he glanced down at the coffee table in front of Will and saw the open box of the pizza he had ordered for him yesterday. One slice had about two bites taken out of it.

'I'm not hungry.'

Ravi sighed. 'You need to eat, Will.'

Will crossed his arms and gazed toward the floor without responding.

'I want to give you some tablets to help you,' Ravi said.

'What?'

'Citalopram. It's an antidepressant?'

Will shook his head. 'I don't need them.'

'You have suffered a hugely traumatic experience for which you are blaming yourself. You need to sleep and eat, and you need to rebalance your mind. I only want to give you a low dose, but it will help. It won't solve everything, but it's a start. You still need to get out and seek some closure.'

'Fine,' Will said.

'I'd love to see you back at work.'

'I've already spoken to them. I'm taking the rest of the week off.'

'How about we hang here for the night? Eat some food together and play some games? I have my laptop and we can sync it up to your PC. We only need to talk about what happened if you want to.'

'Yeah, alright, that'd be good, but I don't want to talk about what happened.'

Ravi nodded and handed Will a box of Citalopram with his name already printed on the prescription label.

'That's fine. And don't worry – no one at the hospital needs to know about this prescription. The records remain locked in my unit. It's between you and me. Doctor-patient confidentiality. I just want to see you get better.'

Will's eyes watered. 'I don't want to feel like this anymore.'

'I know,' Ravi said sympathetically, patting his shoulder.

He took a sip of old water from a glass on the coffee table, swallowed the first of the tablets, and then got up to grab some drinks from the kitchen.

After about an hour of gaming, Will broke the silence.

'I wish I never told Aubrey about the lab.'

'I know, but so many people would be grateful for your gift if they only knew. Think about all the people you saved last year at the hospital without them ever knowing what you did.'

'What do I do now? You know if I get another one. I'm too scared to say anything.'

'I think you need to keep doing what you do. I know you're hurting, but there are people out there waiting to be saved by the things you see.'

'Thanks for coming over. And if you think it will help, I will go to the memorial.'

SIXTEEN

Waking late on the morning of the memorial, a mild stomach ache and a lingering headache greeted Will. Despite the physical discomfort, he harboured no inclination to use it as an excuse to stay home. He still blamed himself for what happened, but the commitment to attend the memorial for the five fallen police officers weighed heavily on him, and he felt compelled to at least honour their memory. He recognised that paying his respects was the least he could do in the face of the events that transpired.

He took a cold shower, followed by another Citalopram mixed with some ibuprofen for his headache, and got dressed in his only suit. Charcoal grey and worn only at weddings and funerals. In fact, the last time he wore it had been at his own mother's funeral a few years earlier. As he fastened his tie, the memories attached to the suit came racing through his mind. The joy he felt during his sister's wedding, and then the grief at his mother's funeral. He wore a crisp white shirt and a thin black tie, which took him several attempts to get right, being a little out of practice. He did his best to flatten his hair down with wax, but a few loose strands were too stubborn to tame.

Stepping out of his apartment building, Will inhaled deeply, savouring the first breath of fresh air in several days. The sensation brought a brief yet welcome relief, contrasting the stale air he had become accustomed to. However, the glare from the sun proved challenging, stinging his eyes, which seemed to have taken longer to adjust after the extended period of indoor darkness.

The memorial was to be held at St Mary's Cathedral in the city's centre. The crowd huddling around the church's grounds was enormous, with thousands of people turning out, including several media outlets. Police officers wore formal dress uniforms, and the mass of civilians and reporters huddled around the large courtyard in front of the church, mourning together. The crowd outnumbered the enormous church's capacity, so the organisers had set up a large monitor in the courtyard to livestream the proceedings inside.

Remaining at the back of the crowd and waiting for the service to begin, Will felt anxious and took shallow breaths amongst the enormous mass of people. While standing by himself, a young woman approached him and handed him a small leaflet, which was information about the memorial. Inside the leaflet, there were the details of who would be speaking, the songs that would be played throughout the service, along with official police photographs of each of the five officers. He flicked through the leaflet and felt a deep and pained sorrow when he looked at the faces of the police officers he was responsible for sending to their deaths.

Detective Sergeant Jason Fredericks

Detective Senior Constable Jennifer Dawes

Detective Senior Constable Philip Jones

Detective Senior Constable Peter Reddy

Detective Senior Constable Belinda Molden

The photographs above each officer's name were old and probably taken in their rookie years. All were in full uniform, with shiny leather jackets and antron caps, as they smiled proudly in front of the blue and white New South Wales Police Flag and the Australian Flag. These photographs, taken at the start of their careers, showed smiles full of promise and enthusiasm.

Will folded the leaflet and put it in his pocket. It was difficult to look at.

As he stood awkwardly at the back of the crowd, waiting for the service to begin, he felt a tap on his shoulder. It was Woods, wearing her full police uniform.

'Hey, Will, Ravi told me you were coming today. How are you?' Will saw sadness written across her face, but she tried to hide it with a weak smile.

'I'm still pretty miserable, to be honest,' he said, 'but coming here was the least I could do.'

Woods had tied her blonde hair in a tight bun, and it sat underneath her dress hat. Normally working in plain clothes, it was the first time Will had seen her in uniform.

Will continued, 'I'm really sorry for ignoring you these past few days, Aubrey. I just felt shattered. I mean, I still do, and I couldn't bear to talk to anyone.'

'I get it. I do. I know how hard it's been for you, and I really hope everything will be okay. You're suffering deep grief, and I want you to pull through. I don't want this to change anything with our arrangement. I'm sure Ravi already told you how amazing it is that you can do what you do.'

'I just need time, Aubrey. I don't even want to think about my visions right now.'

Woods sighed. 'Look, I heard that they ruled the investigation into their deaths as an unfortunate accident at a highly volatile lab. I know it doesn't make you feel any better, but I thought you should know.'

'Yeah, that doesn't really help. I still can't help blaming myself for sending them there. If I had said nothing, the lab may not have exploded, but even if it had, there would have been fewer casualties because no police would have ended up there.'

'What about speaking with Ravi again, or maybe the victim support group at the Pitt Street Church to try to help you manage things?'

'Yeah, and tell them I had a vision and sent five cops to their deaths? That wouldn't go down well, even with that group.'

'I just really hope you can find a way to forgive yourself, because you do too much good to stay hidden away.'

'I just need time,' Will mumbled, avoiding eye contact with Woods.

'Well, I really hope to see you soon. I better get going. I came here with my team to pay our respects. They are already inside.'

'I'm just going to watch from outside.'

Woods nodded and offered a faint smile. 'Bye, Will. Call me if you need anything.'

The memorial lasted for about forty five minutes and Will watched several people talk about the wonderful careers they each had. The service concluded with a montage of photographs over the sound of slow, classical music as the camera inside panned across the faces of several emotional police officers. He felt his eyes water and before the large crowd would disperse; he left and caught the bus back home.

SEVENTEEN

That night, Will struggled to sleep again. Not from the deep grief he felt, which was still there, rather it was from the crippling stomach cramps and an excruciating headache that no amount of pain relief could manage. After several hours of tossing and turning, he sat himself upright in bed. As he tried to hold his upper body still, his head gave out an enormous pulse of intense pain, followed by the sound of people screaming, echoed deep within the back of his mind. His eyes suddenly lost focus, and all he could see were dull colours lost in a thick, grey fog. It was as though his vision was impaired from wearing glass bottles over his eyes. As his mind tried its best to focus, he felt as though his head was going to split open while the screaming continued. When Will saw what he suspected was a shotgun being waved just past his limited field of vision, a powerful wave of nausea hit him before he was thrown back into his bedroom, staring up at the ceiling.

The headache subsided slightly; however, when Will sat up, he felt a cool liquid run over his lips, and when he touched it, he saw it was his own blood, dripping slowly from his nose. He stood up to go to the bathroom, and the dizziness struck him, forcing him back onto the bed to slow the spinning. After a moment, it seemed to have passed, and he cleaned his face up in the bathroom sink before returning to bed, only to stare at the ceiling until morning, unable to get back to sleep and confused about what had just happened. It seemed to have been his mind trying to show him something, but he couldn't work out why he could barely make out the scene and why it triggered a nosebleed. As he lay awake in bed, he remembered something Ravi had said months ago when his visions were first discovered; he wanted to make sure the visions were not causing any physical harm. He wondered if maybe they were now. The brain power he required to project these detailed images was immense, and after every vision, depending on the detail, he always felt a level of fatigue. The thought was frightening, but he guessed they were beginning to impact his health.

The following morning, after no sleep, Will dragged himself out of bed when the rising summer sun pushed through his bedroom window, which only exacerbated his headache. Although confused about his overnight experiences, once he made his way to the bathroom to remove some dried blood from his nose and upper lip, the memories of the police came flooding back to him. He felt the wave of sorrow wash over him once more while he cleaned his face as quickly as he could, and, remembering the prescription given to him by Ravi, went into the kitchen to take another antidepressant. He didn't know how he was supposed to feel after taking them, but they didn't seem to have much of an effect yet. He wondered how long it would be until he felt better and whether his progress would be a result of the drugs or just time. He had been through a lot in his life – the absence of his father, who left when he was just a baby, and the untimely death of his mother, so he knew a great deal about grief and the ability to show resilience. Still, every time he thought about those officers, the crippling feeling that he was solely responsible for their deaths overwhelmed him.

Knowing he needed to eat more than he had been, Will poured himself some cereal and sat down on his armchair with the bowl. Once the last of it was gone, he lifted the bowl to his mouth to drain the rest of the milk, but as the bowl neared his mouth, the headache returned suddenly and with full force. The splitting pain nearly made him drop the bowl, and when he looked down at it to make sure nothing had spilled, he saw ripples in the milk, followed by small waves being created within the bowl. As he gazed intently, his eyes strained, and his vision slowly faded behind a thick, milky fog. His head throbbed, and the sound of people screaming returned.

Through the haze masking his vision, he could just make out what looked like spent shotgun cartridges scattered across a light brown carpet. When he tried his best to focus on what he was seeing, Will caught a flash of what he thought must have been the side of a white panel van speeding off down a street. He could not place his location or any other recognisable surroundings, and his head continued to throb. The pain prevented him from seeing anything more than just the side of the van. He couldn't see any buildings, street signs, people, or anything of any identifiable value.

When Will could no longer tolerate the ache in his head any longer, his mind returned him to his living room. Looking down at his cereal bowl, he winced and rubbed his temples, watching the milk pour onto the carpet as he tried to collect himself.

'What the hell is wrong with me?'

He quickly adjusted the bowl to stop more spillage and continued rubbing his still-tender head.

He fetched some paper towels and got on his hands and knees to mop up the spilt milk. As he did, droplets of blood fell straight down onto the carpet. His nose was bleeding again. He used the wet paper towels to clean his nose up and sat back in the armchair with his head tilted back, trying to understand what was happening.

Two visions, both of which he could barely see anything, and each resulted in intense pain and nosebleeds.

'Why would they suddenly do this to me?' he thought, perplexed.

Then it came to him. It was the antidepressants he had taken. The timing between taking these tablets and when the pain and blurred visions started was far too coincidental to be ignored. There were still a couple of days left in the working week, and he knew Ravi would be at the hospital. Will had already phoned in sick for the week, but he needed to speak with him as soon as possible. This couldn't wait until he finished for the day. He quickly dressed in a t-shirt and chino shorts, took another look at his packet of Citalopram, and threw it in the bin.

EIGHTEEN

By the time Will reached the loading dock area of City South Hospital, sweat soaked his clothes. It was not even 9 a.m., yet the temperature was already nearing thirty degrees Celsius, and the air hung heavy with humidity. He swept his thick, dark hair back from his forehead and quietly entered the hospital through the loading dock doors. He waved quickly at a few nurses and security guards nearby, making his way to the psychiatric ward, while avoiding anyone from administration or maintenance who might be surprised at his return. He found Ravi talking on his phone just outside the locked door to the ward.

Will made eye contact with him and nodded his head urgently.

'I'll call you back,' Ravi said before putting his phone away.

'Hey, what's going on?' he asked. 'You feeling okay? I'm glad you're here, but I didn't think you would be working this week.'

'I'm not working. I need to talk to you, privately.'

'Yeah, sure, let's go to my office.'

Ravi unlocked the ward door, let Will into his office, and closed the door behind them. Rather than sitting behind his desk, he sat on the edge of his desk next to Will.

'Those antidepressants you gave me are making me feel really sick.'

'What do you mean? How so? It's a mild dose and a very safe prescription. Are you feeling okay emotionally with everything?'

'Not particularly, but I'm talking about the side effects of the medication. Physical side effects. I think I had some visions, but they blocked my mind. They gave me splitting headaches, and I even had nosebleeds.'

Ravi raised his eyebrows and looked curiously and carefully at Will. 'That's not a common symptom at all.'

'I'm telling you, I won't be taking them anymore. It's not even about the visions. They are hurting me.'

'I don't think it's the tablets, Will. It might be something else.'

'No, it's not. The blurred and fuzzy visions started right after I took them.'

Ravi rubbed his chin and paused for a moment, looking at Will inquisitively. 'Can I ask you something? How did you feel when you had a vision? Aside from feeling sick?'

'Frustrated. I couldn't see anything properly.'

'That's interesting. I'm sorry I don't mean to make light of your pain, and I don't mean to analyse you, but it seems that you don't want to part with your gift after all. To me, being frustrated when you can't see your visions in the way you normally would may be a sign you want them to return to normal.'

Sinking deeper into his chair, Will met Ravi's gaze with a contemplative expression. The truth in Ravi's words resonated within him – the pain from the drug lab explosion lingered. Yet, even with that pain, Will had a profound realisation: these visions, burdensome as they were, had become a part of his identity. Strangely and paradoxically, Will admitted to himself that he didn't want the visions to stop. Despite the emotional weight they carried, the visions had woven themselves into the very fabric of his existence. They had even become an unconventional companion. Accepting this strange symbiosis marked a shift in Will's perspective, acknowledging that there was a recognition of the unique connection he held with the visions that unfolded in his mind.

'I think you might be right,' Will mumbled. 'I feel sick to my stomach thinking about all those people who died, but deep down, I guess I've accepted they are simply a part of who I am. It's weird, I know.'

'It isn't weird. You're right. It is part of your identity now.'

'It still hurts thinking about the explosion. There are just so many things going through my mind, and I do really wish I never sent those police there.'

'I know it hurts, and I can't imagine how difficult it is to do what you do. The healing process for you won't be overnight, but you will heal.'

'I really hope you're right. I need to stop the meds, though. I mean it.'

'Ordinarily, I would slowly wean someone off Citalopram. However, seeing as you've only just started taking it in small doses, I think it would be okay if you stopped.'

'These new visions I've had scared me. I remembered something you told me when they first started about them possibly hurting me. What if that's happening?'

'Let me look at you,' Ravi said, standing up.

He started a physical examination of Will, looking into his eyes, ears, and nose, checking his blood pressure, and pulling out a stethoscope to listen to his lungs and heart. The examination served not only as a medical assessment but also as a means for Ravi to gauge the overall well-being of his friend. In these moments of physical scrutiny, the bond between doctor and patient intertwined with the threads of friendship as Ravi sought to understand the visible and invisible aspects of Will's current state.

'Everything looks good. If the pain persists another day or two after stopping the meds, or your next vision is hurting you, come to me straight away, understand?'

Will nodded. 'Do you think all this could be happening because of the meds?'

'Normally, absolutely not, but there's nothing normal about your situation. You're a constant surprise, so let's see what happens if you stop taking them.'

Ravi then turned to other things on his mind following his examination of Will.

'How was the memorial yesterday?'

'Heartbreaking.'

'And you?'

'Heartbroken.' Will stood up and turned to leave the office. 'I just need time, Ravi, but you're right. I don't think I want to lose my gift. Losing it would be like losing a part of myself.'

NINETEEN

An air of hushed anticipation enveloped three men gathered around a circular table in the underground cellar of the Golden Bell Hotel in North Sydney. The ambient smoke of imported cigarettes lingered in the air, blending with the heady aroma of expensive scotch that adorned the scene. The dim lighting cast shadows that danced on the walls, creating an aura of secrecy within the clandestine setting. Shrouded in the dim glow, each man maintained a quiet composure, the occasional clink of glasses punctuating the stillness. The stage was set for a life-changing job, and they eagerly awaited the pending instructions that would soon unveil it.

The Golden Bell Hotel, though successful in appearance as a legitimate business, served a dual purpose within the intricate web of the Bianco crime family. While maintaining the facade of a thriving establishment, it primarily functioned as a front for their unlawful operations. The ordinary exterior concealed a world where money laundering thrived, and the secure cellar area served as a storage facility for drugs and firearms. The Bianco crime family, deeply entrenched in illicit activities, specialised in the importation and distribution of illegal drugs. However, their reach extended beyond the confines of narcotics. The family, opportunistic in their pursuits, did not shy away from exploiting any avenue that promised profit, even if it involved preying on the misfortunes of others.

As the patriarch of the family, Frank Bianco had reached the age of sixty-five, marking a pivotal moment in his tumultuous life of crime. Having weathered the storms of a long and violent existence, he deemed it time to pass the reins of the family business to his two sons, Marco and Charlie. While not identical in the traditional sense, the twins shared striking physical similarities — strong jaws, muscular builds, jet-black hair slicked back with excessive wax, and unusually large brown eyes. While Charlie, the older of the pair by five minutes, exuded a reckless and impulsive personality, Marco, equally dangerous, assumed a more reserved demeanour, often content to follow his brother's lead. Together, they formed a formidable duo poised to inherit the mantle of the family enterprise. Frank's decision to entrust them with the family legacy marked a generational transition, setting the stage for the twins to navigate the perilous underworld of crime that defined the Bianco family lineage.

Frank Bianco, following the tradition passed down through generations, initiated his sons into the family business at a young age, just as his father had done for him. Even during their high school years, Charlie and Marco were actively involved in the intricate decisions of the illicit trade, orchestrating the importation of substantial amounts of cocaine from South America.

The turning point in their violent initiation came at the tender age of eighteen, when Frank tasked them with a grim mission. The twins, fueled by the family code that mercy equated to weakness, confronted a mid-level cocaine supplier suspected of embezzling funds that rightfully belonged to the family. Armed with knives, Charlie and Marco executed the order with ruthless efficiency, ending the dealer's life in a brutal display of unrelenting force.

Frank's mantra, *'mercy and weakness go hand in hand,'* became an ingrained philosophy in the twins' upbringing, shaping them into instruments of unyielding resolve within the ruthless world they were born into. The baptism into violence and the family's unyielding ethos laid the foundation for Charlie and Marco to navigate the treacherous path of organised crime. It was this upbringing, surrounded by violence and crime, that groomed Charlie and Marco to the borderline of sociopathy. Now twenty-six years old, both had become cunning and gifted businessmen, especially when it came to managing finances and laundering money. Still, their savagery quickly became well known and feared amongst the criminal underworld.

The family boasted a crew of several hundred loyal employees who specialised in several aspects of the criminal component of their extensive business enterprise and were each fiercely loyal. In return, the family treated them with respect and paid them well. All were of Italian background, and if blood did not connect them to the family, their ties went back generations and were considered as good as family. It was this loyalty that ensured the Bianco's almost monopolised organised crime in Sydney.

Upon assuming ownership of the family business, a subtle shift occurred in the dynamics for the Bianco twins. The relentless exposure to a lifetime of crime had dulled the once intoxicating rush of adrenaline they experienced in the early days, be it in the commission of a business-related murder or orchestrating a successful drug importation. The family's interests remained their utmost priority, but the monotony of their criminal pursuits left a void – an absence of the thrill and danger they had once relished. In search of a different outlet to rekindle the excitement they yearned for, Marco and Charlie, alongside their closest three associates, hatched a plan that promised pleasure, challenge, and amusement. The sole objective was to inject a renewed sense of thrill into their lives, diverging from the routine criminal undertakings that had become second nature. The forthcoming venture, known only to the inner circle, held the promise of being an extraordinary pursuit that would transcend the boundaries of their familiar criminal endeavours.

Now, the three associates sat in the underground cellar, finishing their drinks, eagerly awaiting Charlie and Marco. They had been hand-selected to be involved in something that promised to be amongst the greatest thrills of their lives.

TWENTY

Several weeks earlier, their father summoned Charlie and Marco to his office inside his luxurious Double Bay home in Sydney's east. The twins were in the final stages of the acquisition process to assume control of all aspects of the family business and were reviewing some last-minute contracts. Frank Bianco sat behind a large wooden desk in front of the water-facing window wearing a brand new Tom Ford charcoal grey suit with a thick navy tie. His bald head glistened in the sun as it poured through the office filled with an impressive library and furniture imported directly from Italy. He leant back on an executive style leather chair, looking at his sons dressed equally impressively, sitting on a leather sofa by a heavy marble coffee table. Despite sharing some resemblances to their father, Charlie and Marco bore distinctive features that set them apart. Notably, they still maintained thick locks of jet-black hair. This departure from Frank's appearance was accompanied by their commitment to physical fitness that far surpassed their father's habits, especially in his later years when he had become slightly overweight. Standing at an imposing six foot two and weighing in at a solid one hundred kilos of pure muscle, the twins exuded a formidable presence. Their dedication to a rigorous fitness regimen underscored their commitment to maintaining a level of physical prowess that matched the demands of their chosen lifestyle.

As they carefully examined a pile of documents on the coffee table, two of the family solicitors seated next to them indicated where to initial and sign on each page.

On a legitimate level, ownership was being signed over for several restaurants, hotels and bars owned by the family in the presence of these solicitors. During this meeting, the brothers were also informed that they would have exclusive use of the family solicitors in the future. After completing the legal formalities, Frank Bianco cleared the room and spoke to his sons privately.

'Charlie, Marco, everything is now yours. You have both proven yourself exceptionally competent.'

This statement was about as affectionate as their father could be, and the brothers accepted the compliment, nodded affirmatively, and allowed him to continue.

'You each know all there is about the business. Both the legitimate side and our other side. There is nothing else for me to tell you about all of that. You have both been making the big decisions for months now.'

Frank picked up the landline phone receiver from his desk. 'Ed, come in now, please.'

He sat back in his chair and waited without saying a word. Charlie and Marco had known their father's sole non-Italian associate, Ed, for as long as they could remember. He was a miserable-looking man, cold toward them and cold toward even their father. In fact, they didn't know what he did for the family business except to be at Frank's exclusive service. The bitterness, however, was never subtle, and they actually seemed to despise each other, adding mystery to their relationship, which their father never discussed. Over the years, whenever the twins asked Frank why he kept him around, he ignored their questions or changed the topic.

Moments later, Ed opened the double doors to the office and entered without saying a word. He was about the same age as Frank, with large bags under his eyes and a heavily receding hairline of thinning black hair. He was tall and thin, dressed in tailored grey pants and a matching grey vest over a fitted white shirt, which was no doubt purchased for him by the family. What was unusual about Ed was that he was missing the index and middle finger on his left hand. Because of this, he mainly walked around with his hands in his pockets.

Ed's presence in the room created an air of uncertainty, and it seemed that he was undecided whether to sit or stand as he waited for further instructions. His gaze, devoid of a smile, fixed on Marco and Charlie with an intensity that suggested a preconceived understanding of the nature of this meeting.

'Sit down, Ed,' Frank said, offering him a chair opposite his boys.

He sat down obediently without speaking, and Frank continued.

'Marco, Charlie, listen to me very carefully because what I am about to tell you is very important. It will sound almost unbelievable, but I assure you everything I am about to say is true.'

The twins squirmed around on the couch, wondering where this conversation was going, but their attention was undivided as they continued to hang onto every word.

'You all know Ed has been with me for a long time and it's no secret he doesn't like me, and I don't particularly like him.'

Charlie eyed Ed, looking for a reaction, but he remained completely still as Frank continued.

'But over the years, we have come to certain agreements to work together for the benefit of each other, haven't we, Ed?'

'Yes,' Ed replied indifferently.

Frank seemed not to notice the subtle hostility behind Ed's answer, or if he did, he didn't care.

'But as I am retiring now, Ed's services are better put to use with you two. Now listen carefully and don't interrupt me. I am going to tell you exactly what Ed will be able to do for you and the family.'

TWENTY-ONE

As the clock ticked past 10 p.m., Marco and Charlie approached a large steel door nestled in the hushed alley alongside the Golden Bell Hotel. Unlocking it with a sense of purpose, they revealed a hidden passage leading down a flight of creaky wooden stairs. The stairs descended into the private cellar area the twins had transformed into their designated meeting spot with their trusted associates. Tony, Leo, and Sal looked up in anticipation at their childhood friends and current employers as they made their way down the stairs to join the meeting.

Marco and Charlie, along with their three friends, had been like family since childhood. Their fathers had worked for Frank Bianco, and the twins considered them their most trusted criminal associates. They too were all twenty-six years old and had equally strong builds, spending much of their free time in the gym. Like Charlie and Marco, they were of Italian descent and immaculately presented; clean shaven, wore expensive cologne and had thick black, well-groomed hair, except for Sal who, having begun losing his hair years earlier, shaved his head close to the scalp.

'Not too drunk, I hope,' Charlie said.

'Nope, just excited to go over the last-minute details,' Tony said.

'Excellent. Now listen closely.'

Marco pulled out some large photographs printed on A3 glossy paper and began passing them around while Charlie continued.

'The first bank on our list is the United East Bank at Haymarket. These are the surveillance photographs taken by Leo. The reasons for targeting this branch are that it's risky with a high level of foot traffic and close to the Sydney City police station. The benefits of taking out this bank? Well, it's risky. Just what we are looking for,' Charlie laughed, and the others followed with smug chuckles.

'But seriously, a lot of city businesses trade here, so when we hit the joint we will be looking at an easy seven figures. We won't have the time to make that much, but we'll be assured of a nice little bonus of a few hundred thousand for the thrill when we hit the joint. Now, Leo's done a great job on the internal security systems. So we have no problems with the CCTV system, but nevertheless, we need to be in and out in under four minutes.

'I've tested the silent alarm remotely. We may have four and a half minutes,' Leo added.

'Okay, that's good, but we will still stick to four minutes just in case,' Charlie said. Sal, are you all good with the van?'

'Yep, and with stolen plates, I'm picking it up from my associate later tonight.'

'Perfect, we will meet you at the back of the warehouse we discussed at 8.50 a.m tomorrow morning, then we hit the bank right on opening, 9.30 a.m.'

They all smiled.

'Okay, so get home and get a good night's sleep. We will do it tomorrow.' Charlie said.

***

The white Hyundai iMax van with stolen licence plates came to a sharp halt on Ultimo road at Haymarket directly in front of the United East Bank. The timing was impeccable. Leo's prior surveillance was accurate, and Sal's driving exceeded expectations. The doors were just being unlocked by the guard as the digital clock in the van ticked over to 9.30 a.m. A few early-rising bank customers shuffled inside and created the day's first queue at the teller.

Sal kept the van idle while Marco, Charlie, Tony and Leo pulled black ski masks over their faces and slid their hands into thick leather gloves. The masks matched their tactical boots, cargo pants, and long-sleeve t-shirts in colour, and they had eye slits shaped to allow full peripheral vision while completely covering the rest of their faces. With the sheer physical size of each of them, coupled with the masks, they looked exceptionally imposing. After checking and re-checking their shotguns and collecting a couple of empty black canvas duffle bags from the back of the van, Marco opened the sliding passenger door, and they alighted in single file, bounding towards the glass front door of the bank.

The group entered the bank with speed and ferocity. Instantly, Tony slammed his fist into the jaw of the security guard standing by the doors and knocked him out cold before he could react or even process what was happening. He pulled out a set of cable ties from the side pocket of his cargo pants and tied the guard's hands behind his back. Within seconds, he had completely incapacitated the only threat inside the bank.

As the ominous presence of four shotguns became apparent to the three customers inside the bank, a collective gasp escaped their lips. Fear seized them, and in a reflexive response, they screamed and instinctively covered their heads. The sudden escalation of the situation sent shockwaves through the quiet confines of the bank, transforming it into a tense and harrowing scene. The customers, now hostages to the unfolding threat, braced themselves for the unknown in the face of the pointed shotguns.

'Everyone on the ground now!' Marco shouted as he charged toward the tellers, gun aimed straight at the two young women behind the perspex protected, dark wooden counter.

Leo and Tony pointed their guns at the customers while Charlie stood next to his brother.

'You move, you die,' Leo said coolly.

The three customers, two middle-aged women and one elderly male buried their faces in the carpet and remained as still as possible.

The branch manager, Gary Toland, who was working in his office behind the tellers, heard the commotion and saw the four masked men through a one-sided pane of glass behind the front desk. He triggered the silent alarm under his desk and slowly made his way to the front of the bank to remove the attention from the two young tellers, who were wide eyed and frightened beyond comprehension. He moved slowly, but with purpose.

'Hello, I'm Gary, the branch manager,' he said as he raised his hands above his head in surrender. Gary Toland was almost sixty and wore thick glasses and a tweed suit which was tight on his round, soft body.

'Silent alarm activated,' Leo called out as he checked a small device, which buzzed as the alarm was activated.

Earlier in the morning, Leo had executed a calculated move, syncing an electronic disabler device with the bank's security system. In a strategic manoeuvre, he not only interrupted the CCTV system but also intercepted a record of any electronic data attempting to leave the confines of the branch.

'Thank you,' Charlie replied, looking at his watch. 'I expect we have only a few minutes before the police arrive. You look like a smart fellow, Gary, and you don't want to see your young tellers shot in the head, so be a good man and hand over all the money in the front safe.'

When he didn't move, Charlie walked over to Toland and slapped him hard in the face with an open palm, forcing his glasses to fly off his face.

'Now, we know exactly who is in the office. You and the two tellers. Your other employees will arrive momentarily, so I suggest you hurry unless you want more of your staff to become involved.'

'Okay,' Toland stuttered with a tremble in his lip.

'Bring the money out on the steel trolly in a single trip. At this time of day, there should be around $340,000 inside that safe, so hurry up,' Charlie said.

In just under forty seconds, Toland wheeled out a trolley to the main floor of the bank. Atop it sat a little under $350,000, comprising $20, $50 and $100 notes bundled together with rubber bands.

'Let's go, boys,' Charlie said to Tony and Leo, while Marco took their place holding the three customers still on the ground at gunpoint.

'Back you go. Stand behind the counter next to the girls.' Charlie said to Toland, using his gun to direct the manager.

In a swift and efficient operation, Tony and Leo worked seamlessly, taking precisely one minute and twenty seconds to amass all the cash from the front safe and pack it into the four duffle bags. With practised precision, they sealed the bags with the swift motion of a zipper, transforming the once orderly stacks of currency into compact, easily transportable packages.

'You three, get up,' Marco said to the cowering customers. They immediately complied and stood up, shielding their faces with their hands.

'Move into that corner, over by the side. Stay there and do not move.'

The three customers ran as quickly as they could toward the corner of the bank, just in front of the teller's counter.

The crew swiftly shouldered a duffle bag each and exited the bank with purposeful strides. They briskly made their way to the waiting van without exchanging words, seamlessly climbing in with their haul. The crew accomplished the operation in under four minutes, from the moment they entered the bank to their successful getaway, showcasing an astonishing display of efficiency. They removed their face masks and laughed as the car drove north toward the Sydney Harbour Bridge.

TWENTY-TWO

Police cars raced towards the bank, their sirens blaring. Upon arrival, they encountered a frantic scene unfolding on the street. Gary Toland, his demeanour marked by terror, stood on the roadside, frantically waving down the approaching vehicles.

Within minutes, the bank transformed into a hub of police activity as officers quickly wrapped crime scene tape around the building. An ambulance was called to attend to the aftermath, its presence necessitated by the security guard nursing a headache and a broken jaw. Additionally, three civilians and two more employees awaited treatment for shock.

Ian Yule received the call from the Sydney City police station while enjoying a coffee at police headquarters. He quickly drained the rest of it and called an emergency meeting. Within ten minutes, Yule and the rest of his team, including Woods, were speeding toward the United East Bank at Haymarket.

When they arrived, Yule made his way through a large crowd of irate bank customers who had been denied entry and several curious onlookers. He flashed his ID to the young constable guarding the front of the bank and lifted the crime scene tape. The automatic doors to the bank were sealed tight and locked. Instead of knocking on the glass to get the attention of the police inside, he waited a moment for eye contact with the team already inside. A uniformed officer met his gaze and opened the door with a remote control.

'Thanks,' Yule called out.

He remained in the doorway with his team and called over the Sydney City police station's team leader, who was managing the crime scene. While he waited, Gary Toland approached Yule and introduced himself. Yule, who could be surly at the best of times, was even more so when he was on the job and ignored Toland as he continued processing his investigation plan in his head. While he waited for the uniformed supervisor, he divided his team up, sending Woods to go with Toland and access the CCTV system inside the bank. Then, the others started canvassing neighbouring businesses for witnesses and any security footage they could find.

'Protocol is that the head office accesses the CCTV remotely, and then they provide it to the police later,' Toland said.

'Do I seem interested in the bank's protocol right now?' Yule replied sternly. It was all he had to say for Toland to turn around and lead Woods to his office to pull the CCTV footage. The rest of the team left the bank to begin their canvass.

'Sergeant, run me through what you know,' Yule asked the uniform supervisor, who had finally made his way to the front of the bank.

'The manager told me there were four offenders, with possibly an extra one driving the getaway car. He got a glimpse of a white van as it sped off. They all carried shotguns and wore balaclavas. One of them knocked the security guard out. He was the only guard working with three customers inside and a handful of employees. They took the cash out in large duffle bags.'

'Proceeds?'

'Around $350,000, but we are waiting for the final figure.'

'Were they able to put a tracker in the bag?'

'No, according to the manager, the offenders insisted on packing the bags themselves, and as I said, they bought their own bags.'

'Smart. Okay, descriptions?'

The sergeant flicked through some pages of his notebook. 'Large builds, wearing all black, including gloves. No distinct features.'

'Accents?'

'Australian accents. They spoke perfect English.'

'Okay, let's move onto the crime scene.'

'No one has entered except us and the two ambulance officers. The three customers remain inside, and we have separated them to prevent contamination of their statements. Our detectives are speaking with them now. Do you want them to take their full statements?'

'No, I'll get my team to do all that shortly. We will take ownership of this investigation, but we would appreciate it if your detectives could stick around for a bit. There might be some other jobs to do. Crime scene on their way?'

'Yep, they should be here any minute to process the scene. We can stick around with the unformed crew to guard the crime scene for as long as you need.'

'Much appreciated, thank you. I expect things will get busier on the street. You might want to put another person out with the young constable out the front. He's going to need help managing the crowd. The media will probably catch on soon, so be prepared for the cameras.'

Yule took a deep breath and considered all he knew so far. Whoever had pulled off this job did so with elite proficiency. He hadn't seen a bank robbery team like this in a long time, and he was nervous. These offenders, who were organised and armed, would now be high on adrenaline after their success. Based on his best judgement, he concluded this group wasn't done yet and, given their success here, they would probably plan and execute another robbery soon. He gazed at the high ceiling of the bank and noted each security camera in place. He walked from the front door to the teller and counted thirty-four regular steps. It was a relatively small bank compared to others in Sydney. He looked at the guard, still getting his jaw examined by the paramedic, and it occurred to him, along with the limited staff members and customers in the bank at the time, that the robbery crew had selected this time intentionally. It was clearly their first robbery together, or he and the squad would have heard about it. This first job at a small bank, just after opening, was likely a way for them to test their skills before they moved onto something larger and more dangerous, with the potential for a higher reward.

He closed his eyes and tried to profile these offenders. Most likely adrenaline junkies after a quick fix of danger and a stack of fast cash. They would likely be experienced criminals, not necessarily seasoned armed robbers, but comfortable enough with violence to have no hesitation waving a gun in someone's face.

Woods returned from the office with Toland and walked straight over to Yule with a worried expression.

'There's no CCTV. It's like there was some interference with the system because for about two minutes before and after the robbery, all we got was static on the screen.'

'And there's nothing wrong with the system?' Yule asked.

'No, I checked it before and after, and it worked fine. It's just a five or six-minute period where we have nothing.'

'Take the whole hard drive then, and we will have the tech guys look at it later. Then, give the others a hand on the street.'

Woods marched back to the office with Toland and returned a short time later carrying a large hard drive containing all the footage from the bank. Just as she was bagging it up as evidence, crime scene officers arrived and began by dusting for fingerprints and collecting DNA swabs before starting a thorough sweep for any trace elements like hair or clothing fibres.

Woods sealed the bag containing the hard drive, left it with a pile of other exhibits already collected, and left the bank to join the rest of the team while Yule was speaking with the crime scene officers.

***

After a fruitless canvass, Woods and the team identified the same issue. Every security camera in the immediate area had the same problem as in the bank. They worked fine until moments before the robbery, when it became static. Additionally, none of the people they spoke to could provide any information outside of what they already knew. A few people saw what they believed were men wearing face masks quickly entering a white van.

Still, none could provide any further descriptions or identifiable features of the van or even a partial plate number.

'Sarge, same issues with the CCTV in all the local spots around the bank. Nothing but static on all monitors before and after,' Woods said on her return to the bank.

Yule brushed his beard anxiously. 'Let's just work with what we have, and I'll get a media alert put out about this one requesting for any witnesses, specifically anyone with dash cam footage around the time of the robbery.'

'How are things here with the forensics?'

'They took some swabs and found some fingerprints from the glass doors and countertops, but it's a busy bank, and these guys wore gloves, so they probably won't be a match.'

'Anything else you need done?' Woods asked.

'Yeah, let's start by taking all the statements from everyone here. Just divide and conquer. I want them all collected today while it's fresh in everyone's memories. I want as much detail as they can remember, regardless of how trivial they think something was. Then we will re-group later and work out where we go from here.'

TWENTY-THREE

Will spent the entire day at home. It was the last sick day he could take, and he still felt miserable and lethargic. Although he still felt the sickening grief from the lab explosion, his headaches had stopped, along with the nosebleeds, since discarding the rest of his antidepressants. In the solitude of his thoughts, Will reflected on the strained interactions with Aubrey and Ravi and thought about his unintentional rudeness, that had permeated his demeanour in recent days. Realising the need for reconciliation, Will resolved to extend an olive branch by calling them and proposing a dinner meet up. In this gesture, he sought to make amends and attempt to return some normalcy to his life.

'Hey Aubrey, is this a good time?' Will asked when Woods answered his call straight away.

'Yeah, of course. I've had a busy day, but I'm just getting off work. I've been thinking about you and hoping you're okay.'

'I am. I'm feeling a little better, I guess. It'll take some time, but I'll get there. Listen, I know I already said it, but I really wanted to apologise again for shutting you out and, well, just being rude. I know you were only trying to help.'

'Apologies are not necessary, Will. I know it's been hard on you.'

'Well, I just want to get everything back on track.'

'Glad to hear.'

'Anyway, I wanted to see if you wanted to get some dinner. Maybe pizza or something? I'll ask Ravi, too.'

'Yeah, that sounds great, actually. I had a long day, so I could use a drink, too.'

'Lorenzo's at seven?'

'Great, I'll see you there.'

Will then called Ravi, who said he could also meet them for dinner that night.

'I haven't heard from you all day, so I assume you are feeling okay?' he asked.

'Yeah, no headaches or nosebleeds,' Will said. 'Also, no new visions, but otherwise, I'm feeling back to normal physically, still struggling a bit with the emotional side,' Will said.

'Well, wanting to get out and have dinner is good. In terms of the physical symptoms stopping, it's a little weird the meds may have done what you said, but it's good you're okay. Still monitor yourself though, and if you have a vision soon, let me know. I want to make sure the nosebleeds or headaches don't come back.'

'Of course. I'll see you soon.'

Will was the first to arrive at Lorenzo's restaurant. Being a Friday night, the place was bustling, as was the rest of Surry Hills, with the weekend nightlife starting up. Luckily, though, they could accommodate Will's party if they cleared out by 8 p.m. He sat in the restaurant's corner, facing a large window at a square table covered with a traditional red and white chequered tablecloth, including a candle made from an old Chianti bottle. Ravi and Woods arrived shortly after, and as Will contemplated their appearance, he figured he would have to change his usual ragged look someday. Woods wore tight jeans and a loose-fitting white blouse with her long blonde hair flowing down to the middle of her back. She wore light makeup, and her smooth complexion looked flawless. Ravi had not changed since work and wore light grey trousers and a dark-coloured business shirt, matching the thick, dark rim of his large framed glasses. Will, shaggy and needing a haircut more than ever, wore old baggy jeans and a black t-shirt. Once settled, they ordered beers and a couple of large pizzas to share.

'So, how's work, Aubrey?' Ravi asked after taking a sip of beer.

'I'm pretty busy actually. We had a big job today. Don't know if you guys saw the news?'

They both shook their heads.

'There was an armed robbery at the United East Bank at Haymarket. It was a professional job; a team of at least four or five involved. All armed to the teeth with shotguns. They stole a few hundred thousand in cash.'

'Was anyone hurt?' Will asked.

'No, thankfully, one of them knocked out a security guard, but he will be fine.'

'Any leads or anything yet?' Ravi asked.

'Not yet. It's still early days, though. But forensics turned up nothing, and there was no CCTV because of a glitch. We think they used a signal jammer that disrupted the feeds to all security cameras in the area. As I said, it was pretty professional, but we know they got away in a white van.'

Will absorbed the details shared by Woods. Shotguns. White van. He contemplated the eerie similarity between these elements and the partial, hazy, and painful visions that plagued him earlier.

'But anyway, enough of that. We will keep working on it, and I'm sure something will come up. How are you guys? Ravi?'

'Yeah, work's good, no complaints.'

'And you, Will? I'm glad things are getting better for you.'

'Yeah, I'm getting there. Slowly. But it's good to get out of the apartment too.'

The pizzas arrived on large shared plates. They each took their first slice and started eating.

Will chewed slowly while still considering the robbery Woods described. 'I'm just stuck thinking about what you said, Aubrey. About the robbery.'

'What's that?' she replied before taking a bite of her piece.

'About the white van and the shotgun. I might be wrong, but maybe that's what I saw the other day. You remember Ravi? With all I was saying about the meds?'

Ravi nodded. 'Have you told Aubrey yet?'

'No.'

'Told me what?' Woods asked.

'Well, after all that happened with the lab explosion, and you know, things got pretty bad for me. Ravi gave me some antidepressants.'

'A very low dose, mind you,' Ravi interjected.

'I think they made me sick. I was getting nasty headaches, and then I had a couple of visions, but I could barely see anything of any value. Between the messy scenes, I saw what I thought was a white van and shotguns, but that's all I can tell you. I don't have any context. It was a chaotic vision that didn't make much sense.'

'Oh, okay, wow, that's big,' Woods said. 'Is that possible, Ravi? Could certain meds block Will's visions?'

'Tough question, seeing that Will is so unique, I have no idea. I usually run with whatever he says and try improvising my medical training. I still don't know how these visions work, but hearing they were causing him physical harm, I was pretty worried. I've been concerned about it since they started because we just don't know enough about them.'

'But anyway, I stopped taking the pills, and I'm feeling back to normal. No headaches or nosebleeds,' Will said.

'Have you seen anything else since?' Woods asked.

'No. And it took me a while to want to see anything else, so honestly, I'm glad nothing has really come through recently, but I think I'm ready again. When I was taking the meds and my visions were really grainy, I actually felt strangely irritated. It felt like I was losing part of myself, and that's when I realised it is who I am, and I don't want that to go away, even when it's gut-wrenching.'

'You've got an amazing gift, Will. We both want to see you get better and get back to how things used to be,' Woods said.

'Cheers to that,' Ravi acknowledged, raising his beer.

'Cheers,' they responded, clinking their bottles together before finishing their dinner.

TWENTY-FOUR

That same evening, in the dark and cold cellar beneath the Golden Bell Hotel, Charlie, Marco, and their associates reclined in plush leather chairs, enveloped in the swirling smoke of thick cigars. Their relaxed postures conveyed a sense of triumph as they discussed the seamless execution of their successful bank robbery. With their feet casually resting on a coffee table, the atmosphere was one of complete satisfaction. The four large duffle bags, once filled with the spoils of their heist, now lay emptied, and an impressive pile of bundled cash adorned a small table in the corner of the cellar. Notably, the group displayed a nonchalant attitude toward their monetary gain, as they had yet to bother to tally the substantial sum. For them, the tangible rewards were secondary, overshadowed by the intoxicating rush of adrenaline and thrill accompanying the heist. The focus of their conversation lingered on the exhilaration of the job itself.

'Did you all see Tony drop that guard?' Charlie said. The group immediately burst into laughter.

'Brutal hit,' Marco added, slapping Tony on the back.

'Alright, let's get back to business for a moment,' Charlie interrupted. 'We'll get this money cleaned and then divided up. It won't be able to be traced back to us, so don't worry about that. Leo, how do you think your signal jammer went?'

'I don't think we'll have any problems. All the checks I did beforehand worked as they should, and the feedback it gave during the job was positive. We should be invisible to all the nearby security cameras.'

'Perfect. And Sal, the van and gateway. Anything we could do better?'

'On my end, it was perfect. I suggest using a completely different car for the next job, though, maybe a large 4WD with a little more acceleration and power. I can make the arrangements, of course.'

'Sounds good,' Charlie said. 'Well, I think we can all agree today was a success. Are we ready to hear the details for the second job?'

The team nodded with excitement while waiting to hear what Marco and Charlie had planned for them.

'We are going to hit the Greenspring Bank in the city centre. Another major business and commercial branch. This time, though, we take it during the middle of the day, during the lunch rush.'

'We can't make things too easy on ourselves, can we?' Marco added.

'Cheers to that,' Tony said, raising his scotch glass. They all then drained their glasses at the same time.

'We will go over the plans shortly. First, though, we need to discuss some proper family business,' Charlie said. He cleared his throat and stood up. 'As you know, some imports are pending, and we need to sort the distribution. This shipment will contain high-quality, bulk pseudo and other precursors from Southeast Asia. The short version is I want to get into methamphetamine manufacturing. The problem is we are competing with the Chinese Triads for market share. My sources tell me Zao Ming knows we are trying to move into this market and is far from pleased. Because their meth lab in Sefton recently exploded, I've heard Ming and his people are seeking to intercept this shipment before it arrives at the docks so he can recover his losses. Once it hits our shores, our Customs and Border Protection people will look after us as they always do. We just need to prevent the early interception in open water by Ming's people. Tony and Sal, could you look after this? Ming will most likely use Li Pau to arrange this job. If they succeed, we will lose millions.'

'You got it, Charlie. Leave it with us,' Tony said.

Tony and Sal had been around long enough to know precisely what Charlie wanted.

Pau dead.

'We're familiar with Pau as Ming's right-hand man,' Sal added. 'He's pretty ruthless from what I've heard, but it won't be a problem. The Chinese will react, though.'

'Of course they will. I'd expect nothing less. But we will have the product, and losing someone as valuable to them as Pau will slow them down,' Charlie said.

'We will do it tonight then,' Tony said, while Sal nodded in agreement.

'Good,' Charlie said. 'Okay, now that's all the regular business for tonight. Now, to the next robbery, we need to do some reconnaissance work on this one. Most of the plans are in place, but there are a few things I want to check out first, mostly guard transitions. Plus, I want to scope the area with Leo to get some familiarity. I also want to bring our assistant, Ed, with us to look over things too. He will tell us how we are looking. He hasn't been told about these plans, but I will talk to him after this meeting. Tomorrow work for you, Leo? We need to find the best escape routes for Sal, too.'

'Of course, no problems,' Leo said.

'Well, pending the outcome of the surveillance, we will begin the final plans to hit the joint. It'll be an aggressive rush job. Heavily armed, exactly the same as the first. All the tech seems in place, so Sal, we will need a new car, and then we should be right to go.'

'Sure, leave it with me. First, though, we might leave to look after Pau.'

Charlie nodded. 'Ring the usual people and confirm his address. Let me know when it's done.'

TWENTY-FIVE

After contacting a senior member of the Australian Federal Police on the family's payroll, Tony and Sal obtained confirmation of Li Pau's current address at Strathfield in Sydney's Inner Western suburbs. They confirmed he lives there with his current girlfriend, who was not expected to be home tonight.

Li Pau was in his mid-forties and had been the operational manager of Ming's business for many years, overseeing all aspects of their drug operations. The Triad's structure was predictable, and Charlie was correct in assuming Ming would put Pau in charge of stealing the Bianco family's import. It would be a valuable delivery, and Ming would only put his most trusted associate in charge of such an operation.

Sal parked a stolen black Toyota Camry across from Strathfield Park, and they made the short walk a block away to Pau's residence. Even at 1 a.m., the house was well lit with garden and porch lights illuminating a modern, two-story white rendered brick house. Standing at a distance on the other side of the road, Sal identified the five security cameras at the front and sides of the extensive property. Sal spotted a large window, almost five metres tall, lining the entire front of the house, and a large grand piano was visible on the ground floor. The marble stairs to the upper level reflected the bright light from the luminous perimeter. Undoubtedly, all the lights aided Pau's security at the house, and it appeared he was living luxuriously.

The house appeared to be a fortress, and even though it had several large glass windows, their composition hinted that they were made of two-inch thick bulletproof panes.

'Look over there,' Tony said. 'Alarm system.' A small box on the upper right side of the house was flashing a small red dot every three seconds.

'I'd say it's activated, but only on the ground floor if he sleeps upstairs.

Sal saw a large water heater peeking over a grey steel gate at the side of the house. This would be their way in: up the heater and onto the second level. They would enter the house via the large balcony door he could see from the yard.

They both put on thick gloves and black face coverings, carefully and quietly scaled the side gate, pulled themselves over the side balcony, and faced a locked sliding glass door. Tony pulled out some lock-picking tools from his pocket and, in under ten seconds, had gained entry to one of the spare bedrooms on the upper level.

Tony entered first, followed by Sal, and they carefully crept through the empty spare bedroom. Their heavy leather boots made muffled sounds on the floor, which was covered in expensive, lush white carpet. They moved into the hallway and identified what they believed to be the master bedroom behind large double doors decorated with ornate wooden carvings of Chinese dragons.

Sal carefully tried the door handle. It was unlocked. He slowly twisted the knob all the way around and pushed the two double doors open just enough for him to slide into. Tony followed closely behind. The room was pitch black except for a weak beam of light from the floodlights in the front yard, which had crept through a crack in the thick curtains facing the street. With the small amount of light in the room, they could see a single person lying under white silk sheets on the king-sized bed. It was Pau, and he was alone.

At this stage, communication between Sal and Tony was not required. They had done this many times before and had become dangerously efficient at silent executions.

Tony walked to the left side of the bed, where Pau was facing outwards. As he silently stalked the edge of the bed, he produced a brand new, razor-sharp hunting knife, unsheathed from the back of his belt. The knife would make the job quiet, lethal, and intimate.

In a swift and ruthless motion, Tony drove the knife with lethal precision, plunging it deep into Pau's temple. Pau had no opportunity to react, and death was instantaneous. As he withdrew the blade, a chilling calm settled in the room, interrupted only by the gruesome evidence of the swift execution.

Wiping the bloodied blade on the sheets, Tony observed the crimson pool forming on the bed. The room now bore witness to the silent aftermath, a macabre scene veiled in the darkness of the night.

Tony looked back at Sal and nodded. Kill confirmed.

Sal took a small electronic device that looked like an old first-generation iPod from his backpack, which Leo gave him. Switching it on, he drifted around the room, waving the device around. It beeped when he got close to the wardrobe in Pau's bedroom. Sal opened the door leading to a large walk-in wardrobe. Designer clothes, shoes, and watches lined the shelves, and as he walked deeper into it, the device buzzed louder. He swept aside a rack of suits and located a computer monitor connected to a hard drive.

The small device could detect strong electronic signals, and in this case, Pau's internal CCTV unit. The system looked like at least a dozen cameras were set up inside and outside the house.

Sal looked at the system and recognised the model as one that locally records footage for up to a few weeks and sends a live feed to the user's mobile phone. He unplugged the hard drive and placed it into his backpack. He then returned to the bedroom and located two mobile phones on the bedside table: a standard Android smartphone and an encrypted mobile phone.

Sal collected both devices, removed the SIM cards, smashed the phones with the heel of his boot, and, just for extra measure, placed the wrecked phones in his backpack to dispose of later.

'Clear,' he said. I've got his two phones and the CCTV hard drive. No one will ever know we were here.'

'Good,' Tony replied. 'Let's get out of here. I'll text Charlie from the car.'

They left the house the same way they had entered. The night was dark and calm, and the kill was perfectly quiet. No one would have seen or heard anything. They hurried to their car and drove back to North Sydney.

Tony took out his phone and, via secure encryption, text messaged Charlie. '*Done.*'

Moments later, Charlie replied. '*Good. Prep for the other job now.*'

TWENTY-SIX

Early the following morning, Bao Zu entered the Strathfield residence via the large front door. Bao was only twenty-three years old but had already managed several of the illegal brothels operated by Ming and his criminal network. Along with her professional role, she was also Pau's girlfriend. She was petite and wore a slim-fitted red dress and high heels as she struggled with her keys while handling two cups of takeaway coffee. As she entered the house, an eerie quiet enveloped the space, and her footsteps echoed on the tiled floor. An assumption that Pau had a late night prompted her to move cautiously, treading softly as she ascended the stairs, intending to join him in bed.

A disconcerting shift in the atmosphere greeted her as she neared his bedroom – an unmistakable and foul smell, like rusted iron, lingered in the air. The scent hung heavy, a prelude to the unknown behind the closed door. The promise of a peaceful reunion now gave way to an unsettling tension, and a sense of foreboding settled in as she hesitated, grappling with the pungent odour.

A gut-wrenching sight awaited Bao as she entered the bedroom. The blood-soaked sheets and the lifeless form of Li Pau sent shockwaves through her senses. The coffee cups slipped from her grasp, forgotten, as a scream tore from her lips, echoing in the room. Bao crumpled to the floor. Her stomach twisted in knots, and tremors coursed through her as tears streamed down her cheeks, marking the devastating unravelling of the peaceful moment she had expected only moments ago.

Caught in grief and not knowing what to do, Bao took another look at Pau. His face was ghost white, and the dried blood matted his dark hair. She slowly reached out and touched his upper arm. It was cold. She screamed again, fully aware that someone had murdered Pau. She quickly crawled into the wardrobe and huddled into a ball, fearing his assailants might still be nearby.

After a moment, she took her phone out and called Zao Ming.

During the call, Bao spoke in panicked Mandarin and told him what she had discovered. On the other end of the line, Ming took a deep breath before instructing her on what to do.

'I want you to leave now. Through the front door. Not too fast, not too slow. No tears. Go straight home and stay there. Okay?'

'Okay,' she replied, still sobbing. 'What about Li?'

Through the phone, she heard Ming take another deep breath.

'I will send a team to clean up the house. No police. Then, we will arrange a private memorial for him. No one outside of our people is to find out about this. Do you understand that?'

'Yes.' Whether or not Bao trusted Ming with this decision, she would obey his direct order. She ended the call and left the house immediately after one last glance over Li Pau's body.

***

Zao Ming took a cool shower inside his large Potts Point penthouse in the exclusive Eastern Suburbs. As he let the cool water run over his body, he thought about the death of his lifelong friend. After feeling like he had wasted enough time standing under the water, he turned the taps off and stood in his spacious bathroom, looking back at himself in the mirror. As he looked at his reflection, he promised not to stop until those responsible met the same fate. There would be a time to grieve, but it was not now. He dried himself with a large towel, looking at the giant dragon tattoo on his chest. Strength, wisdom and longevity. The dragon represented these virtues, and each time he looked at his bare chest, he was reminded of these qualities. Ming was forty years old and only 5'6 tall and thin, although his body seemed to be made up entirely of lean muscle. Despite his small stature, he was renowned for his intellect, composure under pressure, and mercilessness towards anyone who challenged him.

Ming dressed in black jeans and a grey linen shirt before calling his cleanup team. Those he employed to make it look as though nothing happened in the house. While the team was there, they would collect samples just as a crime scene officer would, and forward them to the same lab the police use, along with a large payment to the staff on Ming's payroll to process the samples quickly and discreetly. Ming would find who was responsible and, in doing so, use every resource at his disposal.

He also took it upon himself to contact Pau's family, who were still living in Sichuan, China – a task that he did not want but felt responsible for. Before he did, however, he opened his laptop and logged into Pau's Google Cloud account.

The CCTV system connected to his house fed a direct relay to Pau's phone, which also backed up automatically on the cloud in real time and stored there for one week before overwriting itself to save storage space. Pau, Ming, and a few other close associates of the crime syndicate had access to each other's external cameras via shared Could Drive accounts. They believed that having secure and spare copies of data was crucial, so even if something happened to the main hard drive, they could still retrieve copies of the footage until the point the unit was disconnected. After logging in, Ming located the files, which comprised footage from several cameras uploaded to the drive. The system was programmed to record only when motion was detected, and Ming quickly identified the two intruders through the front garden camera and a camera on the upper side balcony of the house.

Upon reviewing the footage, he witnessed the two men scaling the wall and entering via the balcony before the camera was deactivated shortly afterwards.

'No, it couldn't be,' he muttered. He took out a phone and called Feng Cui, a close friend and trusted member of his organisation.

Ming told Cui the news about Pau and gave him a moment to collect himself.

'Who did it?' Cui asked.

'The Bianco family,' Ming replied.

'What? The Italians? Surely they wouldn't be stupid enough to do that. Are they trying to start a war? Are you sure it was them?'

'Yes, I saw the CCTV. Two of them broke into the house. They wore masks and gloves, but I recognised them. Both are close associates of Charlie and Marco. I recognised their builds, the way they moved, and how they dressed. And there's something else that confirms their involvement.'

'What?'

'Pau and I had made plans to intercept a shipment of pseudoephedrine that Charlie Bianco had arranged to import. It was to get our people back on track after what happened at Sefton, and word must have got out through our friends at the Federal Police or Border Protection. The timing is too coincidental, and I don't believe in coincidences. They wanted to take him out to interrupt our plan.'

'So what do we do?'

'First, I need you to clean Pau's house for me. Be gentle with his body, okay? He was a good friend. After that, we will discuss our retaliation. We will not forget this.'

TWENTY-SEVEN

On Tuesday morning, Sydney experienced its first rainfall in over a month. Despite the persisting summer humidity and high temperatures, the refreshing downpour was a welcome relief. The aroma of damp earth permeated the air, signalling the revival of the city's surroundings, and the lush garden beds surrounding City South Hospital received a healthy drenching of natural water, bringing them back to life.

Arriving at work just before the rain started, the downpour thwarted Will's plans for roof repair above the ambulance bay, forcing a priority change. Seeking refuge in the dingy demountable at the hospital's rear, more reminiscent of a large garden shed than an office, Will redirected his efforts. Amidst the array of maintenance tools and machinery, he had carved out a makeshift workspace several months ago following his promotion and used the area to complete paperwork.

Will saved the Excel spreadsheet he worked on as the rain became more intense and distracting, hammering against the light tin roof above. Instead of sitting inside his demountable office, Will collected his tool belt and wandered through the hospital to ensure there were no leaks inside.

Navigating the hospital's hallways, Will, still shaking off the excess water that clung to him since leaving the maintenance shed, felt a sense of satisfied relief as he observed no visible leaks thus far. However, the cleaners did not share his satisfaction, and expressed their displeasure at the muddy tracks left by Will's wet boots, which disrupted their freshly mopped floors. Despite the inconvenience, Will pressed on, avoiding their frustrated glares, and headed for the large emergency department at the front of the hospital.

As Will reached the front of the hospital, the sticky humidity had succeeded in mostly drying the rain on his grey maintenance uniform. However, the lingering moisture and humid conditions made him sweat again. Entering the emergency department, he encountered a scene typical for the time of day – a full waiting room. The area buzzed with activity, populated by individuals nursing limbs encased in bandages, mothers attempting to console crying children amidst the prolonged wait, and elderly patients audibly coughing and sniffling.

He manoeuvred through the crowd and nursing staff, his gaze scanning the ceiling for potential leaks; an unexpected encounter disrupted his routine. He felt a sudden wave of lightheadedness and instability on his feet when a middle-aged, petite blonde woman charged toward him with palpable fear etched across her face. In the blink of an eye, she stood mere inches away, her eyes watering, lips trembling, and her expression a portrait of sheer terror. Without warning, tears cascaded down her face as she unleashed a shrill, high-pitched scream that reverberated through the air. Will, taken aback, surveyed the room in bewilderment, only to be unable to see anything beyond the woman's face beside a foggy greyness.

'My husband is dead! Why? Why?' the woman howled, inches from Will's face.

'Ma'am, what's wrong? Let me get you some help. Here, have a seat. I'll find a nurse,' Will said, gently guiding her to a seat as his vision returned to normal and his balance restored. He scanned the room and could see several people curiously watching.

'Excuse me, don't touch me,' she replied, ripping her arm out of Will's grasp.

'I'm sorry, I'm just trying to help,' Will replied.

'Who are you? Get away from me,' the woman said as she looked down and saw the hospital emblem on Will's shirt. 'Nurse! Nurse,' she cried out.

'Ma'am, please, just try to calm down,' Will pleaded, trying to understand what was wrong with the woman.

'How dare you? Don't tell me to calm down. Excuse me, nurse!'

Two junior nurses came running over to investigate the disturbance, as did a nearby security guard.

'This man just grabbed me. I was just trying to get past to go to the bathroom. He blocked my way, looked at me strangely, and grabbed me by the arm.'

'You were screaming, ma'am. I was only trying to help.'

'I did no such thing. Are you insane or something?'

Will looked around and saw a room full of patients looking back at him, all with confused expressions on their faces, and likely thinking the same thing the woman had just asked. He then quickly realised what had just happened: the lightheadedness and slight dizziness, the foggy vision where he briefly lost sight of his surroundings. The woman's screaming never actually happened – at least not right now, anyway.

'But what could she have possibly meant? Could this woman's husband be at risk? If so, when?'

Will did not know what it all meant, but he repeatedly asked himself these questions as the nurses looked at him as if he was losing his mind.

'What screaming? We were right here?' a nurse asked.

'Will, what's going on?' Rhonda Davidson, the veteran triage manager, asked as she joined the conversation.

Embarrassed at the attention, Will lowered his head. 'Um, nothing, Rhonda. Look, I'm sorry. I must have just been confused. I'm really sorry.'

'Well, just leave me alone,' the woman said.

'Ma'am, I'm so sorry for the disturbance,' Rhonda said. 'Please take a seat; it won't be long until you see the doctor.'

Will began walking towards the exit door when he heard Rhonda say, 'I'm sorry. Look, he was involved in a bad assault last year. I don't think he's been the same since, but please, there's no need to make anything of this.'

He sighed and headed straight back to the maintenance shed where he could be alone.

Will closed the door behind him and sat behind his desk. He contemplated what Rhonda had said, wondering if that's how all his colleagues saw him – as some kind of a traumatised shell of who he once was.

Leaning back in his chair, rocking it on two legs, Will felt a sudden wobble. Just as he was about to regain balance, the room seemed to spin, and his eyes involuntarily closed. In the next moment, as if in a blink, his eyes flickered open to an entirely different setting. Instead of the maintenance shed, he stood on George Street in the middle of the Sydney CBD, facing the recognisable facade of the Greenspring Bank. The distinct concrete columns flanking the heritage-listed building confirmed its identity.

The air felt fresh. It was cooler, with a crispness contrasting the warm, humid atmosphere he had just left behind. Now breaking through the clouds, the sun painted a different scene from the one he had left in the hospital. Bewildered and intrigued, Will took in his surroundings on George Street and saw a large dark SUV pull up directly outside the bank. He felt a pulling sensation in his stomach before he could give the vehicle any further thought.

The transition was disorienting, and in an instant, Will found himself inside the bank. The atmosphere was tense, and he could feel the weight of the situation. Four masked individuals shouted at the bank staff and customers, demanding everyone to get on the floor. The room echoed with the terrified cries of those caught in the chaos. Will, unable to interact with the scene, observed helplessly, feeling the palpable fear and desperation of the surrounding people.

'Get on the ground now!' one of the masked men yelled, pointing his firearm in all directions. The mass of customers immediately complied, throwing themselves to the floor, trying to stay as low as possible.

'Where's the manager?' another asked with a deep and authoritarian voice.

'Here,' a middle-aged man in a black suit and tie identified himself, lifting his head from the ground and slowly waving his hand.

Two of the masked men, with an uncanny display of strength, effortlessly hoisted him off the ground, gripping the scruff of his blazer. The terrified gasps and cries of those still on the ground echoed through the foyer.

Will's eyes were darting around the room, a room which pulsed with terror, and he tried to take in as much as he could. However, before he could process any additional details, his stomach twisted again, and he was dragged to the front of the bank. Now he stood behind the trembling branch manager.

The manager was gasping as the two men had him now in a tight headlock, but he offered no resistance aside from his knees, occasionally buckling, requiring his captors to pull him back to his feet.

'Safe,' one of them demanded.

Will's vision shifted up, and he saw a digital clock behind the teller's counter. It was a rectangular retro flip clock that rolled over a new date, hour, and minute from a stack of cards built into the device. The display on the clock read WED 2 FEB 11:45 AM.

Will's head spun again as his stomach swirled and his vision became grainy. As he lost focus on the scene before him, he heard the loud crack of a shotgun being fired, followed by the piercing screams of those inside. He felt a spray of warm liquid slap his cheek. Involuntarily, his arm was raised to his face. With his vision still grainy, Will couldn't see beyond his hand, now coming into his eyeline, but he recognised the deep red liquid dripping from his fingers as blood.

Before he could see anything else, he was back in the maintenance shed, and his eyesight readjusted to the cheap fluorescent light hovering above.

TWENTY-EIGHT

Emerging from the depths of his premonition, Will found himself abruptly thrust back to reality. As his consciousness reconnected with the shed office, Will's mind still held the vivid echoes of the vision, and he felt shaken from the spray of blood that had splashed his cheeks.

The chair he had been leaning on wobbled almost past the point of balance, and Will quickly grabbed onto his desk to stabilise himself while he processed everything he had seen. The armed robbers kept their faces hidden. There was no way of identifying them, but importantly, he had a time and a place.

'Tomorrow,' he muttered.

As Will continued to process the vivid details of the chaotic scene at the bank, a revelation struck him with a sudden clarity. The haunting echoes of terror reverberated in his mind, particularly the woman he had encountered in the emergency room — her anguished scream mirroring the chorus of fear that had gripped the bank patrons. A connection, previously obscured, materialised in his thoughts. The abrupt closure of his vision following the shotgun blast left him considering the possibility of these two incidents being connected. Questions raced through his mind like a torrent. Could the woman from the emergency room have been present at the bank? Was her scream a precursor to the tragic event that unfolded there? He felt overwhelmed with empathy as he considered the possibility that the woman he had heard in his vision could have had a direct connection to the unfolding tragedy at the bank. In his mind's eye, he again recalled the impact of the gunshot, the spray of blood, and the gut-wrenching screams. Without a second thought, Will ran back through the rain towards the emergency department. He just hoped the woman was still there; he needed to warn her.

He arrived back at the emergency room, sweating and panting. His shirt had come untucked on the run over, and he looked as dishevelled as he felt. As he tried to catch his breath, he scanned the waiting room and saw the impatient yet concerned faces of everyone inside who stared back at him. Will held back a grimace when he made eye contact with several patients. He knew he had made them all a little nervous after his earlier outburst. As his eyes tracked the room, he saw her, still sitting quietly in the corner. The woman was typing on her phone, but she briefly glimpsed up and made eye contact. She squirmed in her seat and, like the others in the room, was clearly uncomfortable at Will's return.

As Will propelled himself toward her, she involuntarily let out a cry, a mixture of surprise and trepidation, bracing herself for an imminent second confrontation with the man she had just learned was grappling with PTSD.

Just as the woman began calling out to security, Will said, 'Please do not go to the bank tomorrow.'

At the very moment when the woman called out for security urgently, Will interjected with a desperate plea.

'Do not go to the bank tomorrow, please.'

He hoped these words carried a weight of urgency and sincerity, but he saw nothing but terror in her eyes, and he didn't think she even processed the grave warning he had delivered.

'Someone help!' she cried urgently.

Will ignored her. 'Please, ma'am, whatever you do, don't go to the bank tomorrow.'

Rhonda came striding over once again, this time with a security guard by her side. She looked furious as she folded her arms. 'Will, what on earth is going on?' she demanded.

'Please, just tell me you understand,' Will repeated, ignoring Rhonda and remaining fixed on the woman, now cowering in her seat.

'Will!' Rhonda shouted.

Just then, Ravi entered the emergency room and headed for the exit. He saw Will surrounded by the triage nurse and a security guard, standing next to a terrified middle-aged woman.

***

At that moment, Ravi, having finished for the day, entered the emergency room and made his way toward the exit. However, he got diverted by the chaotic scene unfolding before him. As he tried to make sense of what was happening, the sight of Will stopped him in his tracks. Enveloped by the triage nurse and a security guard, they stood beside a visibly anxious middle-aged woman. The urgency of the situation was palpable, and the collective unease emanating from the huddled group suggested that something unusual had transpired.

'What's going on?' he asked no one in particular but thought only of Will, who suddenly looked relieved in his presence.

The woman, spotting Ravi's doctor ID tag hanging from his belt, spoke first. 'This man here is crazy. He's assaulted and harassed me.'

'I was just telling this lady not to do her banking tomorrow,' Will said, giving Ravi a look of concern as he nodded his head. Ravi understood exactly what Will meant. Unfortunately, he knew he would be the only one to understand and did his best to calm the tension.

'Ma'am, I'm Doctor Sandeep, one of the psychiatrists here...'

Before he could finish, the woman stood up and headed for the door. 'If you're a psychiatrist, that man needs help. Now, all of you, just leave me alone.'

She stormed out of the building, not looking back.

'Will, seriously, what's gotten into you?' Rhonda asked.

'It's nothing,' he replied, shaking his head and looking at Ravi.

'Maybe Will and I can have a chat?' Ravi said, taking Will by the arm.

'Sounds like a good idea,' Rhonda said. 'Don't you come back here scaring everyone.'

Ravi waved the security guard off and led Will out of the emergency department.

'Sorry about that, folks,' Rhonda said, addressing the confused and concerned crowd still in the waiting room.

TWENTY-NINE

'What did you see?' Ravi asked Will as they walked down an empty corridor towards the psychiatric unit.

'A bank robbery. This time, it was very clear. It's going to happen tomorrow, and it gets worse. I think someone will get shot.'

'Oh geez.'

'Yeah, at the Greenspring Bank on George Street. I saw four people, and they all had shotguns.'

'You need to call Aubrey,' Ravi said.

'Yep, I'll call her right now.'

'What was that all about with the woman?'

'I can't be sure, but she screamed her husband was dead. I didn't see her in the bank, but I think her husband could have been the one shot during the robbery. She freaked out when I told her to stay away from the bank tomorrow.

'Will, make the call now. Do you think the woman will stay away?'

'I hope so, but I'm going to call Aubrey anyway and see what they can do. I'm also going to have a look at the bank after work.'

'What? Why?'

'I don't know. Maybe I'll see something else that might help the police. I have no idea who these people are. They wore masks, so I didn't see their faces. I didn't even get the registration of the car I saw them get out of. I want to be able to give Aubrey more information. I want to see if anything else comes to me.'

'I'm coming with you.'

'Okay, meet you out the front at six?'

'Sure,' Ravi replied.

Will ran back to his office and made the call to Woods behind closed doors.

'Aubrey, I saw the robbery crew strike again. I mean, I assume it's the same group you're investigating.'

'You did? Where, when?' she asked urgently.

'The Greenspring Bank on George Street, tomorrow at 11:45. They arrived in a black SUV, but that's all I have at the moment.

'You're sure of the time?'

'Absolutely. I saw the clock on the wall while I was there. Aubrey, they were armed with shotguns, and I think someone was shot, maybe killed. Please be careful.'

'Don't worry, we will be fine. I'm going to organise a tactical surveillance operation tomorrow. We will cover the entire bank and take them out before they can even get inside that bank.'

'Okay, let me know how you go. Ravi and I are going to have a look at the building tonight. I might see something, you never know.'

'Okay, thanks, Will, leave it with me.'

'How's the investigation coming along, anyway?'

'It's a tough one. There is no CCTV or forensics. They are professionals, but we are working as hard as possible. We will get these guys.'

'Okay, I'll let you know if I see anything else.'

Overwhelmed by the gravity of what he had witnessed, Will could not focus on his usual tasks for the rest of the day. Seeking refuge in the maintenance shed, he grappled with the weight of the vision, with each vivid image playing out in his mind and sending shivers up his spine. In his solace, he sought to connect the dots, with the woman in the emergency room at the forefront of his mind and the crew responsible for the armed robbery only days earlier. The urgency of his warning to the woman weighed on him, and a sense of helplessness gripped him as he considered the possibility that she might not listen to him. Will knew all he could do now was place his hopes in Woods and her team.

THIRTY

'So this is it, then?' Ravi asked, looking at the front of the Greenspring Bank on George Street.

'Definitely,' Will replied.

It was right on 6 p.m., and the Sydney summer graciously extended the daylight, casting a warm glow over the city. Despite the lingering brightness, the once vibrant street was gradually slowing down. The ebb and flow of the nine-to-five trade had tapered off in an area primarily dedicated to commercial business, leaving the surroundings in a subdued calm.

'So what's your plan now that we're here?'

Will shrugged. 'I have absolutely no idea. I've never been able to prompt a vision before, and I have no clue if this will even work or where to start, but I owe it to Aubrey to try. If she and her team are going to take down these guys armed with guns, the least I can do is try to see something else which might help them.'

'Sure. And I guess this place is the best spot to try,' Ravi added.

'That was my thinking. Come on, let's take a closer look around.'

They crossed the road and stood directly outside the bank. Will noticed several CCTV cameras on the roof pointing to the entrance. Heavy iron bars protected the large front doors, which were locked tight.

'Why don't you try touching something?' Ravi suggested.

Recalling an attempt made several months prior, Will reflected on his futile efforts to trigger visions by touching everyday objects around his home. Despite his persistence, the elusive nature of his gift remained beyond his grasp, and the mystery of how to control or induce a vision persisted, shrouding him in uncertainty. Still, with nothing to lose, he tried.

'Close your eyes and think about what you saw in the last vision,' Ravi said, as Will placed both hands on the large round pillar at the front of the building.

He closed his eyes and felt foolish.

'Nope, nothing,' he said, dusting his hands off. 'Plus, I feel ridiculous. Let's have a look around the back.'

***

In the shadows of the George Street laneway, Charlie Bianco stood, fixated on the façade of the bank before him. His attire, a meticulously tailored navy blue pinstripe suit, exuded a sense of authority. The sharp lines of his oxford shoes mirrored the precision with which he observed the surroundings. Nearby, Leo, in stark contrast, sported a fluorescent yellow polo shirt, black cargo pants, and steel-capped boots. Their hushed conversation unfolded seamlessly against the backdrop of the city's bustling rhythm. To any casual passerby, the scene appeared ordinary, reminiscent of a construction manager conferring with a labourer.

Behind Charlie and Leo, Ed, the family associate, maintained a seemingly disinterested posture. His attire, a customary combination of trousers and a grey vest beneath a shirt and tie, suggested a detached demeanour. Standing in quiet observation, he cast a nonchalant gaze at his employer. Meanwhile, Leo extracted a compact electronic device from his side pants pocket. As the small display illuminated, he shared its contents with Charlie, and both engaged in an animated discussion, pointing discreetly at various sections of the Greenspring building.

So immersed in the intensity of his discussion, Charlie remained oblivious to the two slender young men standing nearby. One had shaggy black hair, and the other was wearing glasses and of Indian descent. They pointed discreetly at various features of the bank and whispered to each other. Despite their proximity to Charlie's focused exchange, he paid them no notice, his attention wholly absorbed in the strategic dialogue unfolding with Leo.

***

Will proceeded cautiously, circling the building with a vigilant gaze, his eyes scanning its structure for any details that might offer insights to assist Woods and her team. Every step was deliberate, and he craned his neck, examining the architecture and surroundings, intent on triggering a vision. Meanwhile, Ravi watched Will from a safe distance, waiting for any sign of a premonition occurring.

Locked in a determined trance and leaving Ravi behind, Will continued to survey the building without giving much notice to the small group of people around, mostly businessmen and women, heading home for the day. Straining to prompt a vision, Will soon exhaled and gave up. He turned around to find Ravi but instead spotted a tall, thin, middle-aged man wearing a grey vest. He stood by himself with a disinterested expression and his arms folded.

Will's eyes remained fixed on the man in the vest, and an inexplicable familiarity tugged at him, but despite his best efforts, he didn't know why, and the man's identity eluded him. Still, he was fixated on the man and scanned him up and down, waiting for his memory to connect the dots about where he had seen him before.

The man in the vest suddenly looked back at Will, and for a brief second, they locked eyes. He quickly averted his gaze and started walking away, but was forced to a halt when a large man in a navy suit, standing beside a man in fluorescent worker's clothing, called out to him.

'Ed! Where do you think you're going?'

The man named Ed stopped and turned around in response. He tried to avoid Will's eyes again but appeared obviously uncomfortable, shifting his weight and fidgeting with his hands. He walked over to the man in the suit and said something to him before walking away.

As though sensing the weight of Will's gaze, the man named Ed abruptly halted his steps and pivoted around in response. Despite his attempt to avoid eye contact with him, Will detected the man's continuing discomfort as he twitched nervously. As Ed approached the man in the suit, a hushed exchange took place between them, the undertones of their conversation veiled in secrecy. Having conveyed his message or received instructions, Ed distanced himself and continued on his way swiftly.

Ravi eventually caught up with Will and noticed that something had diverted his attention from the Greenspring building.

'Sorry. I lost you. You're too quick,' he said.

'It couldn't be, surely not,' Will said, as though speaking to himself.

'What?'

'I need to follow that man,' Will said.

'What man? Who is it?' Ravi said, scanning the crowd.

Before Will could answer, he had taken off.

As Will noticed Ed's attempt to elude him, a surge of determination propelled him into a swift jog, closing the gap between them. Ed peered over his shoulder and made eye contact with Will. As though recognising the pursuit, he broke into a sprint. Fueled by a sense of urgency, Will matched Ed's acceleration, running as hard as he could to catch up.

THIRTY-ONE

As Will pursued, he witnessed Ed's abrupt turn into a narrow alleyway. The passage was teeming with construction workers finishing their day's work, with their trucks neatly lined along the confined space. Undeterred, Will ran into the alley, navigating the trucks, but couldn't find Ed. He turned on the spot, wondering where he could have gone, seeing as he closed the gap. Creeping further into the alley and now clear of the trucks and workers, he scanned all directions but saw nothing.

Suddenly, a powerful, blunt force struck Will between his shoulder blades, sending him sprawling onto the ground. The impact reverberated through his body, his knees and wrists absorbing the brunt of the fall. Stunned and disoriented, Will turned his head to the left and noticed a plank of wood that someone had thrown onto the ground next to him.

He groaned in agony and tried to stand himself up. As he did, he turned back and saw his attacker. It was the man who had been called Ed. He was running off along George Street at a high speed and did not look back once. Fighting through the pain, Will strained to keep his eyes on Ed, but the distance and the speed of his escape soon worked against him.

Ravi caught up a moment later and saw Will still trying to find his feet. Rushing over and seeing the pain etched on his face, Ravi helped him stand and hold on to a nearby dumpster.

'Geez, what happened? I wasn't that far behind. Did you fall?' Ravi asked as Will nursed his back.

'I was hit with a piece of wood,' Will grunted.

'Hit? What are you talking about? How?' Ravi asked, startled and confused.

'The man I was following.' Will said through clenched teeth as he straightened his back.

'I'll call the police,' Ravi said, reaching for his phone.

'No, don't,' Will protested.

'Why not? Will, you could have been seriously hurt. Why would he just hit you like that? Is he involved in the robberies?'

'I'm not sure,' Will replied, the throbbing pain mirroring his confusion as his mind raced, as he considered why he was attacked.

'Well, have you ever seen him before? Maybe in a vision?'

Will nodded. 'I think I have seen him before. Ravi, I think he's my father.'

***

'Your father?' Ravi said as they sauntered out of the alley.

'I'm pretty sure,' Will said, still struggling to straighten his back.

'I heard him being called Ed. That was my father's name, and he looked strangely familiar.'

'But I thought you said you hadn't met him. He just took off with no explanation, right? Here, let me look at you,' Ravi said, feeling various spots around Will's upper back.

'Ouch!'

'Sorry. Nothing's broken, though. I'd say you'll have a nasty bruise, though. I've never heard you mention your dad.'

'I never knew him. My mother never spoke about him, but she never said he was dead. I assumed he was because he took off and never tried contacting us. But Ravi, I'm sure that man was my father. I've seen that face before. There's an old picture my sister found when my mum died. She has it at her house, but I've seen it a few times. The photo was of their wedding day. He's aged over thirty years, but I'm sure it's him. The nose, the eyes, they're all so familiar.'

'So why would he run away from you? More importantly, why would he hit you?'

'I have no idea,' Will said. 'I need to know if it's him though. I need to see that picture.'

'The one at your sister's house?' Ravi asked.

'Yes. I'll head down there shortly. It's my niece's birthday soon, and I was asked to come down. I'll look at the photo in person when I'm there.'

'If it was him, I wonder what he was doing?'

'Maybe the guy in the suit he spoke with can tell me. Maybe they're friends or colleagues,' Will said. 'Let's see if we can find him and ask.'

They walked back to the Greenspring Bank and along the side of the building where they first saw Ed. The other man in the suit wasn't there. Will and Ravi split up and walked the entire perimeter of the block, but he was gone.

'Any luck?' Will asked when they met again at the front of the building.

'No, sorry.'

'I have to see that picture again, to be sure. If it's really my father, I need to find him.

'I don't like this, Will. I mean, he beat the hell out of you without so much as acknowledging you. Maybe he doesn't want to be found if it is him.'

'He lost that right the day he walked out on us. I have a lot of questions he needs to answer. I'm going to see my sister this weekend and find out for sure. If it's really him, and he's re-appeared in Sydney, I will find him.'

THIRTY-TWO

According to Ed's wristwatch, it was 11.43 a.m. on Wednesday, February 2nd. Charlie, armed with a loaded shotgun, guided his brother alongside Tony and Leo towards the entrance of the Greenspring Bank on George Street, while Ed's gaze remained fixed on the unfolding scene. Meanwhile, Sal idled inside the dark SUV stationed in the loading zone.

The meticulous planning and reconnaissance carried out in the shadows of the city culminated in this moment. Every detail had been scrutinised, every move orchestrated in advance. The final checks conducted the previous evening had assured Leo's success in jamming nearby electronic signals, rendering them impervious to external interference.

The interior of the Greenspring branch buzzed with more activity compared to the United East Bank, a reflection of the different time of day. The late-morning hustle and bustle created an expected atmosphere, attracting more people to the bank's premises. As Charlie and his crew forcefully breached their way to the centre, the heightened human presence in the bank came as no surprise. Then, the orchestrated chaos unfolded, and as they asserted their control, Ed cringed at the sound of the ear-piercing screams that reverberated through the room.

Ed followed the team closely, watching their every move. Wherever they went, he went. After Charlie waved his gun toward the crowd with a sinister menace, the branch manager nervously identified himself with a trembling raise of his hand. Under the imposing face mask, Charlie snarled as he and Leo snatched him up off the ground and throttled his neck with his free hand.

Suddenly, an unexpected wail of roaring sirens sliced through the air, sending a jolt of urgency through Ed. Reacting instinctively, he sprinted to the front of the bank, his gaze fixed on the window. As he peered outside, he saw a convoy of police cars, their sirens blaring in unison, jammed the street in a formidable blockade. Ed's eyes widened as he took in the unfolding scenario. The unexpected presence of the police now besieged the meticulously planned heist, and escape seemed impossible.

'How?' he thought. 'How could they have known?'

He burst through the bank's doors and onto the street, completely ignored by the surrounding police, armed to the teeth. Navigating quickly through the rows of police cars, he saw several officers huddled around Sal's body. He was bleeding out of several bullet holes in his chest. He was dead. The officers were prying a shotgun out of his grip as others began searching through the SUV parked out the front. He looked up and down the streets and realised in just a matter of minutes; the police had surrounded the bank.

Ed returned inside the bank just as a voice through a megaphone sounded through the foyer;

'This is the police. You are surrounded. You are out of options. Leave now with your hands up, or we will use lethal force.'

Charlie pushed Marco hard in the chest. Ed saw a mix of fear and bewilderment on his face. 'How are they here so quickly?'

'I don't know. Why are you asking me?' Marco said, pushing Charlie back.

'Hey, this isn't going to help,' Leo said, but his words trembled with angst even under the balaclava.

In the midst of the chaos and confusion within the bank, two deep male voices shouted in sync, 'Police, don't move!'

Undercover police, already inside the bank and wearing jeans and t-shirts, had produced their guns and were aiming them directly at Charlie and Marco.

'Shit,' Charlie said in a panic. 'Impossible.'

A sudden eruption shattered the tense atmosphere within the bank. From the corner of the foyer, a startled Tony discharged his shotgun, the deafening blast echoing through the space. Before the police could react, the raw power of the 12-gauge shotgun unleashed a devastating force that tore through the officers. The room transformed into a scene of horror as blood sprayed across the walls and the lifeless bodies of the two police officers crumpled onto the floor.

A wave of nausea and dread swept over Ed as he bore witness to the gruesome outcome of Tony's violent act. The crowd of hostages screamed, and the knot tightening in his stomach mirrored the unravelling of their carefully orchestrated heist, now spiralling into an uncontrollable nightmare.

'Okay, alright, we can fix this,' Charlie said desperately.

'How can we fix this? What were you thinking, Tony?' Marco cried.

'What was I supposed to do? They would have shot you,' he replied.

'Oh no, no, this is bad,' Marco said, crouching on the ground, trying his best to breathe through the warm, thick balaclava.

'Leo, look out the window at the front. Tell me how many there are out the front,' Charlie said.

Leo nodded. He took his shotgun and walked to the front of the building via the left wall, trying to stay protected and away from sight.

'If there are more cops inside this bank, I suggest you identify yourself now. Otherwise, if I find you myself, I will killl you,' Tony yelled, looking at each of the petrified people lying on the floor. No one responded.

Leo reached the front of the bank and stuck to the side wall. He carefully peeled his head to the window to investigate the police response. Crime scene tape was being put up around the perimeter of the building and a tactical team, dressed in all black, were preparing their automatic rifles. The crew was completely surrounded.

Still holding onto his shotgun, Leo peaked a little further out toward the centre of the window to begin a count of exactly how many police officers they were currently dealing with. Ed walked over to the front of the bank and stood next to Leo to share his vantage point.

Leo continued to lean further out of the safety of the solid concrete wall while gripping his firearm tightly. As he made one last full stretch out of the window, a bullet burst through the glass and went straight through the centre of his head. Blood splattered across Ed's face, and he stood frozen in shock as Leo's lifeless body collapsed on the ground.

A chilling silence enveloped the room as Charlie, Marco, and Tony froze in shock, their eyes fixed on the lifeless form of their friend. Time seemed to stand still as the reality of the situation continued to unfurl before them.

Ed reached a sombre conclusion. The grim reality of the unfolding tragedy was undeniable – Sal and Leo lay dead, two police officers fell victim to the violent chaos, and the heist had unravelled into a nightmare. Taking a deep breath, Ed decided he had seen enough. He didn't need to witness any more carnage to recognize the catastrophic path the robbery had taken. The weight of the situation pressed on him, and with a momentary closing of his eyes, he sought respite from the chaos and horror sounding him.

Reality snapped back into focus, and Ed found himself again seated on the same wooden chair in the cold garage where he had initiated his premonition. The stark contrast between the vivid, chaotic scenes he had witnessed in the vision and the stillness of the garage created a disorienting sensation. Echoes of the alternate reality still lingered in his mind as he grappled with the weight of what he had witnessed. The cold surroundings of the garage offered a stark reminder that the events he had glimpsed were a mere projection, a window into a potential future that he now had the opportunity to avert.

Feeling the lingering sting on the vein of his inner left arm, Ed rubbed the injection site. The recent administration of the injection resonated as a tangible reminder, grounding him in the present moment. The sensation served as a connection between the vivid premonition he had experienced and the reality of the garage.

He gazed at Charlie and Marco, who were standing above him, staring blankly at him, waiting for what he was about to say.

Ed's voice trembled. 'You need to cancel today's robbery.'

THIRTY-THREE

Just after 9 a.m. on Wednesday the 2nd of February, Woods and Yule briefed a surveillance team at police headquarters. She sat in a small windowless conference room at the head of a large wooden table, which took up most of the space inside. The surveillance team sat along the perimeter of the room and took notes as Woods provided the details. The team received instructions to covertly surround the Greenspring Bank on George Street. They were told to conduct a high-risk vehicle stop and arrest the occupants of a dark-coloured SUV that arrives and stops idle near the bank before they could enter. Woods reminded the team that they had received information on the robbery from a 'confidential source' and that the crew was highly skilled and, most importantly, would be heavily armed.

'Our intelligence suggests they wear all black, including gloves and face masks while carrying shotguns. I know it isn't much to go on, but despite that, given this unique description, we surely won't miss them.'

Yule added, 'Because we don't know their identity yet, the risk naturally heightens.' We have to assume they will use the firearms they are carrying. Just to make sure I'll send a couple of you inside the bank on the off chance, we miss them on the outside. So be safe everyone and remember, our intelligence suggests the timing will be accurate for 11.45 a.m so I need everyone to be completely alert and covering all points in and out of the George Street area. Let's go.'

'One more thing,' Woods added. 'We have a tactical team on standby, already in the field. If the crew are able to make it inside the bank before we can get to them in time, it'll be up to the two inside the bank to stay calm and remain undercover. They will need to be our eyes and ears from the inside while we rally the snipers and tactical team. It is crucial for us to keep everyone, including police and civilians, safe during this operation.'

The team moved swiftly, in well-practised efficiency, as they prepared to assume their designated positions around George Street.

By 11.20 a.m., the team was in place, and the air crackled with anticipation and adrenaline. Two covert police vehicles parked directly out the front of the bank. One was a small white truck that could park in the loading area directly out the front of the bank, arousing no suspicion, and the other was a white courier van. Two surveillance operatives sat in the back managing hidden high-definition cameras, recording a 360-degree view of the area with a live stream being relayed back to a command post set up in a larger van a few streets away being managed by Yule, who could coordinate each operative through a radio.

The officers parked the remaining cars around the building, covering every likely approach to the bank. They were far enough away not to raise the offenders' attention, but close enough to respond quickly when required. Most of the vehicles used were small, nondescript sedans or construction utilities that blended seamlessly with the city surroundings.

Woods was out on foot and walking through Martin Place toward George Street. She had the front entrance to the bank in her line of sight and wore a relaxed fit blazer and pants with pinstripes to blend in with the city business crowd. Underneath the jacket, she concealed a Glock 23 tucked away at the back of her waist. She quickly brushed the handle of the pistol, checking its position inside her trousers, thinking that soon she might need it. Since last speaking with Will, she had not received any additional information, so there was nothing in her mind to suggest the robbery would not go ahead or that he had been mistaken. As she considered the armed offenders would soon arrive, her heart thumped in her chest, and she tried her best to breathe smoothly and slowly. Woods felt comfort knowing she was in communication with the rest of the team via a wireless radio system set up with a receiver tucked away in her pocket. She wore a small earpiece to hear all updates from the various surveillance points.

The time of Wood's watch told her it was 11.43 a.m. She took another deep breath and put her hands in her pockets. She activated the switch on her radio.

'11.43 team, standby, any minute now.'

11.45 a.m.

There was still no sign of the dark SUV or anyone resembling someone preparing to rob a bank. Woods walked a little closer to the front of the branch, concerned that she may have been a little too far away.

As Woods surveyed the surroundings, her concern grew. There was still no sign of the dark SUV or any conspicuous activity that would indicate preparations for a bank robbery. Navigating closer to the front of the branch, she questioned if she had positioned herself too far away from the potential focal point of the operation. The anticipation of the unknown hung in the air as Woods carefully scrutinised the environment. The city remained unsuspecting, and the absence of any discernible signs of the robbery crew heightened the tension.

11.46 a.m.

Still no approach of a dark SUV.

11.50 a.m.

Woods relayed a further radio message. 'No change.'

11.55 a.m.

'No change.'

12 p.m.

'No change.'

The mounting anxiety gnawed at Woods as the expected events failed to unfold. Thoughts of Will lingered in her mind, and she couldn't shake the concern that perhaps there had been a mistake with the timing or the location.

Faced with mounting uncertainty, Woods contacted Yule, who remained stationed in the command post. Yule's response was to wait a little longer.

12.10 p.m.

Woods broadcasted again, 'no change.'

THIRTY-FOUR

At that same time, Charlie's strategic instincts were sharp as he instructed Leo to engage in counter-surveillance around the Greenspring Bank. Seated at an outdoor table of a small cafe on George Street, Leo observed Woods from a distance of about fifty metres. Leo, dressed in a dark suit, a thick red tie, and highly polished black shoes, seamlessly blended in with the office workers and business clientele frequenting the café for their meetings.

Leo maintained an air of nonchalance as he sipped an espresso. His gaze, fixed on the street, identified Woods amid her anxious pacing. A subtle smile played across his face as he recognized the telltale signs of a police officer working covertly and attempting to blend in with the public. Leo, confident in his ability to read the nuances of the game, noted the occasional shortcomings of those trying to maintain their cover amidst the bustling cityscape.

He pulled out a small device that looked like a mobile phone, but it was a high-powered, high-resolution camera. He used the camera to zoom in on the nervous police officer with startling clarity and sighted the bulge in her hip, which was unmistakably a firearm. The average person wouldn't have noticed this, but it protruded just enough for a trained eye to spot it. He took several photographs of her and forwarded them to Charlie's encrypted phone via a hotspot Wi-Fi connection with the caption, *'Cops are here. Good call cancelling.'*

***

12.20 p.m

'Still no change.'

As anxiety gripped Woods, a rising panic flushed her face with heat, leaving her feeling flustered. The planned arrival of the offenders at 11:45 a.m. had come and gone, yet there was still no sign of their presence. Faced with the escalating uncertainty, Woods took action. Via radio, she raised the two surveillance operatives inside the bank, seeking immediate information on the unfolding situation.

'No sign of anything suspicious inside here,' one of them replied.

'Except us,' the other added. 'We are getting a few odd looks after hanging around inside for half an hour doing nothing.'

'Ten more minutes, everyone,' Yule added over the radio.

The anxious silence stirred Woods' stomach. She ran her hands through her hair as each passing second grew increasingly tense.

12.30 p.m.

'No change.'

Yule got back on the radio and called an end to the operation.

Woods felt deflated. The earlier spike of adrenaline, fueled by anticipation and urgency, now had no natural release. Fatigue settled in, compounded by a tinge of embarrassment. Confidence had accompanied her briefing to the team, grounded in what seemed like solid intelligence that a robbery would happen. Now, as the expected time frame passed without incident, Woods grimaced at the thought of facing the inevitable debriefing with a sense of disappointment.

Thirty minutes later, during the debrief, Woods remained mostly silent, exhausted and feeling a little sorry for herself.

'Thanks for your help today, everyone,' Yule said, taking control of the room. Sometimes, our intel is a little off, and things don't go according to plan, but jobs like this require the highest, most urgent response to ensure we keep the public safe. I know we are all on edge after the first robbery at the United East Bank, but we will keep working on the case and find these people. Does anyone have any issues to raise or questions from today?'

No one spoke.

'Okay, thanks again, everyone's dismissed.'

The officers slowly filed out of the conference room, leaving Woods and Yule alone.

'I'm really sorry. The intel must have been off.'

'Don't worry about it. These things happen. It's hard dealing with an informant, you know. They are often wrong. I use them myself, but I rarely trust them.'

Woods wanted to stand up for Will and tell Yule that this was different, that she trusted him, and that he wasn't like other informants, but today, it wasn't worth it. She felt too flat, and Yule wouldn't understand.

'Everyone's on edge. I get it,' Yule said. We all want to catch these guys, especially before they do another robbery or hurt someone. We are getting pressure from the Commissioner's office, too, but we just need to keep working the case hard. There's no harm done today, okay?'

'Okay, thanks.'

'But your informant, Will, just be careful with the information he gives. All these people have their own agendas, regardless of what they may say.'

It was becoming apparent to Woods that Yule didn't trust or perhaps even like Will, or he had some unpleasant experiences with using informants in the past. Woods ignored this and knew that Will would make up for it. She just didn't understand why he was wrong today.

She walked back to her desk and started combing through a long list of enquiries for the first robbery. When she became too distracted by Will's recent and apparent incorrect vision, she went for a walk and called him.

Confusion echoed through his voice as Woods communicated to Will that the robbery hadn't occurred. On the other end of the phone, he seemed more befuddled than she was, stuttering, struggling to find words to encapsulate the unexpected turn of events before going quiet for a moment. The silence on the line reflected the shared perplexity, leaving both grappling with the stark contrast between the expected heist and the reality of its absence.

'Hang on, I'm in the hospital. Let me just step outside,' Will said, finding his voice again. A moment later, and in privacy, he continued, 'I don't get it. I mean, I'm just confused. I saw the bank and the date and time. Everything I saw told me it would be then.'

'I mean, we waited for a while, and no one turned up. Maybe what you saw was something a little more cryptic.'

'No, I don't think so. It was as simple as seeing a clock on the wall. That time and date had to have meant something. Everything seemed so clear.'

'Look, it's okay. I guess no one got hurt, and the robbery didn't happen for whatever reason, which is good. It just would have been nice to catch this crew before they really hurt someone.'

'I just don't know what to say. I was so sure of this one.'

'And you didn't see anything else after we spoke?'

'No. Ravi and I went to the bank and walked around, but nothing else came to me. Although something weird happened.'

'What?' Woods asked, leaning forward in her chair. She knew when Will said the word 'weird', it surely would be.

'I think I saw my father. I mean, I'm almost positive it was him.'

'Your father? What? I thought you told me he had left when you were young.'

'He did. Until yesterday, I didn't even know if he was still alive, but I'm sure it was him.'

'Well, did you speak with him?'

'Not exactly. I tried to, but he saw me and ran away. Actually, he hit me with a piece of wood and then ran away.

Woods felt her heart race and blurted out a string of interrogating questions in a single breath: 'Woah, Will, are you serious? It couldn't have been your father, surely. I mean, why would he do that? Are you alright?'

'Yeah, I'm fine. I have a bit of a bruise on my back, but I'm okay. I'm more confused than anything.'

'You need to formally report it,' she said firmly.

'No chance. If this person was my father, I'm going to find him on my own and get the answers I've been looking for my whole life.'

Woods voiced her concern to Will, her tone reflecting a mix of worry and frustration. 'I don't like this, Will. He runs away from you and then hits you with a piece of wood! You could have been really hurt,' she expressed, emphasising the potential danger of what Will was proposing.

'But I need to know, Aubrey. I'm more curious than anything. I'm going to my sister's house to find some old photos of him to make sure, and then I'm going to find him.'

'Will, as both your friend and a cop, I don't know if it's a good idea. I mean, I can't tell you what to do, but whatever you do, don't do it on your own. It all seems a little strange. What was he doing hanging around the city and then running away when he spotted you? That's very strange.'

'I know. It's one of many questions I've got. I can't imagine it'll be a pleasant reunion. He probably doesn't even know my mum is dead or that his daughter has a child. I just want some answers, and then I never want to see him again.'

The conversation hung in an awkward pause on the phone, and Woods, sensing Will's sensitivity to the topic, trod lightly. Unsure of what to say and recognising the delicacy of the situation, she opted to leave it alone. Sometimes, faced with personal boundaries and unspoken emotions, she truly believed silence could be the most considerate response.

'I hope your boss wasn't too mad that nothing happened today,' Will eventually said, changing the topic.

'He was okay. As I said, these things happen.'

'He just seems like the kind of guy who doesn't like disappointments.'

'Well, that's true, but it's all part of the job. Sometimes these things don't go as planned, so don't worry. I'm still confused about why nothing happened. I really thought it would.'

'So did I,' Will replied.

THIRTY-FIVE

Amongst their multifaceted criminal endeavours, the Bianco family boasted ownership of a legitimate catering company nestled in Sydney's Northern Shore. This business venture held particular significance, as it was a legacy insisted upon by the family matriarch, Christina Bianco, when Frank helmed the family enterprise. Upon Christina's retirement with Frank, the reins of the catering company transitioned to the twins, Charlie and Marco, who then entrusted their younger cousin, Tania Bianco, with its operation. In a seamless continuation of tradition, Tania undertook the responsibility of running the business, preserving the essence and values instilled by her predecessors, and it continued to thrive.

Charlie and Marco rarely visited the large commercial kitchen. However, tonight, they were hungry and had business to discuss with Ed. Charlie, making a decisive call just before 7 p.m., instructed Tania to clear the kitchen, a departure from the usual routine. Tania, without hesitation, obeyed, leaving a spread of food and wine for five. Ed would not be eating.

When the group arrived thirty minutes later, they used the back entrance via a dark laneway and opened the door with a key Marco kept. They walked in single file on the tiled floor to the large kitchen lined with steel bench tops and several hotplates. Steel pots and pans hung from the ceiling, and they all ducked and weaved their way to the centre of the kitchen. There, they found stools around a steel island workstation with steaming plates of *pasta alla norma* set out with napkins, cutlery, two bottles of wine and five glasses.

As Charlie, Marco, Leo, Sal and Tony gathered around the table, a heavy silence enveloped the room, broken only by the sounds of utensils against plates. Standing near the door, Ed felt a palpable anxiety about the impending discussion. Whenever Frank summoned Ed into a meeting, it was always for critical matters. Ed's apprehension was heightened by the fact that Charlie and Marco, known for their hostility and brash demeanor, were now in charge. Ed had spent a considerable portion of his life working for the Bianco family, a commitment that posed challenges even under the leadership of the seasoned Frank Bianco. However, working under the twins presented a new set of concerns. Unlike the level-headed Frank, Charlie and Marco brought a different dynamic to the table, one that Ed expected might create additional complications.

***

When Ed was called into Frank's office weeks earlier, the twins discovered an unexpected revelation about Ed's role within the family. Frank, with an unwavering seriousness, disclosed that Ed possessed unique abilities, allowing him to perceive events before they unfolded. The revelation initially elicited laughter from Charlie and Marco, who dismissed the notion as impossible. However, their amusement abruptly ceased when confronted with the stern look that Frank directed at them. At that moment, the weight of Frank's seriousness impressed upon them the gravity of Ed's purported abilities, introducing a dynamic that transcended the conventional realms of business and family affairs.

Frank explained in great detail how Ed was first found by the family many years ago and how his abilities have prevented many business catastrophes. He also explained how he discovered a way to force him into visions of the future when it suited him after they were not coming naturally. The twins, while managing their manners in the presence of their father were still not convinced, however, Frank told them that the use of

Ed is not negotiable in taking over the business, and before too long they would thank him for keeping them out of prison when he can show them their future.

***

Despite their initial scepticism, Charlie and Marco followed their father's instructions and tested Ed's abilities before the first robbery. When Ed foresaw the unfolding details of the United East Bank robbery and assured them that there was nothing to worry about, the twins found themselves inclined to trust him. In a validation of Ed's premonition, the job unfolded successfully, solidifying the belief that Ed's unique abilities held a tangible and strategic advantage for the family's illicit operations.

This success affirmed Ed's role within their operations and fostered a begrudging acknowledgment from Charlie and Marco, as they recognised the practical utility of Ed's visions in ensuring the success and security of their criminal endeavours.

Anticipating the upcoming Greenspring Bank robbery, Charlie summoned Ed to his home. In a controlled and coercive manner, Charlie compelled Ed to tap into his unique abilities and witness the details of their next planned heist before it unfolded.

Following his vision, Ed's advice to call off the planned robbery irked Charlie, and he initially responded with irritation and argumentativeness. However, the weight of his father's words about Ed's history of saving him in critical situations prompted Charlie to reconsider. However, still not entirely convinced, Charlie dispatched Leo to the area as a precautionary measure. The aim was to confirm if Ed's foretelling of police presence was accurate, a test to validate the credibility of Ed's premonitions.

However, the pressing issue for this meeting was why the police had been waiting there at all.

THIRTY-SIX

Charlie and his crew finished their meal and stacked the large white plates on each other, leaving them on the stainless steel bench. They wiped their mouths, sipped the last of their wine and turned to face Ed, who was still standing in the corner of the large kitchen.

'Anything you'd like to say, Ed?' Charlie asked.

'What are you talking about, Charlie?'

Charlie rose from his seat and approached Ed with an air of authority. The buttons of his black silk shirt strained against his round and muscular chest, barely containing the powerful physique beneath. With a deliberate movement, he pushed his chest out, further emphasising his physical presence, a gesture intended to assert his dominance.

'From what you described in your vision, we were correct in calling off the job. But that's not what I wanted to say. You were right. The police *were* there. However, from what I understand, there was an entire team of cops there, not just the two you described. Now, tell me, how did they even know about the robbery? The only people who should have known are in this room.'

'Charlie, honestly, I have no idea,' Ed said nervously, backing away.

'You, of all people, know full well what happens if you betray the family?'

'I never said anything, I swear. I told you what I saw. I saved you all.'

'According to Leo,' Charlie said as he rolled his shirt sleeves to his elbows, 'it was as though the police were waiting for us to arrive.'

Ed attempted to move back a little more, but he found himself already trapped in a corner with nowhere to go.

Charlie continued, 'I promised my father I would use you, but I have to say, Ed, I don't trust you.'

'Look, Charlie, please. I just tell you what I see, that's all. I haven't spoken to anyone.'

'And you know full well what would happen if you rat us out, don't you?'

Ed didn't respond. He just looked down at the missing two fingers on his left hand.

'That's right. My father was kind to leave you with the rest of them. I promise you'll lose more than a couple of fingers if you cross me.'

Ed's lip trembled. 'Yes, I know.'

'Good. Because if I find out that you betrayed us, I'll be taking the heads of everyone you've ever so much as thought about. Then yours will be last. Now get out of here. I'll call you when I need you.'

***

Ed didn't wait to be told twice, and he swiftly turned and left the kitchen. Stepping out onto the humid night, beads of sweat formed on his forehead from the tense encounter with Charlie Bianco. He peeled off his vest, slinging it over his shoulder, and took a deep breath. The night air clung to him as he returned to his small apartment in North Sydney, owned by the Bianco family. The fact that Ed lived rent-free in the apartment meant that his existence was intricately tied to the Bianco family. While he enjoyed the perks of having his expenses covered, it came at the expense of his liberty. He was, in simple terms, a slave.

***

Qiang Chen, a twenty year-old Chinese national with cropped black hair and a thick, muscular frame, maintained a discreet vigil, stationed on the dimly lit street inside a dark-coloured Honda Civic, his watchful eyes fixed on the Bianco family's bustling catering kitchen. His employer, Zao Ming, had assigned him this task. Ming's instructions had been explicit: drop everything and shadow Charlie and Marco Bianco meticulously. The objective was clear — be a ghost and gather details on their movements, activities, and associations.

Ming, fueled by a desire to avenge Pau's murder, intended to play the long game to uncover the location of their safe house in Sydney and strike at the opportune moment.

Chen, vigilant in his observation, noted a tall, thin figure leaving the kitchen but paid him little attention. However, his focus sharpened when, twenty minutes later, Charlie and Marco Bianco emerged from the side door, accompanied by three familiar associates. A surge of conviction gripped Chen, as he believed at least two of the five individuals were the ones responsible for the murder of Pau.

He relayed the details to Ming, updating him about the situation. Chen started his own vehicle as each of the five dispersed into their respective cars. Determined to stay close to Charlie Bianco, he followed his grey Jaguar sedan through the quiet Sydney streets.

THIRTY-SEVEN

Will greeted the weekend with an early start, rising to the aftermath of an unusually humid night that left him uncomfortably damp. Despite a refreshing cool shower, the oppressive humidity clung persistently, leaving him in a perpetual state of discomfort. He packed an overnight bag and opted for light and loose-fitting shorts paired with a comfortable t-shirt. Before the day warmed up any further, he left his apartment and made the short walk to Central Train Station, where he awaited the next southbound train bound for Canberra, with a scheduled stop at Queanbeyan.

Will arrived at the train station and was met by the welcoming presence of his older sister, Rosie. Sharing a resemblance with Will in their tall, slender frames, pointed noses, and dark hair, Rosie had her car ready with the air conditioning blasting.

The short drive led them to Rosie's street in a recently constructed estate. Each house was almost identical, all single-story and made of tan brick. The large front yards and backyard pools along the street contributed to the sense of sameness. They were part of a coordinated development, likely housing predominantly government workers from the nearby capital, Canberra.

Will's brother-in-law, Ben Kennedy, had experienced burnout from his demanding law job in the city several years ago. In pursuit of a more balanced lifestyle, he proposed a move down south, away from the hustle and bustle of Sydney, as a better environment to raise their young daughter, Claire.

Rosie pulled into her concrete driveway and parked the car outside the double garage. She said the garage was being used for storage and was full of clutter.

Will got out of the car and saw the front lawn was dry and brown. Ben typically took great pride in keeping a nice and tidy yard, but looking up and down the suburban street, each garden looked dead.

'This drought's killing us, not to mention the local farmers around here. Some of them are really struggling,' Ben said, walking out the front to greet Will with a firm handshake.

'Yep, the heatwave is just burning everything, and there's been a fair few bushfires,' he continued. 'A few of my friends have had to evacuate, and some houses have been lost. It would be great to get a cool change and some rain. Anyway, how are you, mate?'

'Doing good. It's great to be here and see you guys.'

'Here, give me your bag and come in,' Ben said. He was a burly man, almost forty years old, and he kept himself fit by working out almost every day. Today, he wore a white singlet, and his shoulders and arms were bulky and tanned.

Stepping into the house, another refreshing wave of air-conditioned coolness that offered immediate and welcome relief greeted Will.

'Where's Claire?' Will called loudly from the front hallway.

'Here I am,' she said, running toward Will and crashing into his leg for a big hug. She looked like a mini version of Rosie: long black hair, tall for her age, and sporting the distinctly sharp Denham nose.

'Happy Birthday!' Will said, handing her a large and colourful gift bag.

Claire pulled a box from the bag. It was a new Barbie doll, Rosie told him she had been eyeing in the shops for the past couple of months.

'It's a mermaid Barbie. You can play with her in the pool,' Will said.

'Wow! Her tail is purple with sparkles. Thanks, Uncle Will,' she said, giving him another hug. 'Mum, can I go in the pool?'

'After lunch, I'm making sausage rolls for you, and then after, we have a birthday cake.'

'Yay!' she screamed, running off to find a brush for the doll's long hair.

The four of them sat on the deck in the backyard by the pool, where they ate plenty of food and had a long, overdue catch-up.

Despite their deep closeness, there remained an unspoken barrier between them – Rosie was unaware of Will's visions. Engrossed in her work and dedicated to raising Claire, Rosie navigated life's challenges away from Sydney and lived in a separate world from Will. Although they maintained regular communication and held a genuine affection for each other, Will just never knew how to raise the subject, so he opted to keep his gift to himself.

'Hey, Rosie,' Will said, unable to wait any longer to find out what he had been thinking about since he arrived. 'I'm just wondering where the photo is of Mum at her wedding.'

'Why?' she asked, looking a little startled.

Will saw the surprise in her face and tone, so he quickly deflected. 'Well, you know, I just want to look at it, to see her again. I miss her, and that one is a nice picture of her. I thought you'd still have it around.'

'Oh, of course, sorry. I completely understand. I've kept it in the spare room, which I'll put you in for the night. It's somewhere in the cupboard.'

'Thanks, Rosie.'

'And I know you miss her. We all do.'

'Uncle Will, come in the pool with me!' Claire yelled as she ripped off her large T-shirt, revealing her swimming costume underneath it.

'She's practically been living in that swimming costume all summer,' Ben said. 'But the pool has been keeping her busy. Plus, she tires herself out and sleeps better.'

Claire picked up her new mermaid Barbie and jumped into the pool, creating a large splash.

'Come on, Uncle Will!' she yelled.

'I'll dip my feet in and watch you,' Will said.

Will found a shady spot by the edge of the pool and spent a quiet twenty minutes watching Claire's joyful play. Claire, fully immersed in her own world, found great delight in repeatedly tossing her Barbie into the pool and then gleefully diving in after it. Soon, though, the sun moved, and it took away all the shade in the backyard, and Will felt it sting the back of his neck.

'Come on, Claire. That's enough for now. Let's go back inside and have some cake.'

She dragged herself out and quickly dried herself off with a huge smile, looking very excited at the thought of her birthday cake.

Rosie told Claire to sit at the table as she bought out a chocolate cake with five lit candles. They sang Happy Birthday and watched Claire blow the candles out with one powerful, full breath. Afterwards, they sat together and ate some cake, but Will continued to fidget, unable to contain his curiosity for much longer and desperate to see the photo. He excused himself by mentioning the need to put his bag away in the spare bedroom.

Entering the room, Will opened the wooden cupboard and found the old photograph inside a dusty gold-coloured frame. Although it was a colour photograph, the years had frayed the edges, and the dust covering it had muted the tones, even under the thin layer of glass on the frame.

His heart raced, and he held his breath as he stared at the figures in the photograph. There was no doubt the tall man in the black tuxedo standing beside his mother was the same man he had seen by the Greenspring Bank.

It was his father.

THIRTY-EIGHT

Will stared at the photograph of Edward Denham – tall, slender, and endowed with the same thick, shaggy black hair. The uncanny resemblance to Will heightened the mystery that surrounded his father. The photograph, captured on their wedding day, showcased a smiling face that seemed to conceal a multitude of unanswered questions. Edward Denham's sudden disappearance before he could even remember him, followed by his unexpected and violent reappearance in Sydney, ignited both rage and confusion within Will's mind.

He took a photo of it with his phone and forwarded it to Ravi along with the caption *My dad on his wedding day- the same guy from the city.*

'Did you find the picture?' Rosie asked when Will returned to the living room.

'I did, thanks. It was nice to see it again.'

'You know, if there are any of Mum's things you would like to take back to your place, you can. You have just as much right as I have to her belongings.'

Will thought about this and realised he had kept none of his mother's old possessions. They sold most of what she had owned but Rosie kept the more precious or sentimental items.

'It's fine. My place is too small, and if I'm ever looking for something, I know where I'll be able to find it.'

The family gathered for a dinner of steak and salad, and after the satisfying meal, Will took on the role of bedtime storyteller, offering to read Claire a book and tuck her into bed. As they entered her room, an overwhelming sea of pink enveloped the space. From the painted walls and bedspread to the stuffed toys, there seemed to be no other colour to be found.

'Hmmm. Rapunzel?' Will suggested.

'Yes!' Claire said, pulling her blanket to her chin.

By the time he finished reading, Claire was fast asleep. He left the room and turned the ceiling light off, leaving a dull pink night light glowing at the edge of her bed.

Will took a shower and changed into his pyjamas. He checked his phone afterwards and there was a reply from Ravi.

'Looks like him I guess. Are you positive?'

Will texted back. '100%'

The following morning, he woke late and ate a slow breakfast of bacon, eggs, and toast with the rest of the family. Claire was busy eating as fast as she could before running off to get ready for her pool party with her new school friends.

'The pool has huge slides!' she told Will with a glistening excitement.

'Well, I hope you have lots of fun. I have to get back home, though. I have some things to do, and then I'll be back at work tomorrow.'

'Give Uncle Will a hug, Claire and let's get going,' Ben said.

Ben and Claire left, and Will returned to pack up his things and take the train back to Sydney. Rosie drove him back to the station and hugged him when she parked near the entrance.

'Claire was so happy you came down here, Will. It was great seeing you.'

'You too, Rosie. See you soon.'

***

Ed Denham found himself perched at the breakfast bar on the top floor of his waterfront apartment, a space owned by the Bianco family and designed with a simple yet luxurious aesthetic. Despite its relatively compact layout, its design spared no expense. The apartment exuded an air of extravagance, from the imported plush rugs adorning the living room to the Italian marble embellishing the bathroom. Despite the elegance, a stark reality prevailed – Ed owned nothing within the apartment. The grand surroundings were merely a ruse that endeavoured to keep him content and well-rested as he diligently yet forcefully produced vision after vision at the behest of Charlie and Marco Bianco.

Ed's thoughts meandered through his recent vision as he sipped on a steaming espresso. The close call with an enraged Charlie, poised on the brink of blaming him for a potential leak to the authorities, lingered in his mind. He thought again of Will as he had done every day. This time, however, it was different. He couldn't help but wonder why Will was at the Greenspring Bank just before the planned robbery, honing in on the building and circling its perimeter. He often wondered if someday his son would be the same as him – and now he believed it to be true. The timing of Will being at the bank and the police intervening in the robbery during his later vision was too coincidental. He now knew that he had passed on his abilities to his son, and that Will had seen the robbery in his own mind and somehow reported it to the police.

Ed felt sick as the gravity of the realisation dawned on him. He had kept his distance from his family to protect them. Now, with Will being just like himself, he knew if Charlie and Marco found out, he would be in great danger. Ed realised that at any cost, he had to protect Will from being discovered. He now needed to find him and issue a warning that would probably save his life.

THIRTY-NINE

The moment Will opened the door to his apartment late in the afternoon, a wave of stuffy heat greeted him. He switched the fans on and opened the windows, which only provided mild relief. He ate a late lunch of a cold salad and then took a cool shower.

After drying off and dressing, the loud buzzing coming from the intercom startled him. Before he answered through the speaker, he walked over to the living room window and carefully peeked outside, where he could see the mailboxes and the intercom system by the front door.

His heart suddenly skipped a beat, and his entire body felt heavy. There was no mistaking the person downstairs – it was Ed Denham.

A dilemma gnawed at Will's thoughts. While a part of him yearned to initiate a meeting with his father, he wanted it to be on his terms. Now, the unexpected appearance at his doorstep introduced layers of confusion, uncertainty, and then panic. Contemplating the situation, he furrowed his brow, unsure how Ed even tracked down his apartment. Will found himself at a crossroads. He weighed the options, uncertain whether to open the door and confront the mystery or maintain some distance.

The persistent buzzing of the intercom reverberated through the living room, and Will, caught in the whirlwind of conflicting emotions, paced restlessly around the room. Each passing ring seemed to amplify the urgency of the situation, creating a sense of pressure, and it was now apparently clear that Ed would not leave.

Will's mind churned with the weight of decades-old wounds as he confronted the reality that the man who had once abandoned him as a child, resurfaced after twenty-eight years, and who then inexplicably assaulted him with a wooden plank, was now standing at his doorstep, suddenly demanding acknowledgement.

He carefully peeked out of his window again and looked down. Examining Ed, Will thought about how much he looked just like his father, only that he had an extra thirty years on him. Instead of the smart trousers and vest he had previously worn outside the Greenspring Bank, he now wore more casual apparel: baggy shorts and a baggy T-shirt – exactly the same as what Will was wearing. His narrow shoulders were lost under the shirt as it dropped loosely over his thin body.

Will watched as Ed looked up, scanning the building, and eventually made eye contact with him. His gaunt face showed no emotion as Will quickly retreated behind the curtains. But it was too late. They had made brief eye contact for the second time in a week.

Panic then turned to rage at his father's insistence, but before he could over-analyse the situation further, he pressed the intercom, allowing him access to the building. He heard the front door click. He was on his way up. The weight of his absence and a pile of unanswered questions left Will utterly unsure of what he would say or do the moment he was face to face with him.

A moment later, there was a very faint knock on his door. Will stood silent in the centre of his living room. His legs felt heavy, and his heart was pounding through his chest.

Another soft knock followed.

At the moment before the impending encounter, a thought crossed Will's mind – he considered simply ignoring the knock as if he could erase it through stillness and silence. Yet, deep within, a more profound need stirred. He needed to face what was on the other side of his door.

Will took another deep breath and brushed his hair out of his face. He turned the handle and opened the door slowly. He stared long and hard at his father before either said a word.

'Hi, Will,' Ed eventually said. He appeared anxious, shuffling his weight between his legs and biting his lips. He stood in the doorway and kept his hands in his pockets.

'I don't really know an easy way to say this, but I'm your father.'

Will's lip trembled, and he didn't know what to say. A wave of powerful mixed emotions swept over him with so much power he lost all sense of himself. Instead of responding, he reacted in a way that surprised even him. He slammed the door shut.

Will flopped into the back of the door and took a deep breath before turning to look out of the peephole. His father remained standing in front of the closed door. While still looking anxious, he had an air of calm about him, as though he was not ready to leave. He softly knocked on the door again.

'Will, can you please open the door? We need to talk.'

Will took another deep breath and opened the door a second time, looking at the man he had only ever seen in one old photo until last week.

Rage suddenly led to a mix of other emotions, and he pushed Ed hard in the chest. His bony frame recoiled, and he fell back into the wall opposite the door.

'I'm so sorry for everything. Please allow me the chance to explain,' he pleaded, rubbing his chest.

'Yeah, you've really got some explaining to do,' Will barked.

'Can I please come inside?' Ed said.

Will's rage was reaching a new level. His father's visit caught him off guard, and everything he knew he needed to ask him became clogged up in his brain, and Will suddenly became speechless. Instead of speaking, all he could manage at that moment was a pair of clenched fists. He looked Ed in the eyes one more time and nodded. He moved away from the threshold, and Ed passed him and walked into the living room.

'Thanks, Will. Maybe we should sit down? I owe you a thousand apologies, and perhaps nothing I say will make things right, but there's so much you need to know.'

FORTY

In the subdued ambience of Port Botany, Charlie Bianco guided his Jaguar through the labyrinth of shipping containers, finally converging with Marco near the water's edge. The late afternoon sun cast a harsh glow on the water's surface, intensifying the metallic industrial landscape, towering cranes and colossal containers. Against the backdrop of the silent port, the twins stood in contemplation, their meeting veiled in secrecy following explicit orders and a hefty bribe for all dock workers, bar a select couple, to leave the area.

Dressed in tan chinos and polo shirts, Charlie and Marco stood in silent anticipation as they awaited the two port authority workers on the family payroll.

A text message from Sal relayed the imminent arrival of a sizable shipment. With Tony accompanying him, both en route with large trucks, the stage was set for the reception of their crucial delivery of top-grade methamphetamine precursors. Charlie knew fully that this routine yet essential business deal marked a pivotal point in their family enterprise by disrupting the long stronghold of Ming's Chinese criminal network in the meth trade. Though the thrill of the import may have waned with repetition, Charlie approached his duties with a calculated seriousness, recognising the importance of this operation to not only their family's income but also their criminal influence.

Charlie, observing the two approaching port authority workers in their distinctive yellow high-visibility shirts, recognised them as those on the payroll. These workers, easily enticed by the allure of cash payments, had proven invaluable in ensuring the smooth and discreet reception of the family's shipments. Charlie nodded at their approach and discreetly handed over thick white envelopes, the financial incentives securing an unwavering commitment to privacy and security. The port workers, with their loyalty bought, assured Charlie of an uninterrupted operation.

A few moments later, Charlie heard two medium-sized rigid trucks reversing. It was Tony and Sal, backing up with the large sliding door at the back of the trucks already open. They were empty and waiting to be packed.

***

Observing from a discreet vantage point nearby, Qiang Chen positioned himself behind a towering shipping container, silently biding his time. His dark Honda Civic, parked nearby, stood as a vigilant sentinel, ready to tail Charlie and Marco's operation and trace the final destination of the chemical consignment about to be received. Chen, ever patient, harboured no intent to disrupt the delivery; instead, he opted to observe and gather intelligence quietly. He would soon relay the findings to Ming as he continued meticulously surveilling Charlie and Marco's activities.

***

Fifteen minutes later, one of the port authority workers caught Charlie's attention, signalling a thumbs up from a distance. The much-anticipated shipment had indeed arrived. They steered the two trucks through the vast shipping containers and followed the designated route to the storage area, where the bribed workers had carefully stowed their consignment.

Charlie, Marco, Tony, and Sal hustled for the next twenty minutes to load the large blue drums tightly sealed tightly with white lids. Charlie possessed only a moderate understanding of the raw materials required for methamphetamine production. Nevertheless, he understood the value of the ingredients, and he would store and safeguard these barrels temporarily within the Golden Bell Hotel's basement cellar until the carefully selected few associated with the family could retrieve them and begin the manufacturing phase.

Beads of sweat dripped from their foreheads as they toiled vigorously and efficiently in a well-coordinated production line, methodically loading the trucks to full capacity. Once both trucks were tightly packed, Tony and Sal sealed the roller doors and steered away from the Port.

***

Unbeknownst to them, Chen's Honda discreetly trailed behind, keeping pace with their every move.

FORTY-ONE

Will walked over to his leather armchair and sat down while Ed sat on the couch underneath the window. Still consumed by rage, there was an icy silence as Will refused to speak first. His fists remained clenched, and he could barely bring himself to look at his father.

'I don't really know where to start,' Ed said slowly, cautiously. 'There's so much I need to say, and I know you must have thousands of questions.'

Will glared hard at Ed. 'Why don't you start with how you found me after all these years, and why now?'

'Will, I always kept an eye on you. I know I wasn't around, but I have never stopped thinking about you and Rosie. I was watching from a safe distance.'

'A safe distance? What the hell does that mean? Did you even know Mum is dead?'

'Yes, I do know. I'm so sorry she's gone,' Ed replied, lowering his gaze to the floor.

'You left us!' Will screamed.

'I know what I've done, and I'm so very sorry, but you don't understand. I had to do what I did.'

'Then tell me quickly before I kick you out of here.'

Ed sighed as Will sat on the edge of his chair, ready to throttle the man.

'Okay, you have a right to know. I'm going to tell you everything,' Ed said, sitting on the edge of his seat to meet Will's eyes.

'Before you and your sister were born, I was involved in some pretty bad things – mostly petty street crime, fraud, hustles, things like that. I was on a pretty destructive path, heading for prison in a matter of time. I knew some pretty bad people, who I considered friends, and I started using drugs.'

Will gazed at his father's skinny arms and saw scar tissue built up on the inside of his arm. Some scars looked newer than others.

'Your mother nearly left me because she knew where I was going, and it wasn't good. But then she became pregnant with Rosie, and I tried my hardest to change. After a while, though, I fell back into my old habits. I started hanging around with people connected to the Bianco family, a powerful and very dangerous organised crime group. I needed money, and they paid well. Anyway, when I was running around with them, they found out I had certain abilities, and they made it hard for me to leave. Well, actually, impossible for me to leave. These abilities, or visions, are the same as what I know you have now acquired. Many years ago, I actually told Frank Bianco, the former head of the family, about my visions. At first, he thought I was mad or high on drugs until I was able to prove it. I guess I thought it would impress him and give me a higher status in the family and more money, but he just saw me as a piece of meat to be exploited. One day, we were shaking down some low-level drug dealer for money when he suddenly pulled a knife on me and my friend. I had a gun on me, and without thinking, I just shot him. Unfortunately, he died instantly.'

'You left our family, and you killed someone?' Will retorted in disgust, appalled at the revelation and now on the verge of standing up to release his rage directly on his father.

'Yes. It was a terrible thing to have done, and still to this day, I feel sick with remorse when I think about it. Naturally, there was a police investigation, but Frank Bianco covered for me. He used his influence in the media and the police to create a strong alibi for me, and before long, the case went cold. But this came at a price. I was in debt to the family.'

'You could have left, you know. You don't owe these people anything! It's pretty clear to me now, though. You're nothing but a thug and a killer!'

'You don't understand, Will. Rosie was a toddler, and then six months later, you were born. I now had two children I loved so much, but the family held it over me. If I were anyone else, maybe I would have repaid my debt earlier, but the family would never let me go, not with the abilities I have. Trust me, these people are beyond evil. They knew what gift I possessed, and they held it over me. They threatened to kill you and Rosie if I ever tried to run away. Frank Bianco even kept tabs on you, Rosie, and your mother. I was a prisoner.'

Will's emotions were a storm inside, a mix of confusion, anger, and curiosity. He grappled with his father's atrocities and his reasoning for staying away all these years. Yet, filled with rage, a part of him still couldn't ignore the possibility of understanding his own inexplicable visions from the man he inherited them from.

'When I saw you the other day, you ran away and smacked me with a piece of wood! And now here you are! What's wrong with you? Were you high then?'

'I know, and I'm so sorry. I was with the Biancos that day, and when you saw me and then followed me, I panicked. If they knew who you were, they would take you and use you just like they are using me. I had to protect you.'

'I'd never work for them!'

'It's not that simple. These Biancos are the worst kind of people. Psychopathic and money-hungry. Now that Frank has retired, his two twin sons have taken over the family business, and they're even worse.'

'So why are you here now? What do you want?' Will spat as his hostility increased.

'To warn you. As I said, I know about your gift. I've wondered for years if someday you would inherit it, and now I know you have. I know you saw the robbery at the Greenspring Bank and called the police. Nothing else could explain why I saw the outcome I did. You need to trust me on this. Please stay out of their business. If they find out you're involved, the outcome would be terrible.'

This did it for Will, and his fury went to a new level. He launched himself from his chair and stood over his father. 'How dare you come to my home and say that to me! I have no memories of you. All I ever had was an old photo. You ran away, and now, after all these years, this is what you say to me? Stay away from the mafia? Don't interrupt their armed robberies?'

'I know it's a lot to take in, and I can't tell you how sorry I am for what I've done, but everything I have done was to protect you and Rosie.'

'So what you're saying is that an organised crime family is behind these robberies, then?'

'I've already said too much about it. Just please stay out of it. If you see any other robberies, just ignore them, trust me.'

'Trust you? I don't even know you!' Will said, now hovering even closer over Ed.

'You don't know how bad things could get,' he said grimly, holding up his left hand, revealing two missing fingers. 'This is what they have done to me in the past for nothing other than having a mixed-up vision. They don't tolerate any deceit or failure.'

'And what if someone gets hurt by one of their robberies? You can live with that, can you? What I saw in my vision was horrifying.'

Ed sighed. 'If it means keeping you safe. Yes.'

'You're a coward!' Will said, flopping back in exhaustion, glaring at the ragged old man he despised increasingly with every word he spoke.

'How do you even know about my visions?' Will spat before Ed could say another word.

'I always suspected you would one day be the same as me, but it wasn't until the robbery was foiled that I knew for sure. You and I are the same, Will.'

'Don't you dare! Don't you dare come into my house and say you and I are the same! You have no idea how these visions have affected me.'

'Yes, I do. I got my first one when I was about twenty. Before I met your mum, I was driving late one night when I ran my car into a pole. I was in the hospital for about a week, and I honestly thought I was going to die. I had a severe concussion, along with quite a few broken bones. After this, something must have happened in my mind because I started having visions about all kinds of things.'

Will remained silent, folding his arms defensively.

'Look, I got the family's police sources, some of whom I trust very much, to pull your record secretly without telling Frank Bianco. I read about your assault, and I drew my own timeline to find that assault is what would have triggered them for you. Something must be dormant in our family genetics, and once our brains are triggered, they start.'

'So instead of helping good, innocent people, you use your visions to help criminals, correct?'

'I had no choice.'

'You're pathetic. So that's why the robbery at the Greenspring Bank never happened? You saw it too, didn't you? And then you called it off?'

'Yes, I saw it. I saw it after you must have seen it. I learned of the planned covert police operation. I saw the police waiting inside, and well, it would have been a mess if it had gone ahead. I had to tell them to call it off. They agreed, but then they suspected someone leaked the plan to the police, and well, of course, they accused me. After this, I thought to myself, how did the police know there would be a robbery? I knew then it must have been you.'

'Yes, it was,' Will said aggressively. 'I saw it all and called it in.'

'And now you need to stop.'

'You can't be serious? Who do you think you are? And look at you, you're still a junkie,' Will said, pointing to the track marks and scars on Ed's arms.

'I was once a drug user by choice. Not anymore,' he said, looking down and rubbing his tattered inner arms. 'The family experimented on me for years to find out how they can induce visions.'

'What are you talking about?'

'Well, you would know better than anyone that we can't naturally bring on a premonition. They just come on their own. Sometimes, at the worst possible time. This inability to control them frustrated Frank Bianco, and he wanted to be able to see things whenever he chose, so he employed a team of corrupt government scientists to stick probes in me and try to force them out. They gave me so many drugs at one time I thought I was going to die. Then, they found ketamine. They stuck me with a good dose of it, and it instantly brought on a vision. What I saw after being given the drug was

Frank Bianco being shot when opening the door to his home the following day. It was the clearest I've ever seen anything. In fact, it was a lucid vision. I could navigate through it and see what I wanted to see. I quickly became addicted to ketamine, and after a while, I needed higher doses just to see anything. The family started to give me the drugs so frequently that I now can't see anything naturally anymore. I feel like the longer I go on using it, I will eventually need a dose so high it will probably kill me.'

'Ketamine?' Will asked.

'Yes. It seems to put my mind in a trance-like, hallucinogenic state and induces the visions. I can enter and leave them as I like. All I need to do is concentrate hard on what I am instructed to look for, and they just happen. This is why the family uses me. Before a risky job, they sit me down, inject me, and I see how it will play out. I concentrate on them and where they plan ongoing or doing, and I report back on the outcome of their job. I guess I'm part of why they have successfully avoided being arrested over the years.'

'That's nothing to be proud of. It's despicable.'

'I never wanted to do it. They just had a hold of me. Either I continue to work for them, or they kill you and Rosie. What choice did I have?'

'You chose a life of crime before you even met this family.'

'That's true, and not a day goes by that I don't regret all my decisions. And now I'm trying to make the right one here. To protect you. Please look the other way if you see anything. I don't want them finding out about you.'

'So you've stopped by after all these years to give me this warning?'

'I don't want you to get hurt.'

'What about Rosie? Are you going to see her?'

'That would only complicate things.'

'She thinks you're dead. And you know what? You might as well be. You know what, just get out of my house,' Will growled.

'Will, please,'

'Get out!' he yelled, standing up and walking toward the door.

Will held the door open as Ed lowered his head and slowly walked over the threshold without protest.

'Everything I've ever done was to protect you all. I hope you can understand that.'

'You've made all the wrong decisions in everything you've done, and you can't even see that. You've wasted our gift. All the good you could have done, but you hid away with criminals. Never come back here again!' Will roared, slamming the door in his father's face.

FORTY-TWO

Will's mind was a whirlwind of emotions and questions. After the unexpected vision, all he wanted was sleep and solace in the silence of his apartment, giving himself the time and space to process the encounter.

Waking up just before 7 a.m. the following day, after a deep sleep wrapped loosely in his thin sheets, Will had about half a second of contentment. His barely semi-awake mind thought that yesterday's events may never have happened and that his father was still a non-existent figment of his imagination. Still, it all came flooding back to him when he opened his eyes completely. With his mind still churning, Will hoped his daily work routine would offer a distraction.

Will sat behind his desk in the maintenance shed, but productivity eluded him. Instead, his gaze fixated on the clock hanging above the door, counting down the moments until 9 a.m. when Ravi would start work. Despite the night having passed since his father's visit, Will couldn't claim to feel much better. He was desperate to share the details with Ravi and roamed the hospital wings to help pass the time.

'Hey Ravi, you got a moment?' Will asked sternly, after finding Ravi in the cafeteria an hour later.

Ravi looked up from his morning coffee, recognising the seriousness in Will's expression. 'Sure, have a seat. What's up?'

Will took a deep breath and looked around to ensure they were alone. 'My father showed up at my door yesterday.'

Ravi almost spat his coffee out in surprise. 'Your father? What did he want? How did he even find you?'

'Well, first, he said all these strange things like he has been watching me for years, so he's always known where I've lived.'

Ravi's eyes opened wide, and he fired questions in quick succession. 'What did he say? Why did he hit you the other day? What did he want?'

'Whoa, slow down,' Will interjected. 'But yes, that's essentially how I grilled him yesterday. Once I overcame the shock of seeing him at my doorstep, a barrage of questions poured out.'

'Well, tell me what he said,' Ravi said, now on the edge of his seat.

Will spent the next five minutes meticulously recounting every detail his father had shared with him. This encompassed the reasons behind his departure from the family, his involvement in a life of crime, and the revelation that, much like Will, he also experienced visions.

'So his visions also came on because of a traumatic injury? That's interesting.'

'Yeah, he thinks we must have some kind of underlying trait, and it comes out after a nasty knock on the head. He doesn't know for certain, but it makes sense.'

'Yeah, it does. Well, not medically, at least, but the fact both of you started experiencing visions after an injury is fascinating.'

'Well, there's more,' Will whispered after scanning the cafeteria again. 'This crime group he works for, the Bianco family, began experimenting on him years ago to determine if they could induce visions at will. They eventually found that ketamine injections can trigger what he told me were lucid visions, completely under his control.'

'Ketamine, geez,' Ravi said with raised eyebrows. 'That can be really dangerous if they aren't careful. It produces a dissociative anaesthesia, not something to mess around with.'

'I don't think they care too much about him, and since they've found something that works, I'd say they'll stick with it. He also told me the long-term abuse of it has prevented him from having visions naturally. Now, he needs higher doses to induce any vision at all.' Will explained.

'His body is now probably reliant on it, and addiction in high doses is common,' Ravi added. 'So what are you going to do now?'

'Nothing. I kicked him out,' Will said, begrudgingly and without being able to control his whisper or hide his resentment. He glanced around, but no one paid him any attention. Will continued in a fresh whisper: 'I want nothing to do with him, Ravi. He's working for a crime family, and he even had the audacity to tell me to do nothing if I forsee another robbery. I felt disgusted and ashamed of him, to be perfectly honest.'

Ravi, listening intently, remained calm and offered a balanced opinion. 'Well, what if you were putting yourself in serious danger? You said these people he works for are pretty dangerous?'

'Nothing is going to change,' Will protested, sitting back and crossing his arms. 'Aubrey wouldn't let me down, and we've already helped so many people. I think I've finally acknowledged the disaster of the drug lab exploding, and I guess I'm still healing from that, and I'll need more time to forgive myself completely. But, as you said yourself, it's who I am.'

'Now I'm only thinking of you here, Will, but I need to ask this. Do you think these people are capable of something nasty if they find out you've ruined their plans?'

'It doesn't matter. I can't see how this Bianco family, or those involved in the robberies, will find out about me. Unless my father tells them, but he says he's spent years trying to protect me, so I don't think he'll say anything. Ravi, I can't let them rob banks and hurt people though, so if I see something again, I will report it to Aubrey. I can't just look the other way. My conscience will crush me if I let people get hurt again.'

'And your father?'

Will stood up and frowned. 'I'm going to pretend like I never met him.'

FORTY-THREE

Charlie Bianco handed over the final storage instructions for the liquid precursors to Tony and Sal, along with Leo, who had just arrived at the Golden Bell Hotel to assist. The team had successfully transported eighty large plastic drums, each holding fifty litres of pseudoephedrine, totalling four thousand litres. Even by Charlie's standards, this marked a considerable and triumphant import. Once Charlie moved these materials to the manufacturing site, his drug cooks could expect to produce an extraordinary amount of ice, finally ousting Ming's syndicate from the trade.

Charlie pointed to the far end of the cellar, where a space awaited in front of the back wall for storing the barrels. He and his crew began unloading the two trucks and arranging a neat pile of plastic drums stacked eight by ten against the back wall, which was a swift process. Once safely moved and stacked, they concealed the barrels with old painting drop sheets and strategically placed cases of soft drinks and wine in front of the now-hidden stash. Charlie was confident the goods would remain secure behind the heavy-duty locked door in the family's hotel cellar for the next few days.

Marco grabbed five ice-cold beers from a small bar fridge in the cellar and handed them out. They sat at a round table and drank deeply, wiping sweat off their foreheads.

'Any issues with our people starting the cooking?' Charlie asked after taking a long drink.

'Nope, none,' Tony said. 'I spoke with them last night. They are just setting up the final stages of the lab, and they will be ready to take the gear in three or four days.'

'That's fine. The stuff will be okay here until then. What about distribution once it's ready?' Charlie asked.

'I can help there,' Sal said. We use our usual cocaine channels to start off with, but there are also a couple of guys who did time with one of my cousins a few years back. He introduced me a while back. They're reliable. They'll manage a lot of interstate deals, too.'

'You sure we can trust them?' Marco asked.

'They know who we are. They'd be stupid to try anything. Plus, they stand to make a lot of money themselves.'

'So, who did you guys end up finding to cook?'

'Again, they are friends of friends, but trustworthy. They may not be as good as the Chinese, but from what I hear, they have an excellent reputation. They recently worked for a few other groups, but that's fallen over, so they are keen to start working again. Again, they are fully aware of us and our reputation, and I don't think they're interested in returning to prison, so we won't have any problems with their loyalty to us.'

'I'll only say this once,' Charlie started, his tone now stern, 'if I hear a single whisper of these recruits so much as thinking of ratting on us or screwing us around, I'll cut their heads off.'

'I don't doubt that,' Leo said.

They all took a deep drink, sinking into their chairs. Charlie exuded confidence, feeling that this import had been easy. While the prospect of making a substantial amount of money loomed, he still regarded it as a straightforward family business, albeit dull.

'Well, I think we need to talk about other matters,' he said, taking a fresh beer while the others huddled close in anticipation of their fresh instructions. 'We are one bank job behind, thanks to the hiccup at Greenspring. It's not where I wanted to be right now, but while you guys were sorting the trucks out, Leo and I started looking into our next job.'

'We are leaving Greenspring alone for now and moving to the Australian Summit Bank at Martin Place,' Leo said.

'It won't be easy,' Tony muttered. 'It's in a tight, high-traffic spot.'

'No, it won't be,' Charlie said with a smirk. 'Who wants easy, though?'

Tony and Sal exchanged cautious glances, their expressions mirroring a shared concern. Marco, in response, tried to project confidence, though his attempt was evident in the strained expression on his face.

'I'm struggling to picture a quick getaway route,' Sal said, looking at the maps on his phone. He turned his head in every direction while looking at satellite images of the area and bit his lip.

'Yes, it is true,' Charlie said. 'It won't be as smooth as the United East Bank job, but think about it: if it's slow for us to get out, it'll be slow for the cops to get in.'

'Hear me out,' Leo added, opening his laptop screen. 'I've found a way to hack into the traffic light control centre. Right before we do the job, we place a fake armed robbery call to the United East Bank at Haymarket, right near the city police station. The cops will think we are pulling the same job again, and they will all head there, literally on the other side of the CBD. A few minutes later, I'll create havoc with the traffic system. Green lights will be everywhere, south of Martin Place and west of Pitt Street. That way, we create accidents all over the City, completely grid-locking it and giving us a solid head start out of the City, heading north. We take the Cahill Expressway, changing the lights behind us to all green as we go, leaving a trail of carnage on the road while we sail off into the sunset. By the time the cops clear through the mess and arrive at the bank, we will be long gone.'

'Impressive, huh?' Charlie added with a wide smile.

'Yes, it is. There's still a lot of security at that branch. It may be an old building, but I'm pretty sure the internal security is state-of-the-art,' Sal added.

'You aren't wrong there,' Leo said. 'I'll disable phone signals and CCTV in the area, no problem, but we won't have time to get into the vault or counting room ourselves.'

'And you don't see a problem with that?' Tony asked.

Charlie answered this question. 'Every day at 1.40 p.m., the vault is opened, and cash is moved via a steel, locked trolley to an armoured car to be taken away from the branch. Their vault only stores cash temporarily. In terms of the armoured truck staff, there will be three. All armed. One stays in the truck while two wheel out a steel trolley with the day's cash trade. Here, look at this.'

Charlie unrolled the blueprints of the bank onto the table.

'How did you get this?' Tony asked.

'The bank may have updated their security, but the layout is the same. This is an old plan Leo helped pull from the Sydney Council database when they digitised their floor plans years ago.' Charlie continued, 'See here,' he said, pointing at an area on the blueprint. 'This is the small open passageway behind the teller. When the money leaves the vault, it must make the ten-metre journey along the thin corridor to where the cash in transit truck parks inside the compound behind a heavy steel gate. We will take it before then. The minute the truck arrives, the vault will open. They do it every day, and the timings are precise. But our margin for error is going to be very small. Going too early will result in the vault still being locked, while going too late will cause us to miss our chance and the money will already be put in the truck, which again has timing locks we won't be able to bypass.'

'What's so tough about the vault itself? Why don't we do it well before the armed truck arrives?' Tony asked.

'Yeah, why can't we do what we did with the United East Bank?' Sal added.

Charlie said, 'Because they don't have the same kind of day vault as the United East Bank. In order to access this new vault, you first need the manager and assistant manager to open it together, and second, it takes thirty minutes to unlock. The locks are on a timer, so if they unlock it while we're there, we would have no choice but to wait thirty minutes, and then the cops have plenty of time to arrive.'

'There's also no override for that,' Leo added. 'We could punch, shoot and threaten everyone we like, but it won't change the timer on the lock.'

'Okay, so what do we do about the armed guards?' Tony said.

'We take them out. Don't worry about the other one in the truck. He won't be able to get inside. Only the bank staff can let people through the locked door. In fact, it's airtight and soundproof through that door. He won't even know what's happened.'

'The issue is getting behind the teller,' Leo said.

'Exactly,' Charlie continued. 'So Tony, when you get in, you need to grab the greeter at the front of the bank, and I'll grab one of the loan clerks. They usually work at desks near the front of the bank. There are also two security guards employed during business hours. Marco, you take one, Leo the other. I want them disarmed immediately. You all then follow me to the teller, and unless they open the door leading to the back, they all die. It's only the bank's money. No one there will risk their lives for protecting the bank's money, so that won't be a problem, and by this stage, they will be petrified. So assuming our timing is right, which it will be since we will spend no longer than eight to nine seconds doing this, we should then have the opened vault in our sight. I shoot the guards, and we load the cash up. There should be at least one million to one and a half million in cash. We pack it in four bags, and away we go. No cops nearby and no CCTV to record anything.'

Tony smiled. 'Sounds crazy. But I love it.'

'Me too. Nothing worth doing was meant to be easy,' Sal added.

'Sal, we need a van,' Charlie added. It should be like an electrician's van or similar, with ladders and pipes on the roof, the works. It needs to look legit because we are going to be driving right up to the front door, right in the middle of Martin Place.'

'I'll find one from an electrician, so we don't need to forge any signage. I'll find one at least an hour from Sydney, leave it with me. After the job, I'll take it away and burn it.'

'Good. Check the shotguns, check the rest of our gear and sleep well. We do it in two days.'

FORTY-FOUR

Will woke in the middle of a steamy night, his throat raspy and dry. Keeping the lights switched off in his bedroom, he stumbled into the kitchen for a drink. After draining a glass of water, he stood at the kitchen sink, refilling it. In that moment, he felt the familiar sensation of his stomach being pulled forward, as if attempting to detach from his body. His eyes snapped shut, and soon, he found himself in daylight, standing on a bustling street. Before him loomed an old building adorned with a large green and gold Australian Summit Bank sign. Hundreds of people, all clad in suits, hurriedly passed by as he observed the scene.

Will immediately recognised his surroundings. He was standing in the centre of Martin Place in the city's centre.

Parked directly in front of the bank, obstructing Will's view of the entrance, was a white panel van adorned with the words *'Central Coast Electrical'* prominently displayed in large blue text on the back.

Struggling to peer beyond the back of the van, erupting from within the building, the sudden sound of gunshots jarred Will. The two distinct and loud cracks echoed through the air, reaching his ears and causing him to wince in pain.

The next thing Will knew, he was standing inside the bank, right beside the lifeless bodies of two men lying face down on the carpet, blood pooling around them. As he turned around, his gaze met the barrel of a smoking shotgun. The man holding the weapon was large and muscular, clad entirely in black, including a balaclava obscuring his face.

All Will could see were the dark, cold eyes of the assailant, fixated on the body of his victim, and blood speckled the mask and clothes of the menacing figure.

A second later, the masked shooter sprinted past Will, accompanied by three other similarly dressed and masked men, all armed and gripping people tightly as though they were hostages. They rough-handedly dragged them through the bank, displaying a disturbing lack of regard for their well-being. A woman caught Will's attention as her black mascara ran down her face, staining her white blouse. A large man held her in a choke-hold from behind, and she struggled to keep her feet on the ground. Her legs swung wildly as a large man pressed the end of a sawn-off shotgun into her back, causing her high heels to dangle precariously from their ankle straps.

As the captor discovered the woman's iPhone in her hand, he ruthlessly ripped it from her weak hold and flung it to the ground, right where Will stood. Upon impact, the lock screen activated, revealing a photograph of a middle-aged man with two young children – the woman's family. Glancing at the display, Will noted the time: 1:40 p.m., Tuesday, 8th February.

The four men became increasingly loud, but the words they exchanged were unintelligible to Will. His focus remained fixed on the screaming woman and the lifeless body lying at his feet. The realisation hit him – he was in the midst of another robbery, the same crew he had seen in his previous vision. It had to be the group hired by, or working for the Bianco crime family his father had warned him about that was responsible. A surge of rage and sickness overwhelmed him at the brutality inflicted on the terrified hostages by these violent criminals. As he surveyed the room, Will realised he had shifted to a new location within the bank. Now standing behind the teller, he looked out into the foyer. It took a moment for him to register that he was standing in a puddle of thick blood – evidence of an innocent person mercilessly murdered by these thugs for no reason other than robbing a bank. Repulsion and contempt filled Will as he grappled with the emotions of witnessing such brutality and his father's instruction to ignore what he saw.

He knew he couldn't keep what he witnessed to himself, regardless of his father's earlier warning.

Amidst the continuing terrified screams, Will discovered the reason the armed men had hurried past him. Next to the pool of bright red blood lay the lifeless bodies of two men, face down and motionless. The blood surrounding them flowed away, pooling at Will's feet. Coming into focus nearby was a steel four-wheeled trolley, which he presumed the now deceased men had been pushing. It appeared sturdy, all chrome, with several locked panels. Within seconds, two of the masked men, equipped with small tools from their cargo pants pockets, pushed aside their female hostages and effortlessly forced open the panels.

As they revealed the contents of the trolley, they pulled out bundles upon bundles of cash featuring fifty and one-hundred-dollar note denominations. The masked men erupted into maniacal laughter, intensifying Will's sense of illness. They opened large duffle bags, stuffing them to the brim with the cash.

The unfolding vision became unbearable for Will. He had seen enough and couldn't bear to witness what these men were about to do next. Determined to prevent this future horror, he needed to get out and intervene to ensure this robbery would never come to fruition.

A moment later, Will's mind seemed to align with his resolve, and he felt his head snap forward as his eyes opened. Suddenly, he was back in his kitchen, gripping the sink so tightly that he feared it might break. The anger he felt from what he had just witnessed was unprecedented. The gruesome scenes of death at the hands of these thugs fueled an intensity of emotion within him like never before.

FORTY-FIVE

Still rattled and thinking of his father, Will muttered to himself with fury, each word bitten off sharply, 'How could he let those people do this?'

He called Woods immediately.

She didn't answer. Considering it was the middle of the night, Will assumed probably had a long day and was fast asleep. Knowing that she would wake up early for her morning run, he hung up and sent a text message, asking her to alter her usual route and run past his place in the morning. His news was urgent and he needed to share it with her immediately.

Too agitated to fall asleep, Will attempted to at least close his eyes and try to calm himself down. However, for the next five hours, he stared at the ceiling in bed, anxiously waiting for Woods to reply to his text.

The reply arrived just after 5:30 a.m. Woods, gearing up for her morning jog, told him she would swing by his place.

A little before 6 a.m., a red-faced and panting Aubrey Woods rang the downstairs buzzer. When Will let her through the front doors, she sprinted up the stairs. He waited at the door for her and ushered her inside as soon as she reached the top of the stairs. Her face and tied-back blonde hair were sweaty, and her back showed dampness through her white workout tank top. Will offered her a glass of cold water as she sat behind the small round table, covered in clutter, and unfolded washing.

Will continued to pace through the living room, unable to stand still. 'I saw another robbery; that's why I needed you here as quickly as you could,' he explained urgently.

'Another one? When? Where?' Woods replied with a startle. She could barely stop the glass of water from trembling in her hands.

'Yeah, another one,' Will replied. 'I saw it just last night. It was a bank robbery. The Australian Summit Bank at Martin Place, and it was brutal, Aubrey. It will happen two days from now. 1.40 p.m.'

'Was it the same people? What did you see? Tell me everything.'

Will walked Woods through his entire vision, describing in vivid detail the brutal events he had witnessed, including the murders and the stolen cash from the trolley.

'And the time, you're sure?'

'That's what I saw. I mean yes, yes, I'm sure of the time. The screen display was pretty clear on a phone that was thrown on the ground,' Will said.

'Right, I better get on the phone to Yule. This time, we're going to get them! You're brilliant, Will!'

Woods hurried back down the stairs to call Yule. On her way out, she told Will she would discuss the possibility of setting up another surveillance and interception plan, catching them once and for all.

Will pondered once again about his conversation with his father and the shared gift they both possessed, along with his criminal connections. However, considering the urgency of the situation and Woods having a lot on her mind, he had held off on sharing this information with her for now. Woods needed to concentrate on her job, and Will could discuss it with her later. The involvement of Bianco's people didn't deter him; they were going to be stopped in two days, and it didn't matter who they were or what connections they had. Will was determined to use his gift to do the right thing, and soon, he was confident they would all be brought to justice.

FORTY-SIX

C harlie Bianco descended a lengthy flight of wooden stairs leading to a ground-floor rumpus room in Marco's Waverton home in Sydney's Lower North Shore. The house, perched on a steep hill with a view of the water, created the impression that the lower part of the dwelling was a considerable distance from the street level.

Charlie had just finished a weights session, and he still wore his black running shorts and a tight singlet that struggled to contain his pumped-up shoulders and chest. As he made his way down the stairs, he held something of great importance in his right hand, enclosed in a small black leather pouch.

He had arrived in response to a text message from Marco, who had organised a meeting with Ed. In Charlie's understanding, this "meeting" meant forcing Ed to witness the potential consequences of their planned upcoming robbery. The twins were utilising him in a manner aligned with their father's intentions – ensuring their success and safety for the impending job.

Marco and Charlie shared a similar lifestyle, relishing in the bachelorhood of their mid-twenties. Mostly, they kept their business separate from their homes and personal lives. However, with Ed, they deliberately prohibited him from participating in any official business dealings. As a result, they purposely excluded him from the cellar at the Golden Bell

Hotel, where they frequently discussed work matters. Instead, they used Marco's basement for these special meetings.

The door leading to the rumpus room was closed, and Charlie entered to find Marco leaning against the wet bar, with Ed seated on a bar stool. A heavy silence hung in the air; both of them were well aware of what was about to unfold.

***

Knowing there was no use resisting, Ed stood up and methodically rolled up the sleeves of his grey button-down shirt. Marco had already given him enough information about the planned robbery at the Australian Summit Bank for him to focus on the time, location, and details of how the job would unfold. The success or failure of the robbery now depended, in a way, on Ed and what he would convey from his vision.

He settled into one of the large, soft recliners typically reserved for cigar smoking, took a deep inhale, and waited. Charlie unpacked his small leather pouch, revealing a syringe and a small vial of clear liquid. Wrapping a piece of medical tubing around Ed's right upper arm, he pulled it taut, then inserted the syringe into the bulging vein. As the transparent liquid flowed into his bloodstream, the anaesthetic effect of the ketamine took hold.

Ed soon experienced a sense of weightlessness, his face taking on a slightly flushed hue. However, he felt so utterly relaxed that moving in the comfortable recliner seemed like a tremendous effort. It was as if he could sink right through the cushions as he entered a trancelike state. Closing his eyes, a peaceful smile spread across his face. Taking a deep breath, he concentrated as intensely as possible on the details of the robbery that Marco had just briefed him about.

Within seconds, Ed seamlessly slipped away into another world. Standing next to Charlie and Marco, who wore black face coverings, everything felt wrong. Blood splattered the walls, and two bodies lay in a heap in the centre of the room. Looking out, Ed saw police lining the street. Suddenly, gunshots erupted from within the bank. Tony gasped; he had been shot in the chest and clutched his heart as he collapsed to the ground. In the corner of the bank, two undercover police officers had identified themselves and opened fire.

Ed looked on as Charlie roared and returned fire. The police took urgent cover behind a nearby desk and overturned it, knowing their Glocks were no match for his shotgun. In between blasts, Charlie rushed over to the desk, taking one officer by the throat while Marco shot the other.

Ed suddenly realised what had happened.

'Will, you saw the robbery and set this up again. I told you to stay out of it,' he exclaimed, his words a mix of frustration and terror.

Outside the bank, police continued to gather. Witnessing one of their own murdered in cold blood, it seemed like tactical police were ready to rush inside and put an end to the violent robbery. Looking down at the bodies of Tony, the police officer, and the two customers, Ed knew things would get worse for him, and Charlie would be furious. However, he had to stop this from happening. He shook his head sadly, closed his eyes, and reemerged on the recliner in Marco's basement.

FORTY-SEVEN

Ed looked up and saw Charlie and Marco staring at him. Their cold, heartless eyes locked onto his, waiting for him to speak. After witnessing their brutality during the future robbery, he hated them more than ever. He thought about allowing them to go through with the planned crime, facing the consequences of a police set-up, but then he considered the innocent people who would be killed. Keeping Will in mind, Ed couldn't allow innocent lives to be lost. He needed to keep Charlie and Marco calm, convince them to cancel their plans, and ensure they wouldn't suspect him of any deceit that could backfire on him and his family. The tumultuous emotions running through Ed's mind complicated matters, but for once, he wanted to do the right thing.

'Well?' Charlie said. 'Come on, let's hear it.'

'Yeah, sorry, I was still a little dazed. Listen, you can't do this job tomorrow,' Ed stammered, trying to sound convincing while concealing the true reason behind his sudden change of heart.

'What? Why not?' Charlie yelled. 'You're saying this an awful lot lately, Ed. I gotta say, it's getting tiresome.'

'No, it's nothing bad,' he lied, improvising his story. 'It's just... It's the way... It's the vault. It never got opened.'

'What?' Marco asked. 'It opens at the same time every day.'

'I saw you go in. You took some hostages, and the bank manager said the vault would not be emptied today. You even made the manager show you, and it was locked. There were no armed guards waiting to take the money.'

'What happened then?' Charlie asked, glaring at Ed with menacing eyes.

'Nothing. You weren't harmed or caught, if that's what you mean.'

'You're lying,' he spat.

'I swear, Charlie I'm not. I'm just telling you what I saw.' Ed squirmed uncomfortably in his seat. The weight of his decision pressed heavily on him. If they found out he wasn't being forthcoming, they could kill him on the spot or, even worse, track down Will and Rosie and harm them first. However, the magnitude of innocent deaths in that robbery was beyond anything he had encountered with the Biancos before.

'Get out of here, Ed,' Charlie said.

Ed remained still, uncertain of whether his being excused was a trap.

'Go!' he roared.

Ed got up off his chair, still feeling a little light-footed from the drugs. He slowly scrambled up the stairs and made his way out of the house. The air outside felt like a breath of relief as he distanced himself from the intensity within.

***

'What was that all about?' Marco asked once Ed had left the room.

'I don't trust that guy,' Charlie said.

'I know you don't, but what about what he said? There might be some truth to it?'

'I'm not so sure. I don't know what he's trying to do, but something just doesn't feel right.'

'So you still want to do the job?'

'Yes. But we do it earlier. We will do it tomorrow.'

'You don't want to use Ed again? Given the date change now?' Marco asked.

'No. I told you I don't trust Ed and don't want him to know anything about what we're doing. We do it on our own. Call the others and tell them the change in plans.'

FORTY-EIGHT

Charlie and Marco arrived together the following day at the Golden Bell Hotel. As it neared midday, a small lunch rush of eager patrons started making their way inside for the half-price beers and steaks, the lunch special. To avoid the lunch crowd, Charlie and Marco used the side alleyway and entered the cellar through the thick, locked steel door, access that remained solely with them. Following Ed's vision, Marco contacted the crew through their encrypted group chat and informed them of the recent change in plans.

When they entered the cellar, they found Tony, Leo, and Sal loading shotguns and preparing their equipment. The atmosphere in the room was tense, with an air of anticipation lingering among the crew members.

'So what's this all about?' Tony asked, setting his now loaded, sawn-off shotgun down.

'All you guys need to know is that we believe the safe won't be opened tomorrow, so we decided to bring the job forward. Nothing changes with the plan. It's only the date that has changed.'

'No problems,' Tony replied confidently, with a wide grin. A hint of exhilaration was in his tone.

'I won't have time to steal the electrician's van I wanted to use,' Sal said, 'but we can use a standard white van I have. It's a Hyundai iLoad I pinched a few days ago in case of an emergency. It's parked out back under a tarp, and I'll stick a fake company's decal on it so it looks legit. It'll make for a decent and quick getaway. I'll even throw a ladder on the roof before we go to make it look more authentic.'

'Good. Leo, what about electronics on your end?' Charlie asked.

'Everything should be ready to go. The signal jammers are working fine, and I should be able to access the traffic system. It makes no difference to me if we do it today.'

'Okay, well, let's finish up here and then we go,' Charlie said as he changed into dark clothes he had stored in a box at the back of the cellar. He pulled out his dark balaclava from the bottom of the box and stuffed it into his pockets. The other four did the same, except for Sal, the driver, who remained in high-visibility worker's gear. They then made their final preparations, their focus unwavering as they readied themselves for the impending job.

They piled into the van, and Sal drove off, using the alleyway at the side of the hotel to exit. No one saw the van come in, and no one saw it leave. Sal drove at a steady pace from North Sydney, across the Harbour Bridge, and into the Sydney City CBD. To everyone around, it appeared to be just another delivery or worker's van. Even when it pulled up on the pedestrian walkway within Martin Place, stopping in front of the old Australian Summit Bank building, no one really paid much attention. Pedestrians simply walked around the van, and it caused minimal interruption to their day.

In the back of the van, the crew pulled their face coverings on tight and exchanged thumbs-ups with each other. Charlie then slid the door open, and they quickly got out, forming a single file and charging toward the entrance, which was only a few metres away.

With focus and determination, Charlie advanced towards the bank, followed closely by his crew. He checked his shotgun for the last time, knowing he would show no mercy.

FORTY-NINE

Will was having a slow day at work, and concentration eluded him after his last vision. Tucked away in his makeshift office, he feigned busyness on the computer, but remained distracted. For lunch, he opted to eat at his desk, and realising that only something stronger than the instant coffee he had been sipping could get him through the rest of the day, he messaged Ravi, hoping he had time to meet for a proper coffee.

Will ordered a double shot espresso for himself and a regular flat white for Ravi and found a table in the back corner of the cafeteria by a large window that looked out onto a grassed courtyard. A few minutes later, Ravi arrived just as an elderly waitress carried out their coffees. After savouring the first sip, Will shared with Ravi what he had seen overnight and confirmed that Woods was already looking into it.

'That's great to hear,' Ravi said. 'Hopefully, tomorrow is the day they finally catch them. I actually saw a piece on the news this morning. The police just did another press release this morning about the first robbery. They're still stuck trying to solve it, and it's obvious they're worried there will be another one.'

'There definitely will be another one, but Aubrey and her team will be all over it. The vision of it was horrific, actually. I can't stop thinking about it.'

'Anything I can help with?' Ravi offered.

'No. As long as I have you to talk to and unload the burden, it feels better. So thank you, as always, I appreciate it.'

'You're welcome. I know you are the one with the gift, but you never have to deal with it alone. You have Aubrey and I. We are a team, Will.'

They both finished their coffees, and Will was already feeling much better. He went for a walk through the hallways of the hospital with Ravi, aiming to burn off a little energy and clear his mind. Ravi's company provided a welcome distraction from the weighty thoughts that still lingered from his vision.

They walked toward the front of the hospital together, and suddenly, Will stopped dead in his tracks, his feet glued to the floor. Ravi, a few steps ahead, continued walking before realising he had left Will behind. Turning back, he found Will standing perfectly still in the centre of the room, eyes closed. If Ravi didn't know better, he might have thought Will was having a narcoleptic episode, but he understood what was happening. Fortunately, the hallway was quiet, and Ravi stood awkwardly next to Will, ensuring he would be okay.

When Will felt his eyes shut tightly, he found himself inside the Australian Summit Bank at Martin Place once again. There was no mistaking the distinct walls and old pillars inside the building – the smell, the sound. Immediately, he knew where he was, just as he did last time. Standing next to a large, masked man, he witnessed the barrel of a shotgun pointed directly at the chest of a man who panted heavily, lying on the ground with hands raised in surrender. The masked man fired the fatal shot, and blood splattered from the man who had just begged for his life. A woman crouching next to the man began screaming and crying at the top of her voice while clutching his lifeless body. Will stood behind her, seeing only the back of her head as she howled in the face of a large man wearing a black balaclava. 'You killed my husband! Why? Why?'

She turned around, her eyes red as tears drenched her cheeks. Will recognised her straight away. It was the woman from the emergency room last week - the same woman he had warned to stay away from the Greenspring Bank. But it was the Australian Summit Bank she needed to stay away from.

She continued to sob, clutching the still body of her now-dead husband. Will looked back at the killer, witnessing the man walk away toward a group of cowering staff members in the corner of the bank, a smoking shotgun by his side.

His eyes were forced wide open in terror, and he stared into the panicked eyes of Ravi. The abrupt return to reality left Will shaken. The weight of the visions and the brutal scenes he had witnessed horrified him.

'Will, are you alright?' Ravi asked, noticing the frightened and dazed look in Will's eyes. He gripped his shoulders tightly, making sure he found his balance.

'I just saw someone get killed at the bank tomorrow,' Will said, as his lips quivered. 'I thought I saw someone get shot in my earlier vision, but this time I actually witnessed it. I need to talk to Aubrey. They really have to be on top of this one, or people are going to die.'

'Definitely the same robbery?'

'Yeah, it was definitely the same bank and crew,' Will said, leaning against the wall and taking three slow breaths.

'Will, what is it?'

'You remember the woman in the waiting room last week? The one who thought I was crazy?'

'Yeah, I remember.'

'Well, it was her husband I saw getting killed. She was by his side when it happened. It was always this bank, not the last one. It happened at this bank. Aubrey needs to know what she's in for here. These guys aren't messing around.'

FIFTY

While the van remained idle outside the Australian Summit Bank with Sal in the driver's seat, Charlie led his team, bursting through the front door. They screamed with violent aggression for everyone to get on the floor, brandishing their loaded firearms in all directions. Immediately, they had the full and petrified attention of the entire bank. Standing close to the entrance, two security guards panicked and reacted much too slowly to handle the situation successfully. Outnumbering and outgunning them, Charlie, Marco and Leo fired before they could remove their sidearms. The sound of the shotgun blasts exploded through the bank, followed by ear-piercing screams of terror from the customers and employees. Both guards collapsed onto the floor in a messy pool of blood, and Leo casually removed their guns from their clenched hands and put them in his backpack.

After the initial wave of dread and anguished screams reverberating through the bank, a solemn hush settled over the occupants as they collectively huddled on the cold, sterile floor. Charlie smiled to himself briefly. He knew he now had complete control. The bank quickly became quiet, with the stifling silence punctuated only by the occasional whimper that lingered in the air. Amid the sea of terrified faces, one of the bank tellers summoned the courage to activate the silent alarm just in the nick of time, seamlessly blending into the mass of terrified people. Considering the time of day, the bank was bustling with activity, with a diverse crowd of customers and staff totalling at least thirty people.

Leo retrieved a laptop from the depths of his backpack, its keys soon echoing the staccato rhythm of his furious typing. With adept precision, he penetrated the intricate layers of the Sydney CBD traffic grid, his fingers dancing across the keys as lines of code succumbed to his expert manipulation. A nod to Charlie moments later signalled the successful breach. As he continued to work, a few more seconds of rapid keystrokes were all it took to orchestrate the impending pandemonium on Sydney's bustling roads. Leo now had control of the traffic signals, and he activated green lights at every intersection to the south.

The crew quickly navigated the expansive, open foyer of the bank with a sense of urgency, their movements a careful balance between speed and vigilance. Charlie took point, leading the group with a determined stride. The air crackled with tension as he weaved through the crowd, shotgun ready as his eyes scanned the surroundings for any signs of resistance. Any resistance, he knew, would be met with deadly force.

FIFTY-ONE

Ned and Julie Benson, both in their mid-forties, shared the collective tension that gripped every person in the bank, their bodies taut, hearts racing in unison with the disconcerting rhythm of the terrifying events. Ned, a strong and well-built figure, boasted a thick brown moustache that entirely concealed his upper lip, contrasting his closely shaven head. His muscular physique hidden under a dark suit was a testament to his past life as a rugby player, and in the current moment, he stood almost on par in size with the imposing armed robbers who now held the bank in their grasp. He was a stark contrast to his petite wife, who had a narrow face and her blonde hair arranged in a tight bun. In a light-coloured skirt and silk blouse and wearing designer rings on nearly every finger, she hid her hands under her chest and pressed herself close to Ned.

In that tense moment, as the room echoed with collective fear, something within Ned snapped. The looks of pure terror etched on the faces of the staff and customers seemed to fuel a surge of rage within him. Ned propelled himself forcefully off the ground, catching Marco off guard. With a swift and unexpected motion, he seized Marco by the neck, his large forearm closing in like a vice around his throat. The atmosphere shifted as Marco, still gripping his shotgun, found himself trapped in Ned's powerful grip. He choked and squirmed fruitlessly, and Ned's relentless hold tightened. The other three masked men, alerted by the commotion, turned back to witness the unexpected scuffle. All three trained their shotguns on

Ned, the imminent threat demanding their attention, yet they hesitated to pull the trigger. The realisation struck them: firing their shotguns would undoubtedly result in the death of both men. The standoff hung in the air; the room poised on the precipice of a violent escalation that could change the course of the entire ordeal.

From her position on the ground, Julie screamed at the top of her lungs, 'Ned, no! What are you doing? Just let them take what they want. It isn't worth it!'

Ned ignored her and addressed the three masked men with raw fury; 'Get out now! Drop the guns and walk away. I'll let your friend go if you leave right now. Otherwise, I'm going to squeeze the life out of him.'

Ned knew Marco was struggling to breathe. His legs kicked out, and he continued to make a choking sound with every gasp for air. He soon lost his grip on the shotgun, and it dropped by his side straight onto the floor.

With no hesitation at all, Tony charged toward Ned and Marco.

'Stay back, I'm warning you,' he said, squeezing Marco's neck tighter. 'I'll do it.'

'No, you won't,' Tony replied nonchalantly.

Ned's face twitched as the adrenaline continued to surge. 'I will, I swear I will.'

Tony kept moving forward with a rage now equalling that of Ned. He lifted the butt of his shotgun and drove it straight into Ned's jaw, narrowly missing Marco.

Ned's head snapped back, and he grunted in pain while simultaneously relaxing his arm and releasing Marco from his grip. Both men fell onto the floor. Ned looked up at Tony in shock while rubbing his tender face as Marco scurried away on the ground, choking and searching for his gun on the floor.

Tony swiftly shifted the trajectory of his shotgun, levelling it with precision at Ned's chest, who instinctively raised his hands in surrender. The power dynamics in the room shifted once again, and the collective breaths of those present seemed suspended as the fates of Ned and everyone else now rested on the precipice of Tony's decision.

'No, please, I'm sorry,' he begged. The desperation in his voice echoed through the tension-filled space.

Without uttering a single word, Tony fired directly into Ned's chest. The loud report echoed off the walls of the foyer, a jarring sound that rattled those still huddled on the floor. Gasps and anguished cries filled the air, and the lifeless body of Ned crumpled to the ground, obliterated by the force of the powerful point-blank shot. Julie's scream cut through. It was a raw expression of grief and horror.

'You shot my husband! Why? Why?' she howled, tears streaming down her face.

FIFTY-TWO

Will pulled out his phone and called Woods while Ravi stood with him, fidgeting with his glasses nervously. She answered straight away but sounded distant, with an audible distortion in the background as police sirens blared.

'Aubrey, it's Will, about the robbery tomorrow...'

Woods cut him off, 'It's not tomorrow, Will. It's happening right now. It's happening today. We got the silent alarm alert. The Australian Summit Bank at Martin Place. I'm on my way there now.'

'Now? What?' Will said, his body suddenly rigid.

'Yes right now, I've got you on loudspeaker in the car, we're driving there as fast as we can, trying to get there before they can leave, but it's today, Will, I don't know why you saw tomorrow's date. Traffic is mayhem in the city, too. All the traffic lights have gone to shit. I better go, I really need to concentrate.'

'Sure, sorry, okay, bye, um, talk soon,' Will rambled, not sure of what to say and equally confused about how the robbery could be happening today.

Will looked like he had seen a ghost. 'Ravi, the robbery isn't tomorrow. It's happening right now.'

'Now? How could that be when you saw the date and time?'

'Yeah, I don't know, but I'm going there to check it out. I'll meet Aubrey there.'

'No, Will, you'll just get in the way or you might get hurt.'

'I'll stay back, don't worry. She might need my help, and I might see something else.'

Before Ravi could make another protest, Will had left the hallway and sprinted through the emergency department, headed for the front door.

***

Woods, with adrenaline surging through her veins, continued to drive with an urgency matched only by the blaring lights and sirens emanating from her police car. A convoy of marked and unmarked cars followed suit, racing through the city streets en route to the Australian Summit Bank at Martin Place, spurred into action by the triggered robbery alarm.

Green lights illuminated every intersection, transforming the city's usually orderly traffic flow into a disarray of collisions and confusion. The convoy weaved through the tangled mess of crashed cars, each intersection presenting a perilous obstacle. Despite the police's best efforts to bypass the chaos, mounting the footpath and manoeuvring through the mayhem, progress was slow. As they pressed further into the heart of the city, the once bustling thoroughfares had devolved into a standstill, with traffic halted in every direction. Woods, acutely aware of the ticking clock, couldn't shake the worry that the offenders might escape in the ensuing chaotic gridlock.

FIFTY-THREE

As Julie Benson continued to scream and grieve beside her husband's lifeless body, Tony callously ignored her, his attention fixed on the next task. Marco, having recovered from the unexpected scuffle with Ned, retrieved his gun from the floor and joined Tony. Rubbing his throat, he fell into step with the rest of the crew.

They moved with a menacing purpose toward the front of the bank, where they identified three young women huddled in front of the tellers. In a cruel display of authority, all three were callously yanked up off the floor by their hair. Forced to march forward with shotguns pushed into their backs, the women trembled in fear, barely able to stay on their feet.

'Manager,' Charlie barked at the three tellers who cowered behind the counter. The security screen, triggered by the alarm, had automatically ascended, offering protection to those behind the barrier. However, they would do little to shield their customers and colleagues, who were still vulnerable on the other side.

'Manager now, or these three women die. You've seen us shoot already. We will not be wasting time.'

Within seconds, a portly woman, approximately fifty years old, cautiously raised her hand from behind the counter. She sported a short, dark brown bob haircut and was clad in dark trousers and a matching blazer adorned with the green and gold coloured Australian Summit Bank logo stitched on the breast pocket. Her name badge prominently displayed the title *Nikki - Branch Manager*.

Charlie's intense gaze bore into Nikki as he issued his stern command. 'Open the door now.'

'The safe and counting rooms are on a timer. You won't be able to get into it,' she replied, her voice cracking.

'I know it's on a timer. I also know it was activated twenty-nine minutes and thirty seconds ago and is now due to open itself momentarily. I also know at any second now, the armed guards will walk through the back door, having arrived just before we did, so no games or blood will be on your hands.'

Nikki, apparently understanding the stakes and potential consequences, chose not to verbalise her compliance. Instead, she offered a solemn nod and moved toward the left side of the tellers. There, a large steel bulletproof door stood as the gateway to the back of the bank.

As she opened the heavy door, Charlie wasted no time. With a swift, forceful motion, he dropped his shoulder and knocked her to the ground.

As he had anticipated, down a long, concrete hallway leading to the secure loading dock at the back of the bank, two cash in transit guards strolled through the doors carelessly. To them, it was just another routine cash pickup, and the mundane nature of their task betrayed the unfolding chaos within the bank. The silent alarm, usually a fail-safe for detecting unauthorised access, and ordinarily, the rear doors would lock upon activation, but Charlie's meticulous planning had circumvented this obstacle. The cash truck had smoothly gained entry to the loading dock before he and the crew even entered the bank.

The two overweight guards, casually making their way through the concrete hallway, looked up briefly and gasped as Charlie confronted them. However, the moment of realisation was fleeting, and before they could react, Charlie had his shotgun levelled at them. In quick succession, he pulled the trigger twice, and the deafening shots echoed through the confined space. The guards, clearly surprised and unable to mount any defence, collapsed to the ground in a growing pool of blood.

FIFTY-FOUR

Amidst the aftermath of the gunfire, Leo, positioned behind Charlie, discerned a loud clicking sound reverberating through the concrete hallway. It was the unmistakable sound of the vault unlocking, triggered by the expiration of the thirty-minute time lapse they had carefully calculated. Responding swiftly, Leo approached the steel door and grasped the thick, round steel handle. With a firm twist, the handle turned all the way around, and the vault door swung open.

A jaw-dropping sight greeted them inside the secure steel room, just large enough for the four men to stand around a central steel trolley that acted as a makeshift bench. Hundreds of thick bundles of cash were neatly arranged and on display on the stacked steel trolley.

As Charlie, Marco, and Tony immersed themselves in the sight of the accumulated wealth within the vault, Leo crouched down to retrieve the tightly folded duffel bags from his backpack and passed them out. Before joining the others in bagging the cash, Leo's focus first shifted to the dead armed guards lying nearby.

Approaching within two metres, he observed a startling detail – one of the guards had an empty firearm holster. Both men lay lifeless on their backs, blood continuing to flood the corridor leading to their parked truck. The scene seemed static, but Leo's awareness heightened as he suddenly heard a bloody gasp for air. To his shock, the guard with the missing firearm from his holster lifted his head and shoulders, revealing a trembling hand aiming a pistol.

Before he could react, the guard fired at Leo, hitting him in the stomach. The firearm clattered to the ground as the guard choked and his head collapsed onto the floor. His last moments had been spent firing his gun.

The momentum of the robbery came to an abrupt halt as Charlie, Marco, and Tony abruptly rushed to Leo's side. Leo collapsed on the ground and clenched his stomach, where blood was rapidly escaping. His groans of agony filled the air, creating a dissonant contrast to the initial silence that had enveloped the vault.

In an urgent response, Marco moved quickly, tearing off his shirt to fashion a makeshift bandage. In desperation, he packed the wound to slow the bleeding. The gravity of the situation now intensified as the group grappled with the unforeseen complication, their meticulously planned heist now complicated by the reality of an unexpected injury. The atmosphere inside the vault shifted from triumph to terror as they confronted the immediate need to address Leo's critical condition.

'You guys keep going, we have to get out of here ASAP,' Marco urged, still holding onto Leo's wound tightly, trying his best to stop the bleeding.

'We can't pack as quickly without you two,' Charlie said.

'If I let go of Leo, he'll die. You two just keep going. Take only two bags of cash, if that's all we can do.'

Despite the urgency and unexpected setback with Leo's injury, Charlie and Tony exchanged a determined nod, recognising the need to press forward. They returned to packing the duffel bags with cash as fast as they could.

Leo remained huddled on the ground, groaning with every breath. Marco kept tight pressure on his wound, which was all that was preventing him from bleeding out.

'Is it bad?' Leo groaned.

'You'll be okay. Just stay with me, okay? Keep breathing.'

'It hurts.'

'I know it does. We've got to stand you up, okay? We have to get out of here now.'

'I don't know if I can.'

'Come on, let's try, hold on to me.'

Marco lifted Leo's arm over his shoulder and tried to stand him up. The minute Leo put weight on his own legs, he buckled and collapsed onto the ground. Marco's hold on him slipped, and his wound lost the pressure it had just had. Blood continued to pour out of Leo's stomach, and the colour was quickly draining from his face.

'He's losing a lot of blood, guys. We have to go,' Marco called out to Charlie and Tony, who were still furiously stuffing money into the duffel bags.

'Not yet,' Charlie said. 'We still have to keep packing the bags. Otherwise, the job wouldn't be worth it.'

Marco shot a hostile glare at Charlie. 'Who cares about the money? This was never about the money. We need to go!'

'Shut up!' Charlie snapped back. 'Just hold him still, we're not leaving yet!'

FIFTY-FIVE

Sitting in the van, Sal felt the tension rise within him as the wailing police sirens grew louder. He knew they would arrive momentarily, even with the chaos on the streets. He gripped the gearshift, prepared to accelerate at a moment's notice as soon as the rest of the team emerged from the bank.

He strained to peer through the tinted glass of the van's front doors, attempting to discern any movement inside the bank. However, his view was blocked by several stone pillars at the front of the building. He checked his watch nervously, and the current time showed Charlie and the crew had exceeded the expected duration inside. A sense of unease crept over him as he realised something must have gone wrong.

As the first of several police cars arrived in convoy at Martin Place, Sal's apprehension heightened. He watched the unfolding scene with growing concern. Realisation quickly dawned on him that, with the van parked conspicuously in front of the bank and him alone in the driver's seat, the idling engine served as an unmistakable signal, and the police wouldn't take long to identify it as a getaway vehicle.

Sal's nerves surged as he calculated the risk. The van stood out like a beacon, and the impending confrontation with the arriving police loomed large.

With the police swiftly securing both ends of Martin Place, Sal found himself trapped in the van. The blockade effectively cut off traffic in either direction, leaving no avenue for escape while his friends remained inside the bank.

In a moment of panicked urgency, Sal got out of the van. His heart raced, and rational thoughts left him as he grappled with the escalating tension. His decision, while lacking a clearly defined plan, was a desperate attempt to take some control of the unfolding situation. He knew that staying put made him an easy target, and the need for proactive action fueled his impromptu decision. As he stepped out onto Martin Place, carrying a shotgun. His fate and the success of the impending getaway hung in the balance of what he was about to do.

Without a coherent plan, he resorted to wild and frenzied gunfire, aiming at the police officers who had just arrived at the perimeter established in Martin Place. The shots reverberated through the air as Sal, driven by the hope of forcing the police to retreat, unleashed a chaotic barrage of bullets, hoping to buy a small window of time and space for a quick getaway.

FIFTY-SIX

Bullets ripped through nearby shop windows and shattered the windows of several police cars, including Yule's vehicle, which had been the first to arrive, followed closely by Woods. The sudden onslaught prompted the police officers to take cover, crouching behind their cars and returning fire at the shooter. Though outnumbered, he still held a significant advantage with his devastating shotgun. As the wild shooter continued to fire, the pellets cascaded over several police cars and wreaked havoc on Yule's front and rear tyres. However, Yule, undeterred by the hail of pellets, stood tall over the front of his now bullet-riddled car. With three slow and well-aimed shots, he unleashed a deadly response. All three bullets struck the man's body, and he crumpled to the ground.

The smell of gunpowder lingered as the street went quiet, broken only by the blaring sound of police sirens.

'Is everyone okay?' Yule's voice cut through the uneasy stillness that settled over the chaotic scene. Standing amidst the line of smashed cars tightly jammed on Martin Place, he surveyed the aftermath of the confrontation. The firearm remained in his hand, though lowered by his side, as he wiped the beads of sweat from his forehead with the sleeve of his navy polo shirt.

Woods was the only one to reply as the other officers remained dumbfounded with shock. 'Fine, and you?'

'I'm fine. The rest of the crew must still be inside. My bet is this one was the driver. Look at how he parked his van, mounting up on the path, with the engine still running.'

A local uniformed sergeant from the Sydney City police station eventually called out from the western perimeter of Martin Place. 'You okay over there?'

'Yeah!' Yule called back. 'You all stay where you are for now. Tactical units are on their way.' He then whispered to Woods. 'I'm going to drag the body behind his van. I don't want the ones left inside to see what has happened out there. They might panic.'

'Maybe we can ID him,' Woods said.

'It doesn't matter now. We are going to take them all down. They have nowhere to go. They're stuck inside. But that isn't what worries me. It's the other people inside I'm more concerned about. If this guy shoots at us without a second thought, who knows what the crew inside is capable of. Those inside need to be our priority, okay?'

'Absolutely,' Woods replied as she watched Yule run toward the body in a low crouch to conceal the shooter from the view of whomever was still inside the bank. Given the sheer hostility displayed on the street by the getaway driver, her concern grew thinking of what kind of violence those stuck inside the bank faced.

FIFTY-SEVEN

Charlie's ears caught the distant wail of sirens and the unmistakable sound of gunfire.

'Shit, they're here!' Tony cried. 'Charlie, the cops! We've gone way over time here.'

Flustered by the escalating chaos around him, Charlie raised his voice to be heard over the lingering echoes of sirens and gunshots and shouted urgently to his brother, 'Marco, come on, let's go!'

'Leo's not going to make it,' he replied, still holding him and trying hard to control the bleeding. 'He's lost way too much blood. Look, he's white as a ghost.'

'Dammit, Leo,' Charlie grunted. 'Alright stay here. I'm going to have a look out the front.'

Charlie walked out through the steel door beside the tellers and marched past the cowering crowd of people and the lifeless bodies of Ned Benson and the two security guards.

He remained to the side of the foyer and peaked out the front through the thick glass windows.

Charlie positioned himself at the side of the foyer. Peering through the thick glass windows, he strained to assess the external environment and gauge the severity of the police presence.

'Oh shit, no! No!'

The scene outside the bank had escalated, with police officers lining the streets and a tactical operations truck arriving, carrying heavily armed operatives wielding automatic rifles. Charlie also noted the ominous presence of snipers positioning themselves in a building opposite the bank, prepared to take lethal shots if necessary. Charlie ran to the body of the deceased security guards. Frantically searching, he located a set of keys on a keychain and ripped them from the guard's belt with a swift and forceful yank. Returning to the bank's entrance, he identified a keyhole that seemed to control the automatic doors. He used the key, manually locking the automatic doors shut.

'You there,' Charlie said, pointing to a young man in a baggy suit and a thick green and gold Australian Summit Bank tie. 'Did I just lock the doors correctly?'

The young man swallowed and nervously nodded.

'Go over to the doors and see if they open,' he instructed.

The young employee complied. He stood up, his legs trembling, and walked to the front of the bank. He looked out through the automatic glass doors and saw the police out the front. The doors didn't open.

'Good,' Charlie said. 'Now get back on the floor and don't move.'

Charlie marched back to the front of the bank, where Tony was waiting for him at the steel door.

'Is it bad?' he asked.

'Yeah, it's bad,' Charlie replied. 'But we have a bunch of people in here with us though. The police won't just charge in if they think they could all get hurt. They'll try to negotiate with us.'

With a guttural roar, Tony crouched and punched the ground in frustration.

'Manager!' Charlie yelled, spinning around and looking through the crowd.

Nikki presented herself nervously. Tears still pooled in her eyes.

'The cash in transit driver. Can he get inside on his own?' Charlie asked, thinking the driver, delayed in reuniting with his colleagues, would soon suspect something was wrong. He didn't need another armed person entering the bank.

'Not unless I buzz him inside.'

'Okay, if you do that, you'll be shot. Understand?'

'Yes,' she replied immediately.

Marco sprinted back to Charlie. His breaths came in rapid succession, and the visible tremors in his body betrayed his heightened emotional state. 'Leo's dead.'

Charlie squatted on the ground and cupped the back of his head. 'No!'

'We need to find a way to get out of here now. The cops must have Sal by now, and Leo is dead. It'll just be the three of us,' Marco said.

'They do have Sal. I saw our van. He wasn't in it,' Charlie said.

'Shit. Do you think he'll talk?' Tony asked.

'No way, not a chance,' Charlie said. 'Sal would never rat on us. He won't say a word, they won't ID us from him, don't worry.'

'We need a plan, Charlie,' Marco said. 'Otherwise, they will lock us up or kill us.'

FIFTY-EIGHT

Swift and assertive, the tactical operatives assumed command. Their specialised training and equipment showed a readiness to handle the heightened threat within the bank. Despite the potential for civilian casualties inside, the Robbery Squad detectives had to take a backseat and give operational control to the tactical operations unit until the situation could be resolved. Shortly after, police negotiators arrived on the scene and were briefed by the commander of the tactical operations unit.

Woods found herself at a mandated safe distance, standing beside her battered and bullet-riddled unmarked sedan. She positioned herself far enough away to avoid unnecessary risk, yet close enough to be readily available if her team's investigative skills were required as part of the response to the unfolding robbery and hostage situation. Though under control with a coordinated tactical response, the scene held an air of uncertainty as the threat inside the bank remained unknown.

While the tactical team and negotiators worked to establish control and communication, the priority shifted to contacting the armed offenders. The goal was to initiate an open line of communication, striving to resolve the situation with a focus on a peaceful outcome.

Still observing the unfolding scene from a distance, Woods noticed Will sprinting towards the eastern side of Martin Place. His urgency was clear as he disregarded the crime scene tape and rushed towards her location.

'It's okay. He's with me,' Woods called out to a uniformed officer guarding the perimeter, her eyes wide with surprise when she saw Will rushing towards her amidst the chaos. As he reached her, Woods sought an explanation. 'Will, what are you doing here?'

'I came straight from work. In my vision, I saw a man get shot dead in there. I just wanted to see if I could help and make sure you're okay.'

'I'm fine. It's obviously pretty messy here. We believe the robbery crew is all still inside. Unfortunately, the customers and staff who have now been taken hostage are also still inside. So, Will, just stay back. We need to let the negotiators and tactical team take it from here.'

'I'm sorry I got my dates wrong. I really am.'

'Just go, Will, it's too dangerous for you to be here.'

A booming voice suddenly called out from within the centre of the crime scene. It was Yule. 'Hey! What the hell is he doing here? Get out of here!'

His aggression startled Will, and he took a few steps back. 'I thought maybe I could help. In case I see anything else,' he said quietly to Woods.

'You'd better go, but maybe don't go too far. If you see anything else, you can let me know.'

'I'll call you.'

'No, my phone is playing up. All of ours are, in fact. There's no signal around here, which is odd. But please go, Will. Yule isn't exactly thrilled with you at the moment, just with everything that's gone wrong. You know, the Greenspring Bank, and now this and the wrong date. He thinks you're playing games with us.'

'But I'm not, you know that.'

'I know, but just get out of here, please, Will, or it'll make things tougher on me too. Maybe hang out around the corner or something.'

'Fine, I won't be too far away though,' he said with reluctance as he crawled back under the crime scene tape and walked around the block.

FIFTY-NINE

Charlie and Tony grappled with the urgent need to decide their course of action. Meanwhile, Marco remained close to Leo's lifeless body, his presence a stark reminder of the immediate stakes at hand if they fail to take some kind of action.

'Hey,' Charlie said, getting Marco's attention. 'I get it, you're upset, we all are. He was a great friend, but you need to help us find a way to get out of here. We'll mourn for Leo later.'

Marco took a deep breath. 'I think I have an idea.'

After hearing Marco's plan, Charlie and Tony, recognising the urgency of the situation, agreed that while risky and bordering on crazy, it was their only plan. Charlie knew the longer they remained inside and undecided on what to do, the more time the police would have the chance to prepare a coordinated and lethal raid. They had to get on the front foot and fast. The terrified population inside the bank, currently under their control, presented an advantage they needed to leverage effectively.

Charlie marched over to Nikki, who yelped and cowered, covering her face with her hands.

'Stop that and listen carefully,' he said.

She removed her hands from her face, dried her eyes and nodded.

'I want you to show me how to open the back door through which the armed guards enter.'

'The controls are in my office.'

'Lead the way.'

Charlie followed her while Marco and Tony monitored the hostages, ensuring they remained still and obedient.

'Here they are,' Nikki said, pointing to a control panel next to a CCTV monitor behind her desk in the small windowless office. While his mind raced at the prospect of escaping with his life, he felt satisfied when he saw the CCTV monitor showing nothing but static thanks to Leo's electronic disruptor device.

'Where's the button to open only the internal door? The door that would lead to where the armed truck is parked?'

'This one here,' Nikki said, pointing to a small green button.

'And what about the button that would open the external gates to allow the truck to leave?'

'The larger one next to it.'

'How long does it take for the gate to open completely?'

'It's slow, about fifteen seconds.'

'Well done. You've just saved your life. Now go back out with the others.'

Charlie checked his shotgun and pressed the small button to unlock the door to the garage area. He walked out into the corridor, stepped over the body of Leo and the two armed guards, and pulled the now unlocked, heavy door open.

'It's about time!' a voice from the other side of the door said. 'I was going to send out a search party. I think I hear sirens out....'

Charlie walked into the garage and stared directly at the armed truck driver, who was now standing beside it. Before the guard could react, Charlie fired and shot him cleanly in the chest. His body recoiled hard and flopped onto the concrete ground with a loud slap.

He made his way to the side of the truck. The driver's side was open, and the keys were still in the ignition.

He left the truck as it was and went back into the foyer to meet up with Marco and Tony.

'Step one is done,' he said. 'The keys are inside, and the engine is still running.'

'Okay,' Tony said, before turning to face the crowd of people in the foyer. 'Listen up, everyone. You are all going to leave here in a few seconds, completely unharmed.'

A few people lifted their heads off the ground with confused expressions. Others were simply relieved.

'Believe me, it is no joke. I will give the manager the key from the security guard to unlock the front door. When I tell her, she will unlock the doors, and you are all to run as fast as you can out the doors and straight into the arms of the police waiting outside. If you are too slow, you will be shot. I don't care if you trample each other or scream at the top of your lungs, but you will all cause a scene when you leave. Are there any questions?'

No one said a word.

'Is there anyone who has an issue with this?'

Again, there was no reply.

'Good. Wait for my signal.'

Marco left the foyer, collected the duffle bags full of cash, and headed for the garage to take the driver's seat of the armed truck. Charlie returned to the control panel while Tony threw the keys to Nikki.

'Open the door in fifteen seconds, no later, no earlier, understand?'

She nodded.

Tony ran to the back of the bank and met with Charlie in the corridor, who had just activated the opening mechanism for the rear gates.

'What about Leo's body?' he asked.

'We can't take it now. The cops will take him, and we will help collect it later from the morgue. His body alone won't link all of us to the robberies, and after the autopsy, they will have to release him eventually. We will arrange a funeral that is no expense spared. He deserves no less.'

Charlie and Tony entered the armoured truck just when the gates were open wide enough for them to exit. At the same time, on the other side of the building, a crowd of screaming hostages charged out onto the street, straight toward the police.

SIXTY

As Marco punched the accelerator, the heavy truck surged forward, tearing through the back entrance of the bank. A sharp turn through an alleyway brought them face to face with three police cars, positioned as part of a citywide street blockage activated in response to the robbery. However, the officers associated with these cars leaned back lazily, assuming they were far enough away from the unfolding action and that the tactical unit at the front had everything under control.

The unexpected arrival of the truck caught the officers off guard, their initial complacency shattered as the reality of the heist suddenly confronted them. With split-second timing, the officers at the street blockage barely managed to jump out of the way before the armoured truck barreled through the line of police cars. The massive vehicle ploughed through the obstruction with ease, its weight and armour rendering the police cars little more than tiny obstacles. Undeterred, the truck continued its trajectory northward, headed towards the Harbour Bridge.

'Get off at the first exit after the bridge. We need to dump this truck as soon as possible,' Charlie said.

Marco skillfully manoeuvred the armoured truck through the city streets at high speed, deftly weaving through traffic to maximise the distance between them and the inevitable pursuit by the police. Reaching North Sydney, Marco brought the armoured truck to a stop in a quiet residential street. Moving fast, they shed their balaclavas and located a late-model Toyota Corolla. With a lifetime of theft experience behind him, Tony gained access and hot-wired the vehicle within seconds.

Charlie, Marco, and Tony, exhausted, entered the basement cellar by the side door after dumping the stolen Toyota Corolla four streets away from the Golden Bell Hotel. They dropped their duffle bags full of cash and sat down at the round table as they caught their breath. Charlie looked at the two empty seats around their table in sombre reflection, one was Sal's and the other, Leo's. He uncorked a rare bottle of 20-year-old single malt scotch and filled three small glasses. They drank to Leo, offering a silent tribute to his memory.

Still grappling with the uncertainty of what had transpired on the street at the front of the bank, Charlie's thoughts turned to Sal. He suspected the police had apprehended him, but for now, he was left with a gnawing sense of helplessness. He could only hope that Sal was holding up okay.

SIXTY-ONE

The dramatic escape of the robbery crew demanded additional resources as police deployed tracker dogs and a helicopter to aid in the search. The hovering chopper scoured the Cahill Expressway and the lower end of North Sydney, focusing on Sydney Harbour and the iconic Harbour Bridge. Their efforts eventually led to the discovery of the abandoned armoured truck, confirming the path taken by the heist team, although the authorities were too late to intercept them.

Yule, Woods, and the team arrived a short time later, while the tactical squad began searching the wider area. The police issued a further radio broadcast to look out for the three males armed with shotguns and wearing all black, but they had limited information and still had no idea who they were dealing with.

'You guys stay here with the truck,' Yule said to a pair of uniformed officers. He walked further down the street and scratched his head. He then turned and faced some more uniformed officers and highway patrol cars who had parked up around the street and blocked access.

'I want you all to spread out and keep looking for them. I want the dogs to stick around too, and hopefully they can pick up a scent.'

'Who are we looking for?' one asked.

Yule felt a vein bulge in his neck and snapped at the question. 'Three guys with guns! Just start looking. It's better than standing here doing nothing!' Yule shook his head and took a deep breath. 'Woods, you come with me. We're going back to the bank. We now need to identify our dead shooter.'

She nodded but didn't speak. Yule buried his face in his hands. His frustration was clearly evident, and it was quickly turning into pure anger. This crew had been involved in a shootout with the police and made a mockery of their security at the dangerous crime scene and hostage situation. They still had no leads on identifying them, and Woods knew if this crew had hit two banks in a short period, they would strike again.

Returning to the bank, Woods and Yule found themselves confronted by a sea of media personnel and curious onlookers, all kept at bay by the crime scene tape. While the media attention didn't faze them, the arrival of several senior police officers posed a unique challenge. Among them, an assistant commissioner, two superintendents, and a group of chief inspectors signalled the potential for a clash of egos, each vying for control of the evolving crime scene.

'Ignore all of that nonsense,' Yule muttered as they pulled up the crime scene tape and walked past the high-ranking officers and toward the body, now surrounded by crime scene officers wearing full-bodied white hazmat suits, inspecting the scene and taking photographs. 'The brass won't be there helping us actually solve the case, so just focus on your job.'

Yule singled out the lead crime scene officer.

'Got an ID yet?'

'We do. The van was clean, but I just ran his prints. Name; Salvatore Ricci.'

'Any history?'

'Yeah, a bit. Drug supply and street crime stuff. A few assaults. There's some old intel that he's an associate of the Bianco crime family.'

'Okay, thanks, good work.'

'Speak to my colleagues processing the bank. But be warned, it's a bloodbath in there. Two dead security guards, three dead cash in transit officers, a dead civilian and another dead offender.'

'Shit,' Woods said under her breath as she contemplated what went on inside the bank and what she was about to walk into.

The atmosphere in the bank's foyer was thick with an eerie chill, heightened by blood splattered on the walls. Death permeated the air even before Woods laid eyes on a single body, and she felt a tingle crawl up her spine. The snapping sound of cameras wielded by the crime scene officers wearing hazmat suits broke the silence that enveloped the space.

Finding a box of gloves and blue cotton slippers left by the door, Woods and Yule equipped themselves with a pair of each and proceeded forward with a meticulous and measured approach. Even though their shoes were covered, both investigators moved cautiously, acutely aware that they must avoid contaminating the crime scene.

The first two bodies they encountered were those of the security guards, senselessly gunned down in the line of duty, victims of the perpetrators' ruthless determination to eliminate potential threats. The next victim, Ned Benson, as identified by a passing crime scene officer, further underscored the indiscriminate violence that unfolded within the bank. An unarmed civilian, Woods thought it was highly likely Ned had become an unintended casualty of the robbery.

As Woods and Yule proceeded toward the back-of-house area near the large open vault, the scene took a grimmer turn. The lifeless bodies of the two armed guards were in a disordered heap, their forms mingling with the remains of a young, muscular male whose balaclava had been rolled up to reveal vacant, wide-opened eyes. Blood pooled along the length of the narrow hallway in front of the vault. The violence and utter disregard for human life left Woods in a state of shock, the chilling reality of the crime scene sending shivers up her spine.

Woods took a deep breath, a momentary pause to centre herself. The gravity of the situation demanded composure. A mental fortitude to confront the disturbing scene and carry out the responsibilities that lay ahead. Focused on her duties, she steeled herself, determined to catch this crew before they struck again.

She walked over to the crime scene officer, who was taking photos of the face of the man in the balaclava.

'How are you going over here?' Woods asked the officer. A middle-aged woman with bulging, dark rings under her eyes. The result of tirelessly working with death and traumatic scenes every day, Woods thought.

'Yeah, fine, almost done with this one,' the crime scene officer said, looking up at Woods and shifting her face mask down slightly to reveal small pursed lips and a wrinkled face.

'Got an ID for me?'

'Yes, I do. Leonardo Moretti. I looked him up on the system. He's a confirmed associate of the other deceased. History of drug supply, steroid supply, assault, and cyber related crime. The intelligence report on file matches the other guy's - associate of the Bianco crime family.'

Yule walked over, and Woods relayed the identity of the second dead offender.

'So that's how they are connected,' he said. 'They've probably known each other for a while. I think the others are probably connected to the Biancos too,' he said.

'Seems very strange these people would be involved in armed robberies. High risk and no guarantee of a good monetary return. I mean, that's why the Bianco family are involved in drugs, extortion and probably fraud, all for a higher return and much safer.'

'Well, it doesn't mean the family members, Frank, Charlie or Marco Bianco themselves, are necessarily involved, but maybe that's our connection,' Yule said.

He continued, 'I'm looking around here, and something doesn't feel right. I think things got really out of control. Like they thought they had more time than they did. The traffic light issue, especially, can't be a coincidence. I also think someone interfered with the electrical signals of the CCTV, just like at the United East Bank job. We really are dealing with a clever and well-resourced crew.

'I agree,' Wood said. 'Look at our two confirmed offenders, both experienced, lifelong crooks. I bet the other three will have a similar history and have probably worked for the Bianco family at some point.'

'Have a look in the vault, too. There's still money inside. They were definitely rushed, or perhaps the death of their co-offender slowed them down. That, along with the dead getaway driver, it looks like their plan collapsed around them. I think the stealing of the armed truck was an improvisation. You wouldn't plan and rely on such a reckless move.'

Woods looked at the stacks of money still left inside the vault. Yule was correct; large piles of money were still inside the vault, on top of the steel trolley, along with two empty duffle bags on the floor. She surmised they had probably intended to fill these bags but quickly fled the bank in the armoured truck.

'Woods, stay here for a little while longer and make sure you're around if the crime scene finds anything that might help us. I'm going to talk to a few of the witnesses outside.'

For the next several hours, the crime scene officers took DNA swabs, fingerprints, and thousands of photographs. They also bagged hundreds of trace items and exhibits, including the duffel bags left behind, before eventually taking the bodies to the morgue.

With her phone finally displaying a regained cell service, Woods noticed several missed calls from Will. Recognising the urgency of the crime scene, she consciously set aside personal matters for the time being. The pressing demands of the investigation required her undivided attention, and any conversations with Will would have to wait.

As work on the crime scene neared its conclusion, Woods stepped out of the grim confines of the bank. The oppressive atmosphere inside, marked by blood-soaked walls and carpets, had become stagnant and she welcomed the clean, fresh air outside.

Surveying the aftermath, Woods recognised the ongoing challenges that awaited her and the team. While anticipating forensic breakthroughs from the lab, their focus would shift to the meticulous task of interviewing witnesses and untangling the potential connections with the Bianco crime family.

Stepping into the sunlight, Woods saw Yule standing in the centre of the crime scene, strategically distant from the surrounding media.

'Sarge, they collected a load of exhibits and the bodies are on their way back to the morgue. The autopsies will be tomorrow, I expect.'

Yule nodded. 'The statements are coming along, and the local detectives are helping. I've got a pretty good picture of what went on inside the bank, and I'll write up a progress report later that you and the team can read, but first, I need to talk to you, Aubrey.'

'Sure, what's up?' she asked quizzically.

He walked away to a more secluded area within the crime scene perimeter. Woods followed.

'This relationship you have with Will Denham is to stop right now,' he said bluntly.

'Look, I understand he made a mistake...'

Yule raised his hands and cut her off. 'You're a good Detective, Woods. I truly mean that, but you're too invested in this guy. He got it wrong with the Greenspring Bank robbery, and we wasted time on that operation, and now, although he was right about this location, he gets the date wrong. I mean, does he think this is a game? Is he simply wrong? Or is he just messing with us?'

'I trust him, I really do. He was just a little off, that's all.'

'See, that's your weakness. You're too trusting, and I just don't buy it anymore. I gave him a chance, but now we cut the cord.'

'But what about the Taree extortion? He led us to solve that case,' Woods said, pleading her case to keep Will as a regular source of information for the team, but deep down, she knew where this was going. Yule had likely made up his mind.

'That's enough, okay?' Yule said, slightly raising his voice. People are dead in there, and there's no place for him around anymore. I'm cutting him off, and you are not to get any more intel from him anymore. Do you understand?'

'But...'

'No, Woods, that's an order. I have half a mind to lock him up for being a public nuisance and giving us false information, but all I want to do is forget about him and get on with this investigation. I'm not interested in hearing another word from him.'

Feeling deflated, Woods acknowledged Yule would not change his decision. The weight of the investigation, coupled with the challenging circumstances of the crime scene, left little room for argument.

'Do we understand each other?'

'Yes,' she grunted.

'Good. Now finish up what you need to here and then get home and get some sleep; you'll need it.'

Woods nodded, yet she was still silently furious as Yule turned away and returned to the command post.

SIXTY-TWO

The expensive scotch bottle rapidly emptied as Charlie, Marco, and Tony continued drinking. Each shot of the warming liquor served as a solemn toast, a way to mourn the loss of Leo.

'He was like a brother,' Marco said.

'He was,' Charlie agreed. 'Here, come on, another one to Leo.'

They all raised their glasses solemnly and took another shot.

Charlie stood up and turned on his old TV set in the cellar. He was looking to see what the news had to say about their robbery. As expected, it was the major news story for the night.

The clean-looking, middle-aged reporter, clad in a well-fitted suit with greasy hair styled with an excess of product, held up a thick blue microphone. Against the backdrop of Martin Place, he gazed somberly into the camera and spoke in a sympathetic tone as he reported the sombre facts of the armed robbery.

The news camera panned away from the reporter, capturing shots of the police crime scene tape and the front of the bank. A grim procession of bodies, now encased in thick bags, being wheeled out through the front door. The reporter continued his narration over the footage. 'A sophisticated criminal group, who fled the scene in a stolen armoured truck, orchestrated this vicious armed robbery, leaving a path of destruction behind them. Police have confirmed eight people are now dead. Authorities also believe the same group was involved in the recent armed robbery of the United East Bank at Haymarket. A police spokesperson revealed the totality of the death, stating the group killed five security and cash in transit personnel, along with a bank customer. The police have advised that one of the robbery offenders is among the dead, and they later discovered his body inside the bank near the open vault. Police shot dead a second man, believed to be a getaway driver when he opened fire on them right here on Martin Place. Detectives are currently withholding the identities of these males as their investigation continues. Still, there is no doubt they are feeling the pressure to solve these violent robberies as soon as possible, as the remaining offenders are still at large.'

'Oh no! No!' Charlie said, trying to hold back tears at the shocking revelation, but rage quickly took over. He pushed the TV over and stomped on the screen, smashing it to pieces.

'They got Sal!' Marco cried, 'No!'

Tony just sat in silence, his head buried in his hands.

Charlie reached for the nearly empty bottle of scotch, drained the rest in a single gulp, and rubbed Tony's back.

'It'll be okay, Tony. Be strong. We'll all miss him. He was a great man.'

'Sal was like a brother, just like Leo,' Tony replied, choking on his words. 'He must have started shooting to hold them back. He died for us.'

'We won't ever forget what he did to buy us more time,' Marco said.

Charlie found another bottle and opened it. Tonight, they would drink in excess and mourn their friends.

SIXTY-THREE

In the quiet solitude of his expansive living room, Ed Denham sat with the lights off and curtains drawn. The only illumination came from the flickering scenes on his television, broadcasting the late news. Horror washed over him as he watched the camera pan over the crime scene that unfolded at the Australian Summit Bank in Martin Place. Despite a lifetime spent working for the Bianco family, involved in various acts of violence and crime, what he witnessed on the screen was unlike anything he had ever seen.

Working for Frank was inherently challenging, and not a day went by that Ed didn't harbour regret over the life choices that led him to his current predicament. His association with Frank, while lucrative in the early days, now came at a steep cost. Despite the routine brutality of organised crime, Ed had always regarded it as 'just business.' Others may have suffered, mainly rival crime figures, but never civilians. The recent events, however, changed everything. When Charlie and Marco took over the family business, the paradigm shifted, taking their criminal activities to a new and senseless level. These bank robberies were beyond anything Frank would have condoned or even considered.

The weight of his involvement in the planning of the bank robberies bore down on him, and he couldn't escape the harsh reality that eight lives had been lost – six of them innocent civilians. He believed warning Charlie and Marco to cancel their plans would save lives while ensuring Will's safety and preserving his anonymity. However, unbeknownst to him, the twins had circumvented him and pushed forward with the robbery without the guidance of another vision, leading to a level of destruction beyond his worst imaginings. The remorse and guilt now consumed Ed as he grappled with the devastating consequences of his unwitting contribution to the tragic events.

A revelation dawned on Ed as he sat alone, watching the news unfold on his television. Charlie and Marco, whom he had suspected of a darker inclination in their youth, now exhibited a disturbing enjoyment for violence and killing. Whether it was his contact with Will or an escalating hatred for the Bianco twins, a profound shift occurred within Ed. The realisation struck him that mere attempts to have them postpone their planned robberies were no longer sufficient. He couldn't tolerate their brutality any longer. They needed to be stopped.

SIXTY-FOUR

Woods persevered at the Martin Place crime scene until 11 p.m., acknowledging that fatigue had reached a point where she would no longer be productive. They towed away her car for forensic analysis after it had been caught in the crossfire earlier in the day. Rather than securing another vehicle, she opted for a reflective walk home, granting herself the space to clear her mind. The night air was warm, and though the sun had long set, a residual brightness lingered, imparting a subtle sense of invigoration as Woods attempted to distance herself from the horrors that unfolded inside the bank.

As she started her walk, Woods aimed to shift her focus away from the grim circumstances of the day and channel her energy toward propelling the investigation forward. The day's chaos had caused her to forget to return Will's call. Instead of calling him back, she stopped at his apartment on her way home. She wanted to talk to Will face to face where she could share Yule's decision and provide the context, knowing that the news would likely crush him.

The struggle to accept Yule's decision weighed heavily on her, and she picked up her pace to vent her frustration. The realisation that he wanted to sever ties with Will, dismissing the invaluable information he could provide, left her grappling with a dilemma. She understood the pressure Yule faced in solving the robberies and acknowledged the frustration caused by some inaccuracies in Will's information. However, having worked closely with Will, she knew his abilities were often accompanied by a reason behind everything he saw. She knew they were usually frustratingly cryptic, but she truly believed in his visions.

Relieved to find the light still on in Will's living room, Woods arrived at the front of his building. She buzzed his unit, and Will promptly let her in.

'Are you okay? I just saw the late news,' Will said from the doorway as Woods reached the top of the stairs.

'Yeah, it was just a hell of a day,' she replied, walking inside and flopping herself on his couch. 'I'm so exhausted.'

Will sat opposite her in his armchair and waited for her to continue.

'It was horrible there at the bank. There has been so much death, and we still have three of them on the run. Honestly, I don't know how we will solve this before they hurt more people.'

Will sighed and shook his head. 'I can't believe I was wrong. What I saw at the bank was so clear. I thought I had the right time and date. I'm so sorry, Aubrey. The news devastated me when I saw so many people had been killed. I just can't believe I was wrong again.'

'It's not your fault, Will. You can't blame yourself. If you never even had the vision to begin with, these robberies would still have happened, so don't think like that.'

'Well, there is something I have to tell you. I wanted to tell you this sooner, but I'm still kind of processing this myself. I might know why I was wrong,' Will said, almost cautiously.

'What is it?'

'Well, I wanted to tell you sooner, but you were so busy, and I didn't think it would matter. I really thought these people were going to be stopped, regardless. But they got away, and now I know it matters.'

Woods raised her eyebrows, puzzled. Will continued, 'It's about my father. Ed Denham. Remember how I told you I thought I saw him? Well, it was him. He came here, actually.'

Now alert and sitting upright, Woods took a moment to process the news. 'Oh wow, what did he say? Are you okay after talking with him after all those years?'

'Well, he told me some pretty concerning things. He can see things the way I can. It's a family gift, I suppose.'

'Visions?' Now she was completely alert. 'How long has your father known about that? More importantly, how did he know *you* have them?'

'His visions started like mine after a head injury. He worked it out after he saw me outside the Greenspring Bank, confirming his theory he had a vision of the police later foiling that robbery. But Aubrey, Ed's deeply entrenched with the Bianco crime family. Have you heard of them?'

Woods' eyes now opened wide as the puzzle pieces continued to fall into place. 'Of course I have. They are huge players in the underworld drug and extortion trade and are exceptionally dangerous, from what I have heard. In fact, according to our intelligence, we have connected the two dead offenders today with this family. Will, you'll need to tell me everything.'

As Will spoke, he recounted the shocking revelations his father had shared with him, delving into Ed Denham's life of crime and the discovery of his ketamine-induced visions. Woods sat silently, absorbing the weight of the information she had just received.

Finally, she found her voice and said, 'Will, I appreciate you sharing this with me. It's a lot to take in, but it gives us some insight.'

Will continued, 'Apparently, he's been working for the Bianco family for years. Like he had no choice. He said they threatened to hurt me and my sister if he ever left, but I didn't want to hear his excuses, so I kicked him out. We all have choices, and after what I saw in my vision, what these people did by murdering those people at the bank, well, I couldn't even stand being in the same room as someone who would allow this to happen.'

'So they know about his visions and use it for themselves. That's huge. It's why they always seem a step ahead. So people working within the Bianco family are actually behind the robberies?'

'That's what he told me before warning me to ignore anything else I might see about them. He never mentioned specific people by name, but there is a definite connection between these robberies and the Bianco crime family.'

'Woods nodded. 'And what about the ketamine he's given?'

'Apparently, it's the only way he can have a vision now, but they've changed how he sees things. He told me he is completely lucid during the drug-induced visions and can actually control them, entering and leaving them as he likes. He thinks the drugs mess around with the chemical signals in his brain or something.'

Woods took another moment to absorb everything. 'The fact the Biancos are somehow connected to these robberies is huge, Will. These are dangerous people.'

'My father's terrified of them. He also said he saw the Greenspring robbery in a vision after mine. He saw the planned police operation and how it ruined their job, so he was the reason they abandoned the job at the last minute. I bet it's exactly the same as today's robbery. He must have seen the police responding after my vision and made them change their plans.'

'It's like he's one step ahead,' Woods added.

'Yes, and I can only wait for visions, and I have no control over when or if they occur. The real challenge is not knowing what my father sees after my visions and how he manipulates the robberies. I don't even know how I can help anymore. He sees everything I see, giving them the upper hand. How can you catch them when he anticipates every move?'

Woods started fidgeting and scrunched her face, ready to tell Will of the next complication. 'I don't know if you can help, regardless of your father's involvement,' she said.

'What do you mean?' Will said.

'Well, Yule lost it. After the Greenspring Bank robbery didn't happen, and then the change of date with the Australian Summit Bank robbery, he doesn't want me speaking to you anymore.'

'What? Come on, Aubrey, you can't be serious.'

'Yule's angry and frustrated. He wants to work this case traditionally, with hard evidence. He's a brilliant detective, but he's also stubborn. I won't be able to change his mind. I'm sorry, Will. I wish it wasn't like this.'

'But what do I do if I see something? I know Ed's getting in the way, but what if I can still help somehow?'

'Look, I just need to be very, very careful here,' she said. 'If you see something, just tell me, okay? I just don't know how I'll be able to use it, but I still think it's important you pass on anything else you see. I still need to know.'

Will scrunched his face and nodded. His disappointment was evident.

'You said your father never mentioned names, but what about descriptions or other information we could use?' Woods asked. 'Anything that might help us narrow down who is else linked to the Biancos and involved in these robberies?'

'No, I got the feeling he already said too much. He just came to warn me to stay out of it, and I don't want to speak with him ever again.'

'Okay. Look, I hope this doesn't change anything for us. If it were up to me, I'd still follow up on everything you see, you know that, right?'

'Yeah, I do. I honestly understand why your boss isn't happy. I mean, I still feel like I've failed, and I won't say I like it, but I get it. And don't worry, I'll still tell you if I see something else.'

'I'm counting on it,' she said as she stood up. It's late, so I better get going. I have a big day at work tomorrow. Today was a mess, and we have our work cut out for us.'

SIXTY-FIVE

As Will went about his morning routine, the weight of guilt over the previous day's events settled heavily on his shoulders. Yule's refusal to let Woods listen to him lingered in his mind, creating an uneasy backdrop for his thoughts. He had to overcome this hurdle if he wanted to contribute meaningfully to the investigation.

Will made his way out of the apartment building, his thoughts now consumed by his father and his involvement in the robberies. As he walked past the communal garden tended by his elderly neighbour, Mrs. Simmons was tending to. Mrs. Simmons, an elderly, widowed resident dressed impeccably in pressed trousers and a crisp white blouse, stood on the other side of the garden, delicately picking herbs and placing them in a wicker basket.

'Morning, Will,' she said in a perky, pleasant tone, lifting her large floppy gardening hat to see him properly.

'Morning, Mrs. Simmons, the garden's looking nice.'

She beamed with sincere delight. 'Thank you, sweetheart. Off to work, are we?'

'I am. Best get going, bye.'

'Have a nice day. Stop by for a cup of tea whenever you like.'

Will exchanged a smile and a wave with Mrs. Simmons, appreciating her friendly gesture. Everyone in the building knew Mrs. Simmons for her generous spirit, as she would often offer cups of tea and a friendly chat.

Though Will occasionally accepted her offer, he couldn't shake the feeling of pity for her, as he never saw friends or family visiting. Leaving the small front gate, he started on the short walk to the hospital.

Will made his way at a slow stroll. He had plenty of time to get to work and contemplated stopping for a coffee.

Suddenly, a voice he instantly recognised called out to him from behind. 'Will!'

It sent shivers down his spine. He didn't know whether to ignore the voice and continue walking or turn around. He did the latter, slowly looking back, his fists clenched by his sides.

He looked at his father, who was about five metres away, jogging toward him. He was unshaven and looked tired and unkept, his baggy eyes squinting in the glare.

Will panicked, and his heart and breathing rate suddenly spiked, but the adrenaline surged violently through him. He ran toward his father and grabbed his thin neck, driving him backwards into a concrete wall.

Ed gasped and choked, 'Will, stop. Please.'

'Tell me why I shouldn't ring the police right now?' he said, tightening his grip.

'Because I want to help you,' barely audible under the pressure of Will's grasp.

'Liar!' Will yelled.

A few bystanders nearby halted and gasped at what they saw. Aware of the shocked onlookers, Will released his grip on his father. Ed stumbled backwards, catching himself against the wall. A series of coughs escaped him, his hand instinctively reaching to massage his now red and swollen neck.

'It's okay, everyone. It's just a misunderstanding. Everything is fine,' Ed called out as he waved his hands. This explanation seemed reasonable enough, and the onlookers carried on with their morning.

Will glared at his father. 'You made them change the date of yesterday's robbery, didn't you?'

'No, I honestly didn't know they were going to do that. I saw how it ended with all those innocent people murdered. They don't trust me, but

I tried to do the right thing and get them to cancel their plan. I didn't know they would just change the date and do it a day earlier.'

'Well, regardless, because of you, all those people died yesterday. If I thought you were despicable before, you've now reached a new low,' Will said, turning around to walk away.

'Just please hear me out.'

He stopped and raised his arms. 'Why? Why should I? I told you I never wanted to see you ever again.'

'I want to make things right. These robberies are getting out of control.'

'And you have yourself to thank for that,' Will jabbed.

'I know I've done the wrong thing, and I don't deserve your forgiveness, but please, I want to make things right. Since I met you properly and saw how you've used your gift to help so many people, and after what has happened with these robberies, all the senseless deaths, I just need to do the right thing.'

'You've done so many horrible things. I can barely look at you, let alone trust you.'

'Well, let my actions speak for themselves. Let me tell you what I know, and you can pass on everything to whomever it is with the police you are in contact with.'

Will took a moment to think. His curiosity mingled with lingering anger.

'Look, you don't owe me anything,' Ed said. 'If you tell me to go away, I promise I won't ever bother you again. Please, though, just listen to what I have to say. I don't expect to win you over. I truly don't want these psychopaths killing more innocent people. I saw what they did on the news last night, and it made me feel sick. I can't let them get away with it.'

'Fine. I'm listening.'

'Can we go somewhere private? If I'm seen here, we would have a real problem.'

Will let out a deep sigh, his gaze scanning his father with a mix of weariness and caution. Ed's demeanour betrayed desperation and nervousness, and his inability to stand still was clear. Despite his lack of trust, Will entertained whatever explanation his father offered.

'We can go back to my place,' he said. 'But I'm only talking to you so the police can stop these robberies and nothing more.'

'I understand,' Ed replied.

Will walked in silence back to his building while Ed followed closely behind.

'Back already, Will?' Mrs. Simmons asked. 'Who's your friend?'

She didn't intend to be intrusive; rather, Will knew she believed in acknowledging as many people as possible, particularly those entering her building.

'He's nobody, Mrs. Simmons, no need to worry.' Will replied.

'I'm Will's father, Ed Denham,' he said, offering his hand, which Mrs. Simmons accepted after first removing her gardening gloves.'

'Oh, lovely to meet you, and yes, I can see the resemblance.'

Will grit his teeth and glared back. 'Come on.' Ed quickly followed him into the building as Will had already started up the stairs and let the door swing back. He caught it just before it locked him out.

When they walked into his apartment together, Will stood by the kitchen, leaning on the bench, while Ed made himself comfortable, sitting at the round dining table and clearing away a pile of clothes lying on top of it.

'Okay, go,' Will said, folding his arms across his chest.

'Your neighbour seems nice.'

'Don't worry about my neighbours. Just start talking. What you have to say better be worth it.'

SIXTY-SIX

Crossing his legs and leaning back into Will's couch, Ed began. 'I told you the other day that the Bianco crime family forced me to work for them many years ago when they discovered what I could do.'

With his father disclosing things he already knew, Will was still yet to be impressed and remained silent.

Ed continued, 'What I didn't tell you was that the two people who are now the head of the family, twins Charlie and Marco Bianco, are both directly involved in the armed robberies. These men are brash and arrogant, especially Charlie. He is a dangerous sociopath, and I know they will not stop. I was dreading the day Frank's sons would take over the business, and now that it's happened, it's worse than I could have ever imagined.'

'Okay, so they, not just their associates, are directly responsible for the robberies. Fine. I'm sure the police would have worked that out. So what can you give me that's useful?'

'It's true, they use me like an object and divulge very little of their business to me, but because of what I can do, naturally, they need me to know what they are up to so I can focus my visions properly. The thing is, these twins are smart, and even if the police catch on to them, it'll be hard actually to pin the robberies on them. Also, their associates are so loyal that even if they caught one, they won't talk to the police.'

'So the cops raid just their houses then?'

'That's the thing. If that happens, I promise the police won't find any-thing. Charlie and Marco keep their houses clean for that very reason. No business takes place at their homes, and wherever they do business, they don't leave traces of it around for long.' Ed paused and rubbed his throat, now red and likely to bruise. 'Can I get a drink of water or something?'

'No, keep talking.'

Ed sighed and exhaled, but continued. 'They must keep a safe location somewhere local, where they keep their cash and drugs and do a lot of their business. My guess is a warehouse, or maybe one of the businesses they run legitimately. Unfortunately, they never told me. Now, I've tried so hard to have a vision so I could see where they go, but without the ketamine, I can't. Charlie controls the drugs, so I can't just get it myself, and they keep such a close eye on me I can't get it elsewhere. Honestly, I thought I was getting followed out of my apartment building this morning, but I think I'm okay for now. I left my phone behind, which is how they normally track me, and I'm sure it won't take them long to realise I left without it, but I expect they would be tired and hungover at the moment. They drink hard after a successful job, and I expect a little harder, seeing they lost two of their own. But if I'm not back home soon, they'll realise I'm gone and probably punish me for not taking my phone.'

'Well, you haven't even told me much yet.'

'Maybe not, but I overheard something about how they clean their money.'

'What do you mean?'

'Well, if you rob a bank, you can't just go spend the cash. It's too obvious, and the bills are probably marked. So they need to launder it first.'

'And how do they do that?'

'Through cryptocurrency. I recently overheard Charlie talking about it. Two days after a robbery or any job they do involving large cash deals, for that matter, and once the dust has settled, they convert their cash to cryptocurrency and then do a bunch of tumbling to make it vanish. They buy crypto and then move it around all over the world and even transfer it to other currencies before eventually cashing back out or putting the money through their legitimate businesses.'

'I still don't understand how this helps me?'

'Because I know where they convert the money. It's a new cryptocurrency trader on Pitt Street in the city. They'll leave their safe house with the cash, drop it off at the trader and leave empty-handed but with a digital wallet full of their stolen money, now cleaned and untraceable.'

'So the cops can get information from the crypto place? Don't they have to report large transactions as part of regulations?'

'Ordinarily, yes, but not in this case. They own the business, which is managed under a shell corporation, and everything they do there is off the books. The cash goes in the vault at the office, and then later, it gets shipped interstate, held for a while, carefully banked, and goes back to fund the crypto business. It's like a cycle of dirty money. As I said, I overheard them talking about it a few weeks ago.'

'I still don't understand how this helps.'

'Because if you can wait them out and see them leaving the crypto place, you can follow them back to their safe house. They operate a high-powered laptop from wherever their safe house is and spend the rest of that day using it to move their digital money around. I guarantee if you follow them back to their safe house, the cops will then be able to take their computer and probably find all sorts of documents and plans about the robberies. That's the time to take them out, right after the cash drop, when they are the most vulnerable and have their computer switched on. They would also likely store drugs and guns there, possibly even the ones used at the robberies. They would have all the evidence they need to put them away forever. You need that safe house location and the right timing.'

'And this safe house could be anything? Something the police would never expect.'

'That's right.'

'And Charlie and Marco will drop the money off themselves?'

'Yes, they don't trust many people with that much money. They had a tight group with two now dead, so they will do it themselves.'

'How do I find this crypto business?'

'It's called Express BTC, right on the corner of Pitt Street and Market Street in a big office building. It's up there on level ten. Trust me, they'll be there two days from now. I don't know the time, but they'll be there.'

'Okay, it sounds like you might have something there, but I still don't know if I trust you. I mean, why help now?'

Ed sighed. 'Will, I'm done with this life, I promise you. I should have been brave years ago. Brave like you are and just left. I was a coward, I admit it, but I'm trying to make amends. I don't want to live the rest of my life like this anymore. Maybe it was seeing you for the first time since you were a baby. Perhaps that was all I needed to want to get out of this life.'

Something in Ed's eyes and voice told Will he was sincere, but there was still the hurt from the years of his absence coupled with the shocking revelations of his father's long life of crime.

'You know you deserve to be punished for all the crimes you've committed and helped commit.'

'Yes, I know. I also hope one day you will forgive me.'

Will walked over to the door and opened it. 'You should go now.'

'Okay. I hope what I've told you helps. Charlie and Marco Bianco need to be stopped. They haven't approached me to get another vision for a future robbery, and I'm not sure they even will, but it's probably only a matter of time before they do something reckless, especially after two of their friends were killed. Remember, you only have a small window of opportunity to find their safe house.'

Ed walked out the door, and before Will closed it, he turned around and looked at Will with pleading eyes. 'I trust you'll pass this information on to the right people. I promise all I want to do is put a stop to them, but please be careful, Will. They are so cunning and dangerous, you have no idea what they are truly capable of.'

Will nodded and closed the door. As he approached the street-facing window in his living room, he gazed at his father walking down the street, contemplating the authenticity of the man who had built his life around crime and deceit.

SIXTY-SEVEN

After the meeting with his father, Will was half an hour late for work. As he approached the maintenance shed, he noticed Ravi standing by the door. A concerned expression stretched across his face.

'I tried calling you earlier,' he said. 'I saw what happened at the bank on the news.'

Will pulled his phone out of his pocket and looked at the screen. There were three missed calls and two texts.

'Oh, sorry, Ravi, things just got pretty hectic.'

'Well, are you okay? All that stuff at the bank...'

'I stuffed up again,' Will interrupted. 'Well, kind of. I saw the robbery happen, but so did my father. What he saw was the result of my vision leading to the police intervention. He saw how their plan backfired with the police waiting, so they changed the date. They brought it forward a day. There was nothing I could do. Inevitably, people were going to get killed. It was just a matter of when.'

'What? Seriously?'

'Yes, here, come inside,' Will said, unlocking the shed door, leading Ravi inside and dodging the spare equipment. The metal roof had increased the temperature inside by fifteen degrees, which Will tried to ease by switching on an old pedestal fan. It didn't work.

'Sorry about the heat and the mess. I didn't want to talk outside.'

'That's okay. How are you feeling about it all?' Ravi asked, leaning against the old desk at the back of the shed.

'Honestly, a good mix of angry and confused. It's like everything I saw, my father saw too. So, I could never make a difference or help Aubrey. I tried to do the right thing and get her to step in with her team and stop the robberies and the murders, but it still all ended up happening, regardless. I'm frustrated because I don't have the level of control my father has, which is why he's always going to be one step ahead of me.'

'But he's using dangerous drugs, Will.'

'I know, but what good am I if I can't use my gift like he does? They'll just keep changing their plans at the last minute after forcing my father to see what will happen. Anyway, he came to see me again this morning.'

'Who, your father?' Ravi said, looking shocked. 'What for?'

'He followed me and then stopped me on the street. I was so angry I thought I was going to kill him with my bare hands. I had him by the throat, but then something inside me decided to hear him out. He seemed pretty remorseful that these robberies had gotten out of control. They've taken things too far, and now he says he wants to help.'

'Do you really believe him?'

'Yes and no,' Will replied with a shrug. 'I mean, I barely know him, and the very thought of him, with everything he's done, makes my skin crawl. But there was something different about him this morning. He seemed so desperate. He said he took an enormous risk coming to see me, and that he now wanted to do the right thing.'

'I just don't know if you can trust him after everything he's done,' Ravi said, anxiously fidgeting with his thick glasses.

'I don't think I have a choice. I spoke with Aubrey. The police still have no solid leads. I now know the heads of the Bianco family are directly involved, but we'd need solid evidence to get them, something the police don't have right now. If we don't do something soon, more people could get hurt.'

'What about all that stuff he said about how dangerous they are, and how they have enslaved him for all these years? Holding you and your sister over his head to make sure he does as he's told.'

'I don't think any of that has changed. If anything, it sounds like the new heads of the Bianco family are even worse than the old ones, and he despises them.'

'So they could kill him and then come after you? Or find you first, then kill him?' Ravi asked, looking worried about this sudden level of cooperation. 'I really don't know about this. What did he say, anyway?'

'Well, if what he said was true, it wouldn't involve him at all, so they'd never find out he helped. He gave me a tip to pass on to Aubrey. It was about when they move their money around and how to find their safe house. He doesn't know where it is but says if we find that, we find the evidence about their involvement in the robberies.'

'Okay, so have you told her yet?'

'Slight problem there,' Will said, biting his lip. 'Because I was wrong about the last two robberies, her boss won't allow her to get information from me. He won't listen to anything I tell her.'

'What are you going to do?'

'I don't know. I'll talk to Aubrey later and work something out.'

'What can I do?'

'Get me some ketamine. I want to see things like my father does. I think it'll help to be lucid and in control of what I see. This time, the visions will be on my terms. No surprises, nothing cryptic, just me seeing what I need to see.'

Ravi's eyes widened, and he looked both offended and surprised as he exclaimed, 'What? No. Absolutely not.'

'If you give it to me, it would be safe,' Will said, desperately trying to reason with him.

'Will, ketamine can be so dangerous. It can increase blood pressure, make you delirious, damage memory or give you full-body convulsions. I mean, there are so many considerations using it. Even medically. And recreationally, it can be very dangerous. Fatal even.'

'It's not recreational, and you'll supervise. I just need to get ahead. It might help Aubrey track these people down. I'm serious here, Ravi.'

'So am I, Will. As a doctor and your friend, the answer is no. What if your mind isn't like your father's? What if it's slightly different, and you react negatively to it? Your brain is just too unpredictable. I mean, look what happened with standard antidepressants. I won't do it.'

'Please!' Will begged. 'I'm trying to do the right thing here.'

'The answer is no. You'll have to find another way,' Ravi said, walking toward the door. 'If I can help you, let me know. I hope your chat with Aubrey goes well, but I will not give you drugs.'

He left and shut the door as Will booted the leg of his wooden desk in irritation. He sat on the matching old wooden chair and rested his head in his hands. The past few weeks had drained him. The extortion at Taree, to the death of the police officers in the meth lab explosion, to now facing his father for the first time. In addition to trying to stop these robberies, it was all piling up and taking its toll. Although it came across the wrong way, his anger wasn't directed at his friend; he was simply frustrated, but mostly exhausted.

SIXTY-EIGHT

Woods lived in a modern two-bedroom apartment in a serene complex at the rear of Redfern. Surrounded by lush, leafy trees, the building boasted contemporary amenities such as a heated pool and a gym. The stark contrast between her comfortable residence and the dilapidated unit block Will called home was clear.

He hadn't called first, but Will thought Woods would come straight home from work. He had only ever been to her building once before, and that was to pick her up in a shared Uber to go out for lunch together one Saturday a couple of months ago. Will had yet to be invited inside, and tonight, he will have to invite himself in for this important conversation. He walked along a colourful garden toward the entrance doors. When he reached the intercom, he saw the name *A. Woods* handwritten in black ink and sitting underneath a plastic cover beside her doorbell. She answered after two separate and long rings.

'Hello?'

'Aubrey, it's Will. Can I come up? I need to talk to you?'

'Come up? Oh yeah, sure,' she said.

Woods waited by her open door on the top level of the building, wearing loose-fitting shorts and a baggy green singlet.

'Hey, I just got out of the shower.'

'Do you mind if I come in?' Will asked. 'I have something important to tell you.'

'Uh yeah, of course, come in.

The open-plan apartment was furnished with simplicity in mind. The living room featured coordinated furniture, with a cream-coloured couch complementing the dark wood square dining table and four chairs. Matching the dining set, Woods also had a dark wooden coffee table, an entertainment unit, and a tall bookcase adorned with trinkets, candles, photo frames, and a few books. The polished floorboards reflected the meticulous cleanliness of the space, creating a slight echo as Will moved toward the centre of the apartment.

'I'll cut to the chase,' he said. 'My father came to my house this morning and told me some things about the robberies and murders.'

'What, seriously?'

'Yes. Believe me, I wasn't expecting it either. But I wanted to hear him out. Anything to stop them from hurting anyone else.'

'So what did he say?' Woods asked.

'Well, it was about the Bianco family. You said you thought they were somehow linked to the robberies. That perhaps some associates or people working for the family were involved? Well, according to him, the heads of the family are directly involved. Charlie and Marco Bianco are actually part of the robbery crew themselves.'

'What!' Woods spat in surprise. 'He can't be serious. Why would two people, who are well established in a successful organised crime syndicate, who have gotten away with so much and made a fortune over the years, risk doing something so dangerous and stupid? Does he have any proof?'

'Not exactly. Ed said they don't involve him in family business directly, aside from the ketamine injections and being forced to see what they are up to, so I guess he is well aware of what they are doing but not where they go after the robberies. He believes they have a safe house, though.'

'Well, that's not surprising. These organised crime syndicates probably have many, and often they are difficult to pinpoint.'

'He overheard a conversation about how they clean the cash they take from the robberies. They launder it through cryptocurrency at an exchange they recently purchased. Do you know much about cryptocurrencies and how people launder money with it?'

'Not really,' Woods replied.

'Well, from what I understand, they use cash to buy some cryptocurrency, like Bitcoin. It gets sent to a wallet of their choosing electronically. However, if someone knows what to look for, they can still trace it once it is in Bitcoin and on the public Blockchain. So, they would likely use crypto tumblers to make it next to impossible to track. For a small fee, they mix the Bitcoin or whatever alternate cryptocurrency coin they use, making it harder to trace where it came from. They probably then bounce it around different wallets and find some way to cash out, likely using an overseas digital exchange. It is both simple and highly complex at the same time. The final product is money that can't be traced back to the source.'

Woods nodded. 'I've heard money laundering through cryptocurrencies is growing in popularity amongst organised crime.'

'Yes. Well, Ed told me he heard them saying that two days after the robberies, they would go to their exchange on Pitt Street in the city, and complete the transaction. He also said they keep this part of their business between a select few so they would go themselves. After that, he said they would return to the safe house and use a laptop to move their money around. They don't do any business at their homes and said if we could work out where this spot is, and if you time it right, you would find enough evidence to sink them for the robberies. Guns, plans and more.'

'Why is he suddenly talking to you about this? I don't know if we can trust someone who has spent his whole life working for these people.'

'Look, I didn't at first, and I actually don't know if I believe him entirely, but there was something different about him this time. It was like he understood they are getting out of control, and the murders of innocent people are getting too much for him. It's worth at least a look. There's not much to lose. See if they turn up at the crypto place and follow them afterwards.'

'And if it's a trap?'

'He took a big risk in telling me, so I don't think it is. But in case it is, you can keep your distance and just watch them, right?'

'I suppose so.'

'What about your boss?'

'Yule? I don't know what to say to him about this. I can't see him approving the operation if he finds out you gave me this information. He already ordered me not to take any information from you.'

'This could be a huge opportunity, Aubrey, and time is of the essence. According to him, they will be there sometime tomorrow. He doesn't know the time, but assured me they will be there.'

'I'm not working tomorrow. I suppose I could go down there tomorrow and check it out myself.'

'I'm coming with you, then. I'll shuffle my roster around.'

'Will, that might not be a good idea.'

'Why not? We are just going to watch the place and then follow them after. You could use the help. And we keep our distance.'

'These people are really dangerous, though, and probably armed.'

'We would just be two people in the city. I don't look like a cop, so I'll blend in.'

'Okay, fine, we will go together then. But we stay well behind them, okay? I don't want to get too close.'

'And what if we actually find their safe house? What then?'

'I'll talk to Yule. If we find a safe house, I'll have to tell him you gave me the intel. He'll be furious, and he might even kick me off his team. But, so many detectives have been wanting to get the Biancos for a very long time, but no one can ever find enough evidence on them. His bosses will force him to look into it, especially with the link we already have with the ID of two of their associates connected with the family. When we raid the place and we find the evidence your father says will be there; he'll get over it. In fact, he'll probably end up with an award from the Commissioner.'

'Okay,' Will said, taking out his phone. 'I googled Charlie and Marco Bianco so I can see some recent photos of them. Here, have a look.'

He handed over the phone, which displayed a recent news article about the Bianco twins purchasing a new Italian restaurant in the inner west suburbs of Sydney. The photograph showed them standing with a heavy-set Italian chef out the front of the building. With confident smirks, both twins were wearing black trousers and black silk shirts and had slicked-back, greasy dark hair.

'That picture is only a month old. I've looked at it a few times, so I'll be able to spot them if we see them,' Will said.

'Okay, I can't believe I'm trusting your father, but how about I meet you at Pitt Street Mall tomorrow at 9 a.m?'

'I'll be there.'

SIXTY-NINE

In the heart of Sydney, Pitt Street Mall diverged from the conventional shopping centre design. Instead, it unfolded as an open, two-hundred-metre-long strip exclusively for pedestrian use, flanked by stylish boutiques that collectively shaped one of Australia's busiest shopping precincts. As the clock struck 9 a.m., the street pulsed with activity. Professionals adorned in expensive business attire traversed the pavement, engrossed in phone conversations. Meanwhile, leisurely shoppers meandered along the strip, their attention captivated by the latest fashion trends showcased in the windows of each store.

Will arrived first, dressed in chino shorts, a navy T-shirt, black Adidas runners, and reflective aviator sunglasses. He found the large commercial building on Market Street at the southern end of Pitt Street Mall and took a seat on a public bench nearby, which gave him a good vantage point of the front entrance to the building housing the cryptocurrency office.

Woods arrived a few minutes later wearing jeans and a loose floral-patterned blouse and carrying two takeaway coffees. She sat close to Will on the bench and handed him one. She was prepared for an extended stakeout. Together, they appeared to be a young couple on a shopping date, and with the amount of foot traffic around, no one would notice them in the area for a prolonged period.

'Is that the building there?' Woods asked, nodding toward the tall building about twenty-five metres away.

'Yep. Ed said the crypto exchange is on the tenth floor.'

'It's busy.'

'Yeah, but they will stand out. I had another good look at their photos this morning. Thanks for the coffee, by the way.'

'No worries, I figured we might need it. Surveillance can get boring. What are they? Your surveillance shades?' Woods said, chuckling at Will's dark sunglasses.

Will smiled. 'Better than a newspaper with eye holes cut through. It's a clear day today, and the sun will get stronger later.'

'You're not wrong. Now, if we need it, I've parked my car one street over. There wasn't much parking around here.'

They settled in, both taking deep sips of their coffee, preparing for a potentially protracted wait.

'What's that?' Will asked, brushing his hand against Woods' hip.

'I decided to carry my firearm. I don't intend to use it. It's just in case. Better to have it and not need it, over needing it and not having it.' She pulled her blouse down a little further to keep it covered.

Time went by slowly. It seemed like thousands of people had come and gone from the building, but there was still no sign of Charlie or Marco Bianco. It was nearing 11 a.m., and irritation was setting in. The sun was exposing the previously shaded parts of the street, and just as Will stood up to stretch his back, he saw them.

Two men were walking into the front of the building, both carrying large black backpacks. There was no doubt one man was Charlie Bianco. He wore similar clothes from the newspaper article Will had read the day before: black trousers, a black shirt with the sleeves rolled up, revealing his bulky forearms, and what looked like an expensive designer watch and sunglasses. The man with him dressed in similar dark trousers and sunglasses, but he opted for a dark grey polo shirt. He was of a similar appearance to Charlie, only a fraction taller and about ten kilograms heavier. He could have been mistaken for a personal bodyguard.

'Here, look, they're going in!' Will said, sitting back down.

Woods cautiously peered toward the entrance of the building. 'Geez, you're right. Just as your father said.'

'But who is the guy with Charlie Bianco?'

'Not sure, probably a close associate. He was carrying a bag probably filled with cash too. I don't recognise him. Maybe he's part of the robbery crew, too.'

Will's heart was racing. He was confident things were going perfectly to plan and so far, their surveillance had gone undetected.

They waited five minutes. Then another ten minutes.

'What's taking them so long?' Will asked impatiently.

'Just calm down. It'll be okay. They had two big bags and probably had a lot of money to count. It could take some time. Just stay patient. And don't stare at the building. It looks too obvious.'

After twenty minutes, Will saw the two men leave the building together. Their backpacks look deflated and much lighter.

'Aubrey, look there, they're leaving.'

The two men walked neither slowly nor quickly, rather confidently and with a sense of purpose, but without attracting attention. Woods tapped Will, and they both got up and started following, keeping a safe distance behind.

They walked back through Pitt Street Mall, which he thought was perfect. They could blend in amongst the crowd and follow the pair without being spotted.

When they reached the halfway point of the long shopping strip, Charlie Bianco turned around and briefly looked at Woods.

'Shit, I think he saw me,' Woods whispered to Will.

'What? But he wouldn't know who you are?'

'I hope not,' she said, as she adjusted the gun on her hip and checked that it was still concealed. 'Charlie is whispering something to his friend. Look.'

Sure enough, Will saw the pair stop and have a quick chat with each other. The larger of the two turned around, glancing in their direction.

Woods held Will's hand, and he felt their fingers lock.

'Like an actual couple. We need to blend in,' she said as Will felt his cheeks blush. 'Let's just stop and lie low for a bit. We'll go into a shop in case they think we are following them.'

Entering the nearest shop, Crown Jewellery, Will opened the door for Woods. The refreshing burst of cool air from the air conditioning greeted them, providing a welcomed contrast to the outside warmth. Despite their nerves about being spotted following Charlie Bianco and his associate, they feigned interest in the bracelets and necklaces displayed by the window while subtly glancing back at the street to check if they were being followed.

'Can I help you?' a well-dressed young shop assistant asked.

Woods replied with a curt, rather abrupt, 'No.' The sales assistant gave them a curious look and walked away.

'I can't see them,' Will said.

'That's fine. Let's wait for another ten or fifteen seconds, then we'll leave and try to find them again. I just needed to make sure we didn't raise any suspicions. It could jeopardise everything if they think the police are following them.'

After a moment, Woods nodded her head, and they both left the shop and looked in the last known direction of the men. Charlie Bianco and his associate, however, were nowhere in sight. Will looked at Woods and raised an eyebrow, silently questioning their next move.

Woods glanced around, scanning the nearby crowd and storefronts. She then pointed discreetly toward the end of Pitt Street Mall.

'Let's head that way. They might have continued down the street. Stay sharp and keep an eye out,' Woods whispered to Will. They began walking briskly in the direction Woods indicated, blending in with the bustling crowd of shoppers.

'Nothing, Aubrey,' Will said, scanning the crowd as cautiously as possible.

'Dammit. Okay, let's split up, but be careful. If you see them, don't get too close. Text me your location and I'll meet up with you. Likewise, I'll let you know if I see them, but we do not approach them under any circumstances. Do you understand?'

'Okay,' Will said. 'I'll go into the Westfield's shopping centre. Maybe they went through there and parked their car underneath.'

'Fine, I'll keep walking north along the street. And Will, please be careful. Remember who we are dealing with here.'

SEVENTY

Woods scanned every shop she passed before she made it to the end of Pitt Street Mall, where it intersected with King Street. She looked up and down the street carefully, but saw nothing.

Woods checked the cafes and shops lining the street, hoping to catch a glimpse of Charlie Bianco or his associate. The bustling city atmosphere continued, but there was no sign of either of them. As she reached the end of Pitt Street Mall at King Street, she paused and looked up and down the street.

'Where did you guys go? You couldn't have gotten too far.'

Woods moved briskly along King Street, headed toward the vehicular traffic on the one-way street. It was a calculated guess, a decision made on the fly to prevent Charlie Bianco and his associate from putting more distance between her. Her phone remained clutched in her hand, poised for a call from Will with any information about their whereabouts. As she walked eastward, the cityscape unfolded around her - storefronts, cafes, and the constant hum of urban life. Woods maintained a vigilant gaze, scanning both sides of the road for any sign of the pair.

A well-polished and heavily tinted grey Jaguar parked along the side of the street caught her attention a short distance ahead. The rear passenger door stood open, revealing nothing out of the ordinary at first glance. She casually noted it as a nice model and kept walking.

Feeling an abrupt, intense pressure around her waist, Woods was suddenly caught off guard. In a fraction of a second, thick arms enveloped her, forcefully dragging her into the backseat of the Jaguar. The door shut behind her, and a large, powerful hand covered her mouth, stifling her screams as the rest of her body struggled in vain.

Charlie Bianco turned around from the driver's seat and smirked at her.

'Tony, grab her gun and smash her phone,' he said before starting the car and driving away.

***

Will, realising it was a waste of time looking deeper within the shopping centre, abandoned his search. He believed Charlie Bianco and his associate couldn't have gotten this far and that they must have continued walking outside, and was confident Woods could track them down again. Attempting to contact her for an update, he dialled her number, but the call went unanswered.

Concerned by Woods' sudden unavailability, Will returned to Pitt Street Mall and walked north in the direction she had gone. Reaching the end of the street, he looked in both directions, but she was nowhere in sight. He walked along King Street, attempting to call her once more. To his alarm, the call this time went straight to voicemail.

As he had the phone pressed to his ear, trying to reach her again, he looked down at the road and saw a shiny object laying in the gutter. It was Woods' silver wristwatch; he recognised it immediately. The screen was cracked, and the strap was broken, but it was definitely hers. Will picked it up and looked around for any sign of her.

It took a moment for it to register, but Will knew something was wrong. Woods was missing, and it looked like something or someone had ripped the watch off in a struggle. There were a few shops along King Street, but it was far quieter than the busy trade of Pitt Street Mall. Bursting into a clothing shop near where Will found the watch, he frantically called out to the young male shop assistant.

'Have you seen a woman, late twenties, with blonde hair and wearing a floral top?'

The young man frowned, confused at the urgency. 'No, sorry.'

He rushed out of the shop and spun around, looking in every direction, but there was no sign of her. Frustration and worry gnawed at him as he clutched Woods' broken wristwatch.

***

As the grey Jaguar drove away from the city centre, Woods held captive within, Charlie Bianco was too busy to notice Qiang Chen in his Honda Civic following him. In fact, he hadn't noticed Chen carefully watching his every move all morning.

SEVENTY-ONE

Woods fought back, her resistance escalating as Tony forcefully lifted her blouse, exposing her Glock holstered at her hip. Swiftly disassembling her weapon, he removed the magazine and ejected the loaded round from the chamber. Delving into Woods' pocket, he extracted her phone, brutally smashing it into countless shards with the gun's butt. Applying cruel pressure, he bound her wrists together with cable ties, securing them tightly. As her legs continued to thrash, Tony expertly restrained her by fastening another set of cable ties around her ankles. Now, she was rendered entirely immobile.

Charlie observed the chaotic scene unfolding in the rear-view mirror as Woods screamed and wriggled, fiercely resisting Tony's actions. Despite her efforts, it seemed her struggles barely registered with him.

'Why were you following us?' Charlie inquired calmly, focusing on Woods through the rear-view mirror as the car advanced toward North Sydney.

'I'm a police officer, okay, you need to let me go. You've really gone and done a stupid thing now. If you pull over and let me out, you can avoid a lot of trouble.'

'I know you're a cop. I've seen you before. In a photograph hanging around the Greenspring Bank last week. One of my friends was watching you all. So answer my question. Why were you following me?'

'Did you not hear me? What do you think will come from kidnapping a police officer?'

'I'm not worried about that. What I am worried about is why you were following me. I won't ask again.'

'I wasn't following you.'

'You know I spotted that Glock sticking out of your hip from fifty metres away. I am a very vigilant person. In my line of work, there have been many people who have tried to kill me over the years, so I can spot someone concealing a firearm. What I can also spot from a mile away is a cop on surveillance.'

'You really need to let me go. Things are only going to get much worse for you.'

'See, that's where you're wrong. You don't get where I am by making mistakes. What I'd like to know is what is a cop doing in the city following someone, without backup or without even so much as a radio or surveillance comms kit?'

Woods didn't reply.

'You see, I know how you people work. I also know you perform surveillance in teams and I couldn't spot any other cops around. All I saw was the skinny guy you were with, who I'm sure wasn't a cop, so what, are you working alone then?'

'I'm part of a large team. They'll find me.'

Charlie stared deeply into her eyes and laughed. 'I don't think so.'

Woods felt the tight grip of the cable ties around her wrists, and her panic increased. Alone and uncertain if anyone knew about her abduction, she contemplated bluffing the men to frighten them enough to potentially secure her release. In reality, she knew she had been dragged into the car unnoticed, and wondered if Will was even aware she was missing.

She did her best to think on her feet, 'I have my whole team out with me, I swear. I suggest you let me go now before they find out that you've kidnapped me.'

'If your entire team is around, where are they now?' Charlie asked with an even bigger smirk, lifting a large radio. 'Police radio here that I liberated several years ago. It still works, and one of my old pals added a device that scans all the encrypted police frequencies over every channel for any emergency calls. Nothing about a surveillance operation. No one knows you're here, so let's stop pretending. I don't know why you are working alone here, but I will find out what you're up to.'

'What are you going to do to me?' Woods said, choking on her words. She was now really struggling to remain in control of her emotions.

'First, I'm going to find out what you were doing following me. I like to be very cautious. Depending on what I find out, depends on what happens to you.'

'I've already told you.'

'Well, I have some trust issues, and certain occurrences within my business have been strange lately, so I'm even more paranoid than usual. Anyway, I have other ways of finding things out. Tony, please send a message to Ed for me. Send him the address of our destination. I want him there in twenty minutes.'

'You sure you want him where we are going?' Tony replied.

'Yes, these are special circumstances. Just send the message.'

'Will do,' he said, taking out his phone.

Woods sat quietly for a moment and thought carefully. *Ed, Will's father. This must have been a setup! They'll want him to have a vision about what we know, and then the Biancos will destroy all their evidence. I've played right in their hands. Ed played us.'*

'Where are you taking me?' she eventually asked.

'Never mind that. What's your name?'

'I'm Detective Senior Constable Aubrey Woods.'

'Okay, Detective,' he said. Woods saw him smirk in the rear-view mirror.

'Just reminding you I'm a police officer.'

'I get it. Tony, now.' Charlie said.

Tony produced a black scarf and gripped Woods' face. Despite her attempts to wriggle free, the grip was relentless. He bound the scarf tightly around her head, plunging her into darkness as the conversation ceased, and the car's engine roared.

Woods was terrified. Despite her attempts to conceal it, underneath the blindfold, her eyes were watering, and her legs, still locked together, were trembling. There was no way out now.

The Jaguar slowed down about fifteen minutes later, and Woods felt it travelling along an uneven surface. When Woods felt the ignition turn off, she flinched. Tony held her down and remained in the back seat. Still shrouded in darkness, she listened intently, although all she heard was Charlie fumble with a set of keys, then the sound of a loud steel door swinging open. Trying to absorb as much of her surroundings as she could proved impossible underneath her blindfold and Woods heard nothing except her own breathing. Although she couldn't see, she sensed she was alone with her two captors.

Suddenly, someone lifted Woods out of the car and draped her over a thick shoulder. Even with her kicking and screaming, she knew no one saw or heard her being dragged out of the car. A moment later, she smelt stale air and the feeling she was being carried down a flight of stairs.

SEVENTY-TWO

Tony dropped Woods onto a hard and cold wooden chair and forcefully removed her blindfold. Charlie Bianco's associate grinned back at her as she struggled fruitlessly.

Her back was aching and the cable ties were digging into her wrists and ankles, rubbing them raw and stinging with every movement. He then wrapped a thick piece of rope around her torso and pulled tightly against her chest, holding her firmly to the back of the chair. As the last knot was secured, Woods watched as Charlie poured himself a large glass of whiskey, sat at a table on the other side of the cellar and opened a laptop screen.

Woods looked around at her new surroundings while her eyes adjusted. She figured she was in some kind of basement cellar. A single hanging fluorescent bar was swinging from the ceiling in the centre of the room, giving just enough light for her to identify the room. She saw a few old glass refrigerators, stacks of beer and wine in boxes, several old filing cabinets, a large steel safe and a huge sheet draped over something big in the corner. At either side of the room were two flights of wooden stairs, one smaller set at the side of the cellar leading to a steel door with light creeping in underneath. Woods assumed this is where they entered from, coming in quickly from the bright outdoors. The other flight of stairs was longer and led to another closed steel door above. Woods assessed that this led to another area in the building directly above them.

She continued to observe her surroundings quietly. She knew screaming and yelling at this stage would only cause problems and agitate her captors. Charlie remained working on the laptop, slowly sipping his drink, while the other man leaned against one of the side walls, staring at his phone indifferently.

Abruptly, the steel door on the side of the cellar unlocked and swung open. Woods immediately identified the man descending the wooden stairs as Charlie's brother, Marco Bianco. Their eyes met for a fleeting moment, and he visibly recoiled, as if her presence took him by surprise.

Charlie walked over and turned him around, whispering in Marco's ear. After a moment, Woods watched Marco nod. Woods figured he was unaware of her capture, and Charlie had just given him the update. Marco then poured himself a drink without saying a word and sat opposite Charlie, who had resumed his work on the laptop.

A short time later, she heard a knock on the door leading to the area above them. Charlie closed the laptop screen, finished his drink, and walked up the stairs to answer the knock. He opened the door and Woods got her first look at the third man entering the room. Tall, thin, with shaggy hair, wearing trousers and a vest. He looked somehow familiar. In fact, he looked like Will.

'Come in, Ed,' Charlie said, walking back down the stairs.

Ed? Woods thought to herself. *So this is Will's father?*

He looked nervous. He was fidgeting with his fingers and gazing around the room anxiously, looking at everything surrounding him. If Woods didn't know any better, it was as though this was the first time he had been in this room, too.

'Urgent matters, Ed,' Charlie started. 'That's why I had to call you here. Sit down.'

When he reached the bottom of the stairs, he looked directly at Woods. His eyes widened and gave a look of both horror and surprise. She met his stare and returned the terrified look. It was as though they were communicating with their eyes, and Woods read his body language. She actually believed his eyes. Ed didn't set them up. He was just as scared as she was.

'Sit down!' Charlie repeated loudly.

Ed took a seat on an old wooden chair next to Woods.

'I needed you here, Ed, because we might have a problem. This young lady is a police officer who followed me in the city. I want you to tell me why. I want to know if anything is coming my way soon that I need to know about.'

Ed didn't reply, but his body trembled.

'Hey! Did you hear me?'

'Sorry, Charlie. Um, yes, I heard you.'

'Good, let's get started.'

***

From his parked Honda, opposite the Golden Bell Hotel, Quing Chen watched as Charlie arrived in his Jaguar. He saw his associate, whom he knew only as Tony, carry a blindfolded woman, kicking and screaming, down the cellar doors beneath the hotel. He remained idle and patient, then, a short time later, he saw Marco Bianco enter the cellar. Chen then took out his phone and called Zao Ming.

'They are all inside the cellar below the hotel.'

'Good,' Ming replied. 'Good.'

'Do you still think our stuff is inside?' Chen asked.

'Yes. You wouldn't have missed them moving something as large as those barrels. Plus, I think there'd be more inside, probably cash, more drugs and likely guns. You've been watching them for a while now. After their homes, it is the place they spend most of their time, yes?'

'Correct. Plus, it's very private. Entry is possible through a quiet and private laneway. There is a steel door, which is heavily reinforced. The whole area is well concealed by a cluster of trees.

'Then that must be it. Charlie Bianco's fortress.'

'What do we do, boss?'

'Stay there. I'll be there shortly. First, I need to make some important phone calls. We'll get back what's ours and avenge the death of Pau.'

SEVENTY-THREE

Will's Uber arrived promptly, and he quickly entered, slamming the door shut. The middle-aged driver, sporting a thick Eastern European accent, proudly claimed to maintain nothing but five-star ratings. Will, desperate to reach his destination swiftly, challenged the driver to get him to City South Hospital on the other side of the CBD as fast as possible. The driver nodded, accepting the challenge, as Will settled into the backseat, tapping his feet anxiously and running his hands through his hair, consumed by thoughts of what might have transpired with Woods. Every scenario playing in Will's mind painted a grim picture of Woods being in distress. Was she involved in an accident? Did something happen at work requiring her immediate attention? Will didn't think so. She would have told him or answered her phone. No – the shattered watch on the road hinted at something far more sinister and unsettling.

Will sent a text message to Ravi, *'Meet me in your office in five minutes. Very important!'*

As promised, the driver made it to the hospital two minutes faster than his GPS said it would.

'Five stars, yes?'

'Yes, five stars,' Will said, quickly exiting the car.

Will rushed through the emergency doors, sprinting toward the psychiatric ward. Ravi, recognising the urgency in Will's eyes, promptly opened the sturdy, lockable doors leading to the unit, allowing him entry. Ravi followed closely behind.

'I thought I'd wait for you here. Your text seemed urgent. Are you okay?'

'Come on. Your office now.'

'What's the matter?'

'Not here. Hurry.'

They reached Ravi's office at the back of the ward, and Ravi closed the door behind him.

'What's going on?' he asked.

'Look,' Will said, holding up Woods' broken watch. 'It's Aubrey's. I found it in the gutter on King Street in the city. We were there looking into the things Ed said. We followed the Biancos and split up because we thought they saw us. Anyway, a bit later, I went looking for her and this was all I could find. I think something's happened to her.'

'So you actually saw them at the crypto place? Like your father said?'

'Yes, but now it's gone wrong. I don't know where she is, and I'm really worried something's happened to her.'

'Have you tried calling her?'

'It goes straight to voicemail. Her phone is switched off.'

'And you really think something bad has happened? Maybe she just had to hurry off to do something?'

'No, she would have told me. Plus her watch, Ravi. Look at it. It's broken. I know something bad has happened.'

'Maybe you should call the police.'

'Ravi, she wasn't even supposed to be working today. Her boss didn't even know she was out with me looking into the Bianco money laundering thing. They won't be able to help.'

'They can triangulate her phone. They would have her details.'

'No, they can't. You can only get a cell tower location if the phone is switched on. Even so, if something bad has happened, we may not have time. I need to find her myself. Then I can call the police and tell her where she is.'

'Yeah, but how are you going to find her?'

'You're going to help me. You're going to give me ketamine. I'm going to do exactly what my father does.'

'No, Will. I will not have any part in that. I already told you it was too dangerous.'

'Ravi, don't make me beg. This is about Aubrey. Our friend. I really think something terrible has happened. I've been trying to think of everything that could have happened, and it must be the Biancos. We think they saw us following them, and now I'm worried they have hurt her. I need to do this, Ravi.'

'Will I... I just don't....'

'Ravi, please,' Will begged. His desperation growing. 'I need to help her, so I need your help.'

'I could lose my licence, you know that, right?'

'No one will ever find out. This is important. We need to do something. Please.'

Ravi sighed and looked into Will's eyes. They were watering and strained with desperation. He paused and sighed.

'Fine, follow me.'

Ravi led Will out of his office and down the hallway, past the reception desk managed by one of the psychiatrist nurses and past the security desk attended to by a sleepy guard. The ward was quiet, and no one seemed to notice or care that Ravi was leading Will to a small room at the end of the hallway.

'We should have some in here. There should be some palliative care stores,' Ravi said as he reached for a set of keys on his belt and unlocked the door.

The room looked like a regular examination room painted a crisp white. It had several wooden cabinets, all painted white, and an examination bed reclined to forty-five degrees. Ravi sat on a small stool on wheels and pulled himself over to the side of the room. He started digging through drawers and cabinets and pulled out medical tubing and a new syringe before unlocking a sturdy metal cabinet and sorting through a range of different vials, tablets, and liquids. He pushed several of them out of the way and began examining the labels, and eventually selected the one he was looking for.

'Okay, sit back in bed and try to relax.'

He wrapped the tubing around Will's right arm and pulled it tight. His veins popped out from his skin, ready to receive the injection. After turning his back on Will and fiddling with his equipment, he was ready.

'Thanks for doing this, Ravi.'

He shook his head. 'I can't believe I am doing this, to be honest. I'm doing it for Aubrey. I just really hope this doesn't hurt you. I have some adrenaline and other things ready to go if something happens. Still, if things get bad, I'll have to get you down to emergency. Then I'm in trouble.'

'I promise I'll cover for you if anything happens, but don't worry, it'll be okay.'

'Are you sure there's no other way?'

'No. We may not have time. I need to focus and somehow find her and then call it in, okay?'

'I don't even know how much to give you, so I'm just going to go with a low dose, okay? It'll be what I would consider a low recreational dose.'

'I'm in your hands.'

'Just lay back, take a deep breath and try to relax.'

Ravi pierced Will's skin in his inner arm and entered his vein. He slowly hit the plunger and let the liquid enter his bloodstream. He removed the tight tubing and withdrew the empty syringe as Will's eyes closed.

SEVENTY-FOUR

Will immediately experienced an overwhelming sense of relaxation and euphoria. A blissful smile spread across his face, and he felt as though his body might float off the bed. Closing his eyes, he focused his thoughts on Woods. In his mind's eye, he conjured images of her face, her smooth skin, long blonde hair cascading, and her perfectly straight white teeth. He immersed himself in the mental picture, envisioning walking side by side with her through Pitt Street Mall. The thought of her occupied every corner of his mind.

His eyes snapped open in less than a second, and he found himself standing next to Woods. She was tied to a chair, her wrists bound behind her back. The realisation hit him like a punch to the gut - she had been kidnapped. This was worse than what Will could have imagined.

'Aubrey, can you hear me?' he whispered as he crouched beside her. 'I'm so sorry they took you.' He knew he wasn't really there and that she couldn't react or respond, but his words still comforted him in the dire situation.

Will experienced a newfound clarity during the vision, unlike any he had felt before. It was as if he had transcended the boundaries of a typical vision; his perception was crystal clear, and he felt unprecedented control over everything he saw. The boundaries between the vision and reality seemed to blur, making it feel like he was physically present in the room with Woods.

As Will observed the scene, he noticed Ed Denham, who seemed asleep, seated in a wooden chair beside Woods. Despite the urgency of the situation, Will instinctively reached out to shake Ed's shoulders, momentarily forgetting that he was not physically present, and his actions held no sway in the vision.

Will noted the wooden rafters overhead and the dual sets of wooden stairs leading to distinct doors. As he wandered through the room, he noticed a collection of stacked boxes, old refrigerators, cases of beer and wine, and a round table where Charlie Bianco and another person he recognised as Marco Bianco were seated. Charlie engrossed himself in his laptop, and as Will peered over his shoulder, he discovered a screen displaying numbers and charts. It was a cryptocurrency digital wallet, revealing a balance of $351,500 in Australian Dollars.

Will heard Charlie say to Marco, 'Hopefully, Ed doesn't take too much longer, then we will find out exactly what the cop knows and who she's been talking to.'

'Oh no, no, are you going to rat us out?' he said aloud as he walked past Charlie's muscular associate he had seen earlier in the day. The man was just casually sipping whiskey, ignoring the fact he was standing next to a tied-up police officer.

He crouched in front of his father and examined his face and body. 'God help you, Ed. Don't tell me this was all a setup.'

As he stared deeply, his father's eyes snapped open fast. This startled Will, and he fell backwards. Ed called Charlie over.

'What did you see?'

'She knows nothing, Charlie. She hasn't told anyone about you either. I looked as far forward as I could, and nothing is going to happen to you,' Ed said confidentially.

'You sure?' Charlie said, looking directly into Ed's eyes and then back at Woods.

'Yes, I'm sure.'

Will smiled. His father had revealed nothing. He saved Woods.

Remembering his complete control, Will looked around and spotted a gold coloured analog clock on the wall. 1.05 p.m. Half an hour from now.

He walked back over to Woods and crouched down to meet her eyes, and although he knew she couldn't see or hear him, he said, 'I'm going to get you out of here. I need to find where you are first, but I'm going to save you.'

He walked up one of the flights of stairs and, at the top, found a closed door. The handle moved freely, and Will slowly pushed the door open.

Light poured into the room as the door swung open, revealing a spacious area with tall wooden tables and chairs. Will stood behind a bar, surrounded by glass refrigerators stocked with various types of beer. The assortment of glasses and taps showed a selection of beers on offer. He realised he was inside a pub and surmised that the stairs he had climbed likely led to the cellar below, used for storage.

With his profound sense of control of the vision, he confidently exited the pub and stepped onto the street. Turning around, he examined the facade of the building before him.

Will studied the building and read the large, bright yellow sign above the entrance - 'Golden Bell Hotel.'

He had seen enough. He knew the exact location and could now have the police urgently get to the hotel. Just as he was about to close his eyes to picture himself back in the examination room with Ravi, he saw about a dozen men wearing black helmets, face coverings, cargo pants, long-sleeve t-shirts, tactical vests, and automatic rifles. They were climbing out of a black van parked in the alley and shuffling down the driveway in single file.

'Police?' Will thought. '*Aubrey must have somehow contacted them.*'

He followed them to watch their raid on the building. When he got to the side of the building, he heard a loud crack and a steel door pulled open on the side of the building. The tactical team entered, and Will followed behind quickly.

Without warning, the team opened fire on the room. Without warning, they aimed their automatic rifles in no particular direction and they unloaded a spray of bullets as they made their way to the centre of the room. Will watched on in horror as Charlie, Marco, and the third male fought back, dropping two tactical officers, but they were outnumbered and outgunned. In the chaos, bullets continued to fly, and Will witnessed

Charlie being shot multiple times in the chest, collapsing to the ground, followed by Marco and the third man. The gunfire was deafening, and the gruesome sight of blood splattering on the cellar walls was beyond anything Will could have envisioned.

He covered his ears while considering what the hell was going on. *'How can the police just open fire so carelessly like this?'*

As the magazines were emptied and the final shots reverberated through the air, Will rushed over to Woods, only to find her left arm bleeding profusely. In the midst of the chaos, she had unwittingly taken a stray bullet.

Lying on the floor beside Woods, Will witnessed his father clutching at his stomach. Ed Denham had also been shot, and blood was rapidly pooling around his curled body. His condition appeared far more critical than Woods'. Will realised that the tactical team was focused on the immediate threat posed by Charlie and Marco. They seemed to overlook Woods and Ed in the chaos.

Will had seen enough and felt a sense of urgency. He knew he had to act quickly to prevent the events he had just witnessed. He thought about the hospital's examination room, where he had slipped into his new vision a moment ago. His eyes opened wide, and he was back, staring at Ravi, who gazed down at him with furrowed brows in a look of deep concern.

SEVENTY-FIVE

'How do you feel?' Ravi asked, desperately gripping Will's shoulders.

'Never mind that, I've got to go,' Will said, startling himself back to coherence, brushing him away, swinging his legs around, and jumping off the examination bed.

'Woah, not so fast, wait. What happened?'

'I know where they are. They're in the cellar of the Golden Bell Hotel, a trendy place in North Sydney. Aubrey is there being held in the cellar, and so is my father.'

'Okay, so call the police and get them to go there. Don't you go.'

Will was jittery and moving around quickly in the room, but struggling to hold his balance. The effects of even the low dose of ketamine were clearly still present.

'I can't because someone already called them. Maybe Aubrey somehow got a message to the police, or maybe someone saw them drag her inside. Maybe Ed called them. I don't know. But I saw them come in, and they shot everyone in the cellar. A whole tactical team charged in and took out Charlie and Marco Bianco. Still, they also accidentally shot Aubrey in the arm and Ed in the stomach. It was a total mess. Interestingly, I think Ed was just coming out of a vision when I was there, but he didn't warn them about it. He actually covered for Woods and lied to the Biancos, but surely he saw what I saw. I just don't know why he wouldn't warn them and save himself.'

'Will, wow! Slow down, okay? Are you actually feeling alright? I need to make sure you're not going to collapse on me because you're talking very fast right now, and look, your arms are shaking.'

'I feel fine, Ravi. My father was right. That ketamine gave me the clearest vision I've ever had. It was phenomenal. All I had to do was direct my focus on Aubrey, and I saw her. I don't know what else the ketamine would allow me to see if I had the time, but I saw what I needed.'

'Well, I am not giving you any more. I don't care what you say.'

'It doesn't matter now. I need to go.'

'Go? Go where? What are you going to do?'

'I'm going to get there before the cops arrive and make a mess of it. When they arrived, I saw what they did, and now I need to make sure my father and Aubrey are alright. I'm going to deal with it myself.'

'Are you insane? These people obviously kidnapped Aubrey. They've killed people, and now what? You're going to walk in there and rescue her?'

'Yes.'

'Will stop and think about what you're saying. That ketamine must have warped your mind. I knew I shouldn't have given it to you.'

Will continued to fidget in a panic. His speech was still rapid and desperate. 'It's not the ketamine talking. I just know what I need to do.'

'What can you possibly do? They would have guns in there!'

'They won't hurt me when they hear what I have to say. I'm going to go there and warn them about the cops. When I tell them who I am, they'll believe me.'

'No way! That is the worst possible plan.'

'Trust me, Ravi. I'm going to trade myself for Aubrey. They'll want to have me once they know what I can do, just like my father. I would be worth more to them than Aubrey. Plus, Ed told them she knew nothing important about the robberies, and it seemed like they believed him. I'll tell them a raid is coming, but it's about a money laundering investigation or something, not the robberies. They are involved in that with their dodgy cryptocurrency business, so they should buy it, which might save her. By giving them a heads-up that the police are on their way. They'll need to escape quickly, and I'll see that they leave Aubrey behind and take me instead.'

'That's literally suicide. You've heard what this crime family has done to your father over the years.'

'Yes, except two things are different. First, Aubrey won't quit on me; she'll track them down and find me. And second, I won't be their slave. If Aubrey can't find me, as soon as I can, I'll give them a fake vision and lead them straight into the arms of the police. I have nothing to lose, Ravi, and I will not let them win.'

'But how can you trust them? They'll likely take you and still kill Aubrey. These people are violent criminals.'

'I'll tell them the police raid is imminent and get them to leave right away. They won't have time to worry about Aubrey.' Will took a deep breath and felt his heart still pounding. 'Ravi, I have to do something, and I know she would do the same for me.'

'This is beyond crazy. You need to think about this more rationally. I can't let you do this.'

'My mind is made up, and I am running out of time, so I'm going. I have less than half an hour before the police raid the place.'

'We'll call the police right now, together. It'll put a stop to this.'

Will shook his head furiously. 'Weren't you listening? The police were already called!'

Ravi blocked the door. 'I can't, Will. You'll get yourself killed. Sit down, and we will think of some other way to get them out safely.'

'Sorry,' Will said, running past him and bursting through the door. He ran down the hallway and waved at the security guard, who, thinking nothing of Will aside from him just being the maintenance guy on the ward, buzzed him out of the locked door before anyone could stop him.

SEVENTY-SIX

The Uber drive to the Golden Bell Hotel was the most anxiety-fueled trip Will had ever taken. He tapped his fingers on his legs quickly and took forcibly deep, slow breaths to calm his racing heart rate. Will felt confident in his plan, yet he knew he was heading straight for the lion's den. He convinced himself that there was no other way to ensure that Woods, and even his father wouldn't get gunned down during the messy raid.

The car stopped in front of the hotel and Will saw the building just as he had a short time ago. The sky was clear, and there was no breeze, so the humidity felt stagnant and sticky on his skin. He thought about going through the main entrance of the hotel but decided to remain unseen, and headed straight for the thick steel door at the side of the building.

The large trees lining the alley at the side provided a shaded canopy over the uneven and broken concrete driveway. As he walked along, Will felt the temperature drop a few degrees, or perhaps it was the shiver running down his spine. He knew time was now of the essence.

He knocked three times on the closed door, took a step backwards and waited.

But there was no answer.

***

Qiang Chen, sat in his parked Honda Civic, and observed the unfolding situation keenly. He knew that any unexpected development could significantly impact the carefully laid plans. Pulling out his phone, he swiftly composed a text message to Ming, updating him on the arrival of the unknown visitor to the Golden Bell Hotel.

The text read, ' An *unexpected and unknown male just arrived at the hotel. He could be trouble. Keep an eye out.*'

With the message sent, Chen remained vigilant, ready to adapt to the changing circumstances and communicate effectively with the rest of the crime syndicate.

***

Will knocked again, louder. This time, he heard heavy footsteps walking up the wooden stairs behind the door. His heart raced as he heard the loud sound of someone sliding back the heavy deadbolts to unlock the door. The door swung open slowly, and a blank-faced Charlie Bianco greeted him.

'Entry is around the front,' Charlie said as he began closing the door.

Will blurted, 'I'm here to warn you about the police currently on their way.'

'I beg your pardon?'

'I know Detective Woods is in there, and I'm here to make a trade with you.'

Charlie looked at Will inquisitively. 'You're the guy who was with her following us before?'

'Yes. My name is Will Denham.'

'Did you say Denham?'

'Yes, Ed Denham is my father, and I know he is inside, too. I think we need to talk.'

Charlie opened the door wider and waved Will inside. Before closing the door, he stuck his head out and looked up and down the alleyway, confirming that Will was alone.

Will did his best to appear confident, but his legs nearly buckled as he took the stairs down into the cellar. He looked around and recognised the room from his vision. He saw the round table with the open laptop and Marco sitting opposite it. The other larger man he saw at the crypto exchange was inside, sipping a glass of whiskey. Ed sat in the corner of the room in a wooden chair with his arms folded, while Woods was tied to another wooden chair.

As soon as they made eye contact, Woods struggled aggressively against her restraints and screamed. 'Will! Get out of here!'

Will glanced briefly at Ed Denham, who sat rigid in his chair, seemingly unresponsive to the sudden turn of events.

'Isn't this interesting?' Charlie said.

'Who's this?' Marco asked, rushing over.

'This here is Ed's son. I can actually see the resemblance, too. Dad always said this was the guy he would track down if Ed ever played up on us, and now here he is. He says the police are on their way.'

Charlie turned and faced Will. 'And how would they know about us being here?'

'I don't know. Someone must have called them,' Will replied.

'They have nothing on us. They can't prove anything,' Charlie said, and Will detected a slightly anxious inflexion in his tone.

'I'm just telling you what I saw.'

'What you saw?'

'That's right. I can do what my father can do. I had a vision of this place being raided. You all get shot and killed. My father gets shot, too, and so does Detective Woods. In my vision, I heard the cops say it's about your Bitcoin and money laundering,' Will lied, 'but they know you're all heavily armed, so they too are coming in armed.'

Will was impressed with his quick-thinking story and now felt quite confident in his plan. He hoped this would convince them that the police did not know about the actual robberies and murders, so by default, they would believe Woods also knew nothing about them.

'Is that so? I never knew there were more people like Ed. I guess it runs in the family.'

Will shrugged nervously 'I guess.'

'So why are you telling me this?'

'As I said, I saw you all die in less than...' Will checked his watch. 'In less than ten minutes now. I want to make a trade for this information.'

Charlie smirked but didn't reply straight away. He paused and then turned around.

'Ed, come here,' he called out, ignoring Will's demand.

Ed stood up slowly and walked over towards Charlie. His eyes locked with Will's.

When Ed got nearer, Charlie grabbed him by the back of his hair and pulled his head back roughly. He winced as he felt the force almost lifting him off his feet.

'Why is it, Ed, that this guy here, who says he is your son, tells me the police are about to raid this place, but you told me moments ago that everything would be fine? All you told me was that the cop knows nothing about us. You must have seen the police, though. Decided to keep that to yourself, did you?'

Will's expression went flat. *'Oh shit,'* He was too late. He had hoped to get here sooner, but his father's vision had already happened. He had already told them he saw nothing.

'I uh...I.. I...' Ed was panicking, his eyes twitching back and forth nervously.

'Someone is lying to me. So who do I believe?'

Ed didn't reply. Charlie tightened his grip and pulled his head back tighter.

'Are you trying to get me killed, Ed? I know you've always despised me, and believe me, the feelings are mutual, but this is particularly nasty. Even for you. Anyway, lucky me, I guess. Saved by your son, and now I have two Denhams to work for me. Marco,' Charlie called out. 'We can use them both. We will keep them separate and get them to tell us about their visions independently. A good way to verify their information, I think.'

'No, you won't,' Will said, still panicking but improvising and trying to fix the damage already done to get his plan back on course.

'Excuse me?' Charlie said.

'You will not have two of us working for you. In exchange for my reliable information and future services, you let Detective Woods and my father go. He's old. I'm young and can do a better job. You said to yourself, he despises you. I've given you accurate information. You can trust me.'

'Will, be quiet!' Woods screamed.

'Shut up,' Charlie said to Woods as he yanked Ed's head back harder. 'You don't come here and make a deal with me. You have no idea who you're talking to.'

'I've come here willingly, and I'm going to work for you. I've told you about the raid coming, so let these two go.'

Woods remained in a struggle against her restraints and tears welled up in her eyes.

Charlie continued, 'So let me get this straight. The cops come? And kill me, my brother and my friend? And here you are to warn me. Why?'

'I don't want anyone to be killed. Especially Detective Woods. So that's why.'

'That's very noble of you. Okay, well, like you said, we should get out of here then. But all of you are coming with us.'

'That's not part of the deal.'

Charlie clenched his teeth in anger. The large muscles in his arms twitched and tensed. 'What deal? There is no deal! You all do as I say! I'll figure out what to do about the detective in due course, but you two are both staying with me.'

He produced a small handgun from his pocket and pointed it at Will. He gasped while his stomach did a backflip, and sweat dripped down his forehead.

He had made a terrible, terrible mistake.

'Please, just take me, let them go,' he begged. Any remaining confidence he thought he had was gone. Will had lost and greatly underestimated Charlie Bianco. He looked back at Woods; tears were now running down her cheeks. He had no idea how they would get out of this now. His plan had backfired tremendously.

'No. Sit down over there, next to your cop friend, and be quiet,' Charlie said, waving the pistol around. 'You too, Ed. Get up and sit over there with them. I'll deal with you later.'

He turned back around and prepared for a quick exit. 'Marco, you get the cash, Tony, the guns and the laptop. Forget the stuff in the corner. All six of us are getting out of here together right now. I'll be damned if they find we've kidnapped a cop. Also, there's no way they can pin the robberies and the murders on us. If it's only money laundering they have on us, that's no trouble. The lawyers will get us off any charges, and if they find the drugs, let them take them. They won't be able to prove they're ours. This is a busy pub cellar, and as far as they know, many people have access to it. The charges will never stick. So for now, we get out, lie low and distance ourselves from this place.'

Marco and Tony both nodded in agreement.

While they scurried to collect as much as possible before the raid, Ed leant over to Will. 'I knew you'd come. Just stay calm, trust me. Everything will be okay.'

'Save the reunion,' Charlie said, cutting Woods free from the chair and walking past them with a heavy duffle bag he had just filled with firearms. 'We are all going now, so get up. And thank you, Will. I think we will all work well together for a long time.'

SEVENTY-SEVEN

A large black panel van turned sharply into the alley at the side of the Golden Bell Hotel, and the side door quickly slid open. A team of a dozen masked men wearing all black, including balaclavas and thick heavy boots, left the van in single file. Each carried heavy automatic rifles attached to straps and slung over their shoulders. Moments ago, they were driving slowly and carefully toward the hotel. However, new information about an unknown person arriving caused them to hit high speeds and arrive as quickly as possible. They didn't know who this new person was, but they would risk nothing interfering with their plan.

One of the armed tactical men removed a small device from the pocket of his cargo pants and carefully attached it to the lock on the steel door at the side of the building. The team took a few steps backwards, and seconds later, the lock cracked loudly, releasing smoke from its remains. Pushing open the heavy steel door, they stormed the cellar with military precision, their guns tracking in every direction of the large room.

***

Will looked up at the top of the stairs, astonished at what he saw. The tactical team from his vision was five minutes early. They charged into the cellar and opened fire in every direction. They had the true element of surprise in their favour. Charlie dropped the bag he was carrying and returned fire with his handgun. Still, the sheer power behind the automatic rifles overmatched him, and he succumbed to a hail of bullets. His limp body collapsed onto the ground as a pool of blood spread across the floor.

***

'Nooooo!' Marco screamed while returning fire with a shotgun. His emotions led him to react carelessly without thinking of taking any proper cover. He let off two powerful rounds, which boomed over the sound of the rifles. He hit two of the armed intruders, and they collapsed against the wall. A trail of blood tracked them on their way to the floor, where they slumped together. Marco was still outnumbered, and his shotgun was too slow to keep up with the powerful automatic weapons leering over him. No less than twenty rounds hammered into his chest, shooting him down.

As the bullets continued to scatter through the room and ricocheted off the walls, the sound was deafening. Will stood frozen, trying to comprehend what was taking place and how this could have happened.

'Will! Get down,' Ed called out.

He snapped to attention and then heard the scream. It was Woods. Will rushed over to her, and she was gripping her left bicep. A stray bullet had hit her, and blood was leaking fast out of the wound. As the bullets continued to fly around the room, Will pushed Woods onto the ground and clenched her arm. He ripped part of his t-shirt and used it to clean up the blood and then to tie a tourniquet around her upper arm.

'I'm so sorry, Aubrey, everything I saw is happening, but I don't know why they're early. Here, I'm going to put pressure on your arm.'

As they continued firing, Will kept low and still. Ed had moved into the back corner of the room and was trying to hide from the wild flying bullets. Suddenly, he curled over, and blood trickled out of his stomach. He had been hit.

'Get on the ground and out of the way.' Will cried to Ed, still crouching by Woods, gripping her bleeding arm.

'Go make sure he's okay,' she groaned. Her face was becoming pale and her breathing erratic.

'No, I can't let you go.'

'It's okay, it's just my arm. You put the tourniquet on for me, and the bleeding has slowed down. I'll be okay. Go.'

Will nodded, and his hand was covered in blood as he helped Woods lie down. He kept low, covering his head as he made his way to the other side of the cellar toward Ed.

Will watched as the last standing member of Charlie's crew found cover behind an old refrigerator and a pile of boxes of beer and continued to fire. Glass shattered, and amber liquid flooded the ground as bullets rained down in his direction. As he raised his body to continue firing back, a single precise round struck him in the centre of his forehead. He hit the ground hard on top of the shattered glass and warm beer.

Ed was still groaning in pain, and Will suspected Woods was close to passing out, but the shooting had finally stopped.

Will looked around. There was blood on the walls and shattered glass littered the floor. Suddenly, a man, with his face concealed, charged over to Will and pointed his rifle inches from his head.

'Who are you?' he demanded.

Will raised his hands quickly in surrender. 'Nobody, I'm nobody.'

'You work for the Biancos?'

'No, I don't. I swear, they were holding us against our will. I came here to get these two out, I swear!'

The man scanned the room, his rifle still positioned and ready to fire. A moment later, he turned around, his balaclava lifted slightly at the back, and Will saw a small Chinese character tattooed on the side of his neck.

Will remained huddled and watched the man walk over to the dead bodies of Charlie and Marco Bianco and squatted by their lifeless bodies covered in blood, their limbs in disarray. Undoubtedly dead.

'You've got to help us. Get an ambulance down here now!' Will cried.

Ignoring him, the man rejoined his team in the corner of the cellar where they had discovered a stack of blue barrels tucked away beneath a cover. The man then yelled out in a foreign language.

'Hey! Please! Help!' Will cried. Ed's face grew paler, and he struggled to maintain consciousness between short, staggered breaths. He continued to clutch his stomach, and Will helped apply pressure, but the blood was still pouring out fast.

In a matter of minutes, the group cleared the cellar, removing all the barrels. One of the operatives also collected all the firearms scattered around the room, as well as a bag filled with cash found in the corner behind where the barrels were stored.

'Wait, where are you going?' Don't leave us here!' Will called out as the men began to leave the room.

The man with the Chinese tattoo on his neck turned around and looked at Will. With the balaclava still covering his face, all he could see were two piercing brown eyes. He paused briefly and then spoke again in a foreign language.

Will yelled again. 'Help us!'

The entire team walked up the steps and outside, closing the cellar door behind them without saying another word.

SEVENTY-EIGHT

Zao Ming, the man with the Chinese neck tattoo, had successfully achieved his objectives. The rest of his crew piled back into the van while they loaded up another van with barrels of pseudoephedrine.

'Pau has been avenged, but let us take a moment to honor our fallen friends.' They died with honour, and in doing so, we have destroyed our competition, and we now have what is rightfully ours.'

They swiftly removed their face coverings and drove away as quickly as possible.

Police sirens sounded in the distance and were probably approaching at a high speed, Ming thought, but they would be long gone before they arrived.

***

'They weren't cops,' Woods said slowly, still clutching her wounded arm.

'What? But Ravi gave me ketamine, and I saw them in my vision. They were a tactical team.'

Will detected surprise and perhaps a little disappointment from Woods at his disclosure of the use of ketamine, but she continued without addressing it. 'No, cops don't work that way. They were reckless and ruthless, and they spoke Mandarin.

Woods stood up slowly, pain etched across her face. She stumbled to one of the bodies lying still on the floor and pulled up his balaclava, which revealed the face of a Chinese man with the same small tattoo on the side of his neck.

'See that tattoo?'

Will looked at the man's neck and saw the familiar marking. It was the same tattoo he had seen on the other man.

'It's a symbol for the Chinese Triad.' Woods said.

'Chinese?'

'Yes, there's a stack of intelligence to suggest they are the major rivals of the Biancos. I just have no idea why they stormed the place.'

'Will,' Ed groaned.

Will quickly looked back down at his father and put more pressure on his wound.

'I thought they were cops, but they were still here earlier than I first saw them,' Will said.

'I saw them too,' Ed whispered through clenched teeth. 'They came earlier because they saw you come inside. They thought you were here to move the drugs in the barrels or somehow interfere with their own plans. Charlie and Marco Bianco have been trying to move in on their meth territory. This was a revenge hit.'

'I don't understand. Why couldn't I see that? I even took ketamine like you.'

Ed gasped again; this time, blood leaked from his mouth. 'Because what you first saw later changed due to your response to the vision. Like the many things you have done after seeing something, your actions have caused an effect. Whenever you have a vision and prevent something from happening, you change what would naturally occur. I also saw what happened here. Only my vision showed me what happened after you intervened. I saw everyone get shot. They only changed their timings because you came here.'

Ed groaned as more blood leaked from his stomach.

'They sped up and got here quicker, thinking you were a threat to their operation,' he continued. 'Don't you see, Will? You can't always change what's going to happen. These ketamine visions aren't natural. You possess an amazing gift that will help many people, but there are times when fate cannot be altered.

'Why didn't you stop this, though? You must have seen them come at the new time.'

'It was the only way for the Biancos to be stopped. Who knows what they would have done to you? Or to other innocent people through their reckless crimes.' Through his obvious pain, Ed managed a weak smile. 'You inspired me, Will. I've done so many bad things in my life, but this was my chance to finally do something good. To stop these people from getting away with the robberies and the murders. If it meant I had to go too, well, I probably deserve that.'

'You sacrificed yourself? You saw it all happen, and you sacrificed yourself?'

Ed coughed and spat up more blood. 'Yes. It was the only way to protect you from them.'

'But Aubrey?'

'She only got shot in the arm. She'll be okay, just as I knew you would be when I allowed everything I foresaw to continue. Listen, Will, sometimes people are just not meant to be saved. Don't make the same mistakes I did. The drugs won't help you. You can't force what should just come naturally to you. If destinies align and you are meant to see something and help someone, you will. Remember, you can't just see the future. You can also make it. I know it's tormenting, and I know you want to understand why you can see what you do, but I'm afraid I can't give you a reason. But if you are meant to intervene, you will.'

Still full of adrenaline, Will's frustration and fear caused his arms to tremble as he held his father's head upright while he gagged on the blood pooling in his mouth.

'How does my mind choose to show me the things it does?' Will asked desperately. 'Why do I see some things and not others? Why are they cryptic and sporadic? There are terrible things happening every day, everywhere. I just don't understand.'

Ed coughed and choked some more. He was clearly in pain, but as difficult as it was, he kept talking. 'I don't know, son, but remember, you're only one man, and you can't help everyone, but you have and will continue to do so much good. Whenever you are able, just embrace your gift; don't take it for granted as I did. I'm so glad I got to meet you properly.'

Ed choked as more blood poured out of his mouth. Will tried to hold his head up as he uttered his last words.

'I'm proud of you.'

Will then felt his father's body go limp. He was gone.

SEVENTY-NINE

Woods stood up and slowly walked over to Will, tightly clutching her arm. 'I'm so sorry,' she said.

Will nodded. He felt conflicted in his feelings. Until moments ago, father or not, he held a deep disdain for the man because of his long life of crime. Now, however, witnessing his sacrifice and bravery, Will suddenly felt warmth and gratitude toward him. 'My father was right. He did a lot of bad things in his life, but he showed a lot of courage today. For once, he actually did the right thing. I'm just sorry it ended up costing him his life.'

'Are you okay?'

'Yeah, Aubrey, I'll be fine. I'm just glad it's over now.'

In the distance, the sirens grew louder.

'The police are almost here.' she said. 'They probably got a lot of calls about the loud gunfire. Just stay calm when they get here. I'll tell them what happened.'

Woods winced and gripped her arm, prompting Will to help her sit down. She looked up at Will and sighed. 'You should never have used ketamine, Will. That was reckless and dangerous.'

'I only did it so I could find you.'

Will thought he saw Woods smile slightly in what he hoped was an understanding of his reasoning, but he could have mistaken it for a grimace of pain at her injured arm.

'It's alright, Will. As you said, it's all finally over now. I'll be honest, for a moment there, I thought I was going to die.'

'I think the way things turned out, we're both lucky to walk out of here alive.'

The police quickly arrived and began clearing the cellar with their guns drawn. Will raised his hands while Woods identified herself and explained what happened, referring to her kidnapping and the Chinese Triad's shooting of the Biancos.

A few police helped Woods stand slowly and walk up the stairs where an ambulance was just arriving. Will took one last look at the lifeless body of his father and followed them outside.

Woods spent some time in the back of the ambulance, receiving proper bandaging and pain relief. As more police vehicles arrived, including a convoy of detectives, to assess the scene of carnage below, Will paced around the street, anxiously waiting to ensure Woods was okay and avoiding the crowd of curious and frightened onlookers. When the paramedics had finished, he found her standing by the side of the van, getting some fresh air.

'How's your arm?'

'It'll heal up fine. I really am sorry about your father, Will. You're right, though; he eventually did the right thing.'

'Yeah, he did. He actually said something interesting to me right before he died. About my visions. He said sometimes you can't always control people's fate. I know now I should never have taken ketamine. If I am meant to see something, he said it will come naturally and that I can't interfere with what is meant to be. So I guess my gift is there to help people whenever I can, but sometimes I won't be able to see everything, and I won't be able to help everyone.'

'Maybe like the police at the lab explosion? And those inside the Australian Summit Bank who were killed?'

'I guess so. It doesn't make it easier, but in time, I'll just have to accept what I can and can't control.'

Woods nodded and checked her heavily bandaged arm again.

I was really worried about you,' Will said.

'I'll be okay, don't worry. But thank you for coming here. I knew you'd do whatever it took to find me.'

'You would have done the same for me.'

'You're right, I would have.' Woods slowly leant forward and kissed Will, and he kissed her back.

With no need to speak, they both just smiled as though nothing else seemed to matter.

ABOUT THE AUTHOR

Born and raised in Sydney, Max grew up with a passion for storytelling, however, it was not until a few years ago he turned one of many ideas into his first novel – Altered Sense. Altered Sense was the first novel to feature Will Denham and was born from a single idea – what would it be like to see into the future? Who would believe you? Would you even believe yourself? With no plans to stop writing, Max strives to create gripping and fast-paced stories, with relatable characters thrust into extraordinary situations. Max still lives in Sydney with his wife and son. When not writing, he enjoys spending as much time as he can with his family.

Q&A WITH MAX JEFFRIES

Why did you write Deadly Sense?

Upon completing Altered Sense, I immediately began plotting ideas for a sequel. Even as the author, I was captivated by Will's strange visions and the intricacies of his relationships with Ravi and Aubrey, and I knew there was still so much to explore. Altered Sense, in essence, laid the groundwork for Will's journey, granting me the freedom to delve deeper into his visions and explore the interesting concept of cause and effect stemming from his supernatural interventions. With Deadly Sense, I found myself venturing into darker territory, a progression that unfolded organically rather than by design. My aim was simple: to continue challenging Will's character, pushing him to confront ever-heightening stakes and grapple with the consequences of his actions.

What does your writing process look like?

I'm quite meticulous when it comes to plotting my books. Before I even start writing, I outline the entire story, envisioning major turning points and the ending. Despite this structured approach, I am also flexible, allowing the characters and storyline to organically evolve as I write. It's remarkable how characters seem to take on a life of their own, often leading the plot in unexpected directions, and this is why I will always leave room for smaller side plots to emerge naturally as the characters develop. It is this momentum that the characters develop which keeps the writing process exciting! Once I've outlined the plot, I dive into writing without dwelling on previous chapters. Despite the temptation to edit as I go, I prioritise getting the entire story down on paper before revisiting and refining it later. This approach allows me to compartmentalise the writing and editing processes, ensuring that each phase receives the attention and focus it deserves.

What are your plans for your future book(s)?

While I do have some ideas brewing for another Will Denham novel, my focus has shifted to a variety of other projects, each of which I am very excited about. Venturing into writing for younger audiences has always interested me, particularly as I seek to captivate readers in the age of streaming services. Currently, I'm working on a suspenseful, post-apocalyptic novel and also a fantastical adventure geared toward middle-grade children. Despite the divergence in genres, my passion for crime thrillers remains, and I also have a crime thriller set in Sydney in the 1860s I have just about completed. Juggling these diverse projects keeps me really engaged in my writing journey, and I really look forward to all the possibilities that lie ahead.

ALTERED SENSE

The loyalties of those closest to him will be tested...

When an unprovoked and vicious assault leaves William Denham at a Sydney hospital with serious head injuries, he soon begins to experience strange visions.

Forced to question his sanity at the realisation that he is experiencing premonitions of violent and horrific crimes yet to occur, those closest to Will are confronted with his newfound abilities, causing fear for his state of mind.

As the visions of these brutal crimes continue to plague Will, he must turn to his friends for help to save the lives of the unsuspecting victims...

"An unnerving and thought-provoking new novel from a talented writer who grips the emotional tension with both hands and doesn't let it go..." Trevor, Indie Book reviewer.